SALT ROCK MYSTERIES

A NOVEL WITH MURDER

Magdalena Zschokke

New Victoria Publishers

Norwich Vermont

Published by New Victoria Publishers Inc., PO Box 27 Norwich, VT. 05055
A Feminist Literary and Cultural Organization founded in 1976

Cover Design Claudia McKay
Printed and bound in Canada
1   2   3   4   5   2003   2004   2002   2001   2000

Library of Congress Cataloging-in-Publication Data
Zschokke,   Magdalena,   1950-
    Salt rock mysteries/ by Magdalena Zschokke.
            p.   cm.
    ISBN 1-892281-07-4
        1. Americans--Travel--Caribbean Area--Fiction. 2. Women historians--Fiction.
        3. Caribbean Area--Fiction. 4.Drug traffic--Fiction. I. Title.
PS3576.S75 S25 2000
813'.54--dc21

                                                        00-025378

Acknowledgements

A novel is very much a communal creation as people and places trigger the writing mind in conscious and unconscious ways.

Providenciales exists and a real Club Med was built on its northern shore in the mid-nineteen eighties. In the same way, seventy-six tons of marijuana were found behind the customs dock one sunny dawn and two American suspects escaped just as I have described it here. Much of the quoted historical facts can be verified and women passing as men are easily found in history books. This does not make "my" Providenciales a real place, nor does it make any of the mysteries in this book "true."

This book would not have come about had I had not lived on Provo during the custom-house find. But neither would it have come to be without the support and critique of my friends and readers Connie Chin, LaVerne Coleman, Elizabeth Drowne, Ann Miya, and Ann Pomper. Or the crucial input from everyone at New Victoria Publishers.

For CSR who showed me the world,
and my sons Henry and Ben who taught me about love.

Chapter One

When the little plane had landed on Providenciales, bumping along the uneven strip, Janet was torn between worry about crash landing and laughter. Peering out the plane's round porthole she read, stenciled on an aluminum trailer, Luddington International Airport. What a ridiculously inflated name for what, in reality, was a short, potholed landing strip with an open-sided aluminum shed for passengers about midway along, and a trailer. She assumed the latter represented the airport operational facilities when a tall man with a clipboard emerged from it. He walked toward the plane while a gaggle of tourists stood disconsolately in the sun guarding their various bags and looking doubtfully at the shuddering little aircraft.

As soon as she had stepped on the ground, a young man with the permanently peeling look of red-haired European ancestry grabbed her duffel bag, mumbling, "Hi, I'm Billy, here to welcome you. Let's get out of here."

"Hello, I'm Janet McMillan and how do you know you're my welcoming committee?"

"Oh, sorry. I'm… Well, there was no one else that fit the description. You're going to stay at the Old Turtle Resort, aren't you? My parents own the place. And you're the one who's come to see Francine Stone and Hamilton House. Sorry, Francine is on South Caicos, so she couldn't come to welcome you. But she'll be expecting you on Thursday and—"

"OK, OK, enough," Janet laughed. "I believe you. But what about customs and immigration? I haven't checked in."

"Never mind, you can do that later. And here's the letter she wrote for you."

"Hey, Ricardo," he yelled loudly, and when the tall uniformed mahogany-colored official turned, he went on, "It's OK to go ahead, right? Just tell Morris when you see him, will you?"

The man nodded, waved them off and turned back to his conversation with the pilot of the plane.

"Ricardo is customs," Billy explained. "They're not really interested in tourists, they deal with imports and exports, the big stuff. I mean, how much could you smuggle in one bag?"

Leading Janet away from the facilities, he went on. "Morris's police and immigration and he'll come down to the bar to stamp your passport if you want him to. But it's not like you could get lost on an island with 977 residents. People mostly want the stamp for a souvenir kind of thing. Here, this way."

They passed a white container of the kind cargo ships carry with a big lock on the door, cut across the rocky sand and headed directly for a parking lot. It was dominated by a coral rock sculpture of a biplane on a pedestal labeled 'In honor of Fritz Luddington, discoverer.' Janet had read about him having 'discovered' Providenciales in 1967, and, with the gall typical of American tycoons, called it his own island.

In fact, Provo, part of the Turks and Caicos Islands had been discovered many times over, reputedly by Christopher Columbus himself, maybe even during his first landing in 1492.

"I guess you never have to worry about losing someone in the airport, or about people not getting picked up."

Billy nodded, seriously. "Yeah, everybody comes out here when the scheduled flight arrives, even if only for the excitement. You can tell by the cars, too. See the reddish truck—that's customs. Our resort van has come and gone. Old Johnson dropped off last week's guests and went on back. He doesn't like to drive it because it uses so much gas. But it's the only island car with air conditioning and mainland people always seem to want that. And that," here Billy resorted to adolescent mumbling, "the big Olds is Rudy von der Koll's, our local real estate dealer. Then there are a few of the caretakers' cars here for mail, orders and stuff. And here we are."

With a proud sweep of his arm he invited Janet to admire his recent model white pickup truck. He swung her duffel bag in the back, opened the driver's door and got in. As soon as she had settled he roared off on the wrong side of the road. "Don't worry, I drive safely," he assured her, blushing under her worried glare.

"Billy, how old are you, if I may ask?"

Goodnaturedly he answered, "Almost seventeen and, yes, I'm driving on the right side of the road. We are, after all, a British dependency even though we use American cars and American dollars."

He waved at every one of the few people moving in the midday heat and seemed to be continuing conversations begun at some other time. The only time he came to a complete stop was when a young woman hailed him from the sidewalk.

"Hey, Michelle, what's up?"

About thirty to thirty-five with perfect, caramel-colored skin that looked soft to the touch, Michelle was slim and small-boned with short black hair, curly rather than tightly kinked, showing the influence of European blood. Her dark eyes were almond shaped and large above her high cheekbones, her nose wide and expressive. When she noticed another person in Billy's car, she flared her nostrils like a large cat sniffing danger.

For one moment her dark, liquid eyes focused on Janet with the intensity of a searchlight. "I did not know you had someone with you. Please come talk with me later. Maybe sunset? *Oui*?" Her voice was low, close to sultry, especially with her liquid French vowels. Billy smiled widely and agreed. He drove off. Before Janet could comment he said, "That's Michelle. She's a down islander, from Martinique, and her husband's our chef." Blushing at his use of the possessive pronoun he added, mumbling again, "at the resort."

Martinique, the French Caribbean, was an island with generally higher educational and economic standards than the rest of the area. Like all French colonies it was a place of beautiful, graceful women in all shades of brown.

"Billy, why didn't Johnson give me a ride if he was at the airport with the resort van?"

"When he's by himself he doesn't use the air conditioner. Besides, he said, he drives tourists and since you're going to stay for a month you don't qualify." He shrugged, apologetic but not overly bothered by the argument's logic.

Leaving the settlement, the truck rattled down a slight hill, raising a thick dust cloud on what was either a formerly paved road which potholes and dirt had taken over, or a dirt road with patches of asphalt. Janet breathed deeply and tried to imagine knowing this island intimately, its potholes, its history.

"Did you grow up here?"

"Well, yes, my first twelve years. I went to school right over there."

He pointed toward a small clump of buildings on the ridge, the houses covered with warped, cracked shingles so weathered they looked like hammered silver.

"This used to be the old settlement, with the school on one end and the police on the other. But then things sort of moved toward the airport. Just back there, at the end of town, is the new police station. But the school stayed."

His gaze narrowed and Janet followed the direction of his eyes. There was movement up by the buildings, people milling. The shimmering heat made it seem as though bodies surged together in an unstable heap.

"Hmm." Billy said, wonderingly, then appeared to lose interest and continued with his previous topic. "After that I went to school in Miami. It was that or Kingston. And I wanted to get off the islands."

He took a left onto a single-lane path through brush and scrub land, heading for four coconut palms.

"Here we are."

Janet climbed from the truck and stretched exaggeratedly, which gave her the chance to look around without having to declare an opinion right away. A path of blinding white coral stones led through the palms from the parking area. The buildings which showed behind the coconut palms were low with red tiled roofs and fresh whitewash. Most of the windows sported push-out shutters painted a dark blue and, as a whole, the vision appeared colorful, rustic, tasteful and somewhat self-conscious.

On a wider view, the island stretched out flat and low, covered with sand and brush. A few casuarina trees hosted hundreds of dryly rattling crickets and the dull pounding of waves crashing filled the air.

"Are you coming?"

Billy stood poised on the coral path, a packet of mail under one arm and Janet's duffel under the other. A last crick of the neck and Janet followed without further resistance.

Chapter Two

The reception area, an airy, tiled room with louvered windows and a few overstuffed wicker chairs, was cool and dark after the harsh brightness of the coral path. A couple of sunburnt tourists with peeling noses were loudly complaining and gesturing at the desk attendant. Before Janet could figure out their upset their voices were drowned by the noise of a motor approaching, then four doors slammed and the air suddenly felt heavier.

Four black men, their authority weighing on their shoulders as though they were wearing sashes of medals, walked into the room and were intercepted by a white woman coming out of a side door who clearly looked to be Billy's mother. In the sudden quiet the tourists' voices whined overly loudly. "We paid for an all day dive and we don't intend to spend it sitting on the dock waiting for the guy. This is an outrage…"

Clearly, the desk attendant was not paying as much attention to them as to the mumbling, tense conversation in the other corner.

"Corinne," Billy's mother said in the direction of the front desk, "would you come here for a minute?"

The attendant stood up and moved away from the counter, shaking off the demanding voices as if they were water drops. Standing, Corinne was at least six feet tall, muscular and broad, her obsidian skin glowing against a printed loose caftan dress in oranges and yellows. Passing her, Billy's mother lay a comforting hand on Corinne's arm before she efficiently took over the front desk.

The men huddled around Corinne and the five of them moved toward the door like an amorphously shaped animal. The impatient divers soon walked off in the opposite direction toward the marina, while Janet watched Corinne climb into the back of the car with the four men folding themselves around her.

Billy's voice cut in. "This is Janet, Mother. My mother, Sophie."

"Yes, pleased to meet you," Sophie's eyes strayed back outside where the car sped off in a cloud of dust.

"A family tragedy. A brother of Corinne's. They just found him. Dead." Sophie sighed and, as though a switch had been flipped on, became energetic and efficient. "Billy, would you take Janet's duffel to her room while she signs in, please." He hesitated as though to protest, looked at his mother, and left. Sophie opened a large leather-bound book and turned it toward Janet for registration.

Janet asked, "How old was he?" Sophie's eyes lit on her as though she wondered who had been talking. Janet persisted. "What did he die of?"

After a long pause during which Janet wondered if Sophie had even heard her, Sophie said slowly, "Drugs. There's just too much of them everywhere." Her body straightened and she began tidying piles of invoices, lining up pencils. Her voice turned hard. "Midway Island, they call us. Halfway between Colombia and the U.S., we are the ideal refuelling station. They've got it down to eight minutes, I hear, to refuel a mid-size cargo plane."

Shaking her head, Sophie reached behind her with a foot angling for the stool and, once seated, said, "Sorry about this reception. Usually this is a very quiet place. If you need anything, Corinne knows all that's worth knowing and she's usually here at the desk. Or you can try to find me or Billy. One of us is almost always on the grounds."

Janet's room clearly had been a maid's lodgings in the days of servants and plantations. For a resort room it was narrow and rather spartan. One small window at the long end looked out on dry scrub land which sloped uphill toward the single road. Its only furnishings were a narrow bed, a small bedside table, a chest for clothes, and a chair by the window. But it was quiet and the window was screened.

Janet only took the time to find her bathing suit and she was off down to the marina. Time to try out a windsurfer. Billy the chauffeur turned resort recreation manager rigged the sail and yelled a few helpful suggestions from shore. When it seemed she wouldn't get in trouble inside the lagoon, he wandered off to some other project.

The water was perfectly still, the wind light and steady, and Janet was quite pleased with herself. Not too long into the initial numerous, dunkings, she found herself sailing by the outer edge of the lagoon. She reveled in the sense of quiet speed...until she fell off backwards onto a shallow bed of sea urchins.

She had seen the small black balls with their waving spikes on and around the shallow rocks. She had decided they looked like chewing gum passing as hedgehogs. But she had never landed on them. Nor expected the pain to be quite as fierce.

She hauled herself onto her board and lay stunned. Her whole body pulsed with a pain that made her eyes water. Finally unable to tolerate it any longer, she pulled the mast from its attachment, laid it on top of the board, and began paddling in direction of shore.

The unwieldy load kept slipping off and pain made her clumsy. One of the first boats she reached was a chubby gray concrete schooner with an unpainted hull and tarred telephone poles for masts. An anxious young face peered over the stern at her and a hand reached down. "Do come up and take a rest. I saw your spill—you must be in pain."

Slowly, inelegantly, and with multiple groans, Janet pulled herself up the rope ladder which he had lowered over the topsides. She tried to inspect her back while her host tied off the windsurfer.

He turned to her. "Nice to meet you, even at such a painful moment. My name is Johnny and this is *Rosinante*," proudly indicating his fiefdom.

She shook his hand, nodding in acknowledgment, and said, "Janet. I think I landed on a colony of sea urchins."

Still holding her hand, he craned to look over her shoulder. He was about six feet tall and gangly. His wispy blond hair fell to his eyes but did not manage to cover the freely flying ears. He nodded, reached below and produced a mug. "Here, you can use this. Pee in it and I'll pour it over your back. You can have the cockpit for privacy."

Janet thought it might be his accent which made her misunderstand. Feeling an almost irresistible need to sit down she said, "Excuse me?"

"Sea urchins! As you said yourself. Your back is indeed full of spines. Didn't you know that urine is the remedy of choice?"

In response to her incredulous look, he insisted, "Believe me, it's the only thing. The acid in the urine dissolves the protein in the broken-off spine, or something. I forget exactly how it works."

"You are telling me pee dissolves the barb or that it lessens the pain? And why should I pee in your mug? But wait. I can't argue, it hurts way too much." Before she gave in, accepting the mug, she hesitated once more, "Why not extract the spines with a pair of tweezers?"

"You can't. They break off. You have to dissolve them in your skin."

"OK, fine." Her tone indicated she wasn't convinced, but the pain made her disinclined to argue further.

He returned from the foredeck only after she called to him, her voice sheepish.

"Right-oh," he said, reaching for the mug, "It would probably be best if you lay down on your belly here and I'll pour the stuff over you."

It took a couple of rum toddies, which she drank lying on her stomach, before she could laugh about her predicament, and a couple more before the pain had receded enough to make her attempt the sail back to shore. By that time she had begun to like her host thoroughly and had agreed to go sailing with him the next day.

When Janet brought the windsurfer back in she found Billy out behind the shed smoking a joint the size of a small cigar, having reached the stage of contentment where he kept giggling at her misfortune, no matter how he tried to keep a straight face.

Chapter Three

Despite the pain she fell asleep immediately and did not wake until early morning light streamed through the small window. She couldn't recall having set out her book before falling into bed, even less having read. She was just barely conscious of the booming surf already a noise, a physical entity, a part of island living.

Janet turned in the narrow bed with a groan, her back sharply reminding her why she had avoided motion for so long.

Behind her closed eyes the image of a large thick white mug with steam rising appeared. The coffee was hot, strong, sweet, and sand colored, with milky foam clouds circling lazily on its surface.

"Why is paradise always at least a coffee away," she grumbled and stretched a long arm in the direction of the night table, reaching for her book and reading glasses folded between its pages as a bookmark. She had determined that in addition to writing a book on the economic history of the Turks and Caicos islands this summer, she was going to read the latest publication by each member of her committee in preparation for the tenure review. Having hefted the book, a definitive analysis of Charlotte Bronte's life and letters written by the chair of the senate committee, next to her pillow, she buried her head once more. It was really too early to work on one's future, especially after just having landed in the tropics. The memory of her first view of the island made her smile. A flat, bluish horseshoe of low land nestling in glittering turquoise water, the island dotted with bright white houses with red and silvery roofs.

"Providenciales," she tasted the name which sounded foreign, promising and fateful. "The forgotten paradise within the Tropic of Cancer." She began composing the introductory paragraph to her proposed book, liking the rhythm of the words.

When she next raised her head, her neck was stiff. With renewed determination she reached for her book.

The smell of coffee meant they were serving breakfast out on the veranda. She kicked off the sheet, swung her legs over the side of the bed and dug for shorts and a t-shirt without looking at her bare skin. "Too much dusty indoors. Bookworm white!" She noted with relief that the comment had lost much of its power. When Tony, her live-in lover of three years had said it shortly before he left the country, she had felt mortally shamed and exposed. That was nine months and seven days ago.

Downstairs, on the porch surrounded by hibiscus bushes and flame trees the tables were still empty. Insect hummings provided a harmony with the background pounding of waves against the reef. In the middle of the dining room a large linen-covered table held the buffet which shimmered and flashed. Papaya slices competed with pineapple, kiwis, and luscious mango squares. Scones were piled high, surrounded by balls of lemon curd. Fried plantains lay next to mounds of snow white taro, alongside reddish link sausages. Glass jars full of white coconut milk, bright red punch and golden pineapple juice glistened. Janet sighed with contentment, breathing in the welcoming scents.

Nobody else was around and she had the whole magic place to herself. The place would be filling up though, because it was Wednesday, buffet day, designed to welcome the new guests who had arrived the previous afternoon. Tuesday was known as turnover day; tourists left on the weekly shuttle which had deposited its new human crop, as well as mail, groceries, and any other items purchased by mail order.

Having piled her plate with fruit and grabbing a cup of coffee, she wandered to the edge of the deck and claimed a table overlooking the lagoon. While the hotel guests had not yet stirred, life on the boats seemed already in full swing. Someone rocked in a bosun's chair to the gentle swells, legs clutching the top of the mast, concentrating on something. Someone was cleaning a waterline, a woman was hanging wash, and a young man slowly raised a sail. Another more leisurely part of the harbor scene showed a boat with three dinghies tied off the stern and the cockpit full of couples drinking, eating, talking. Two men were shouting to each other from adjacent boats, hanging onto their respective stays in identical posture.

"So much activity to so little effect," said a voice behind her. Janet swivelled in her chair, immediately regretting it as her tender, tired back spasmed, and coldly stared at the interloper who appeared not in the least fazed. While she considered herself a social person, she intensely disliked having her food interfered with.

As the man was clearly not going away, she tried to discourage him by disagreeing. Turning back to the harbor scene, she said, "I enjoy the dailiness of life on board—" Her honesty drove her to add, "—as long as I watch it from shore."

"I should not say anything against the boaties. They are our most consistent customers and bring in a steady influx of tourist dollars. Though many of them are cheap and not above stealing, the majority are rich and they have friends and relatives who might come and settle here. But I resent the waste of potential."

Janet noted in fascination how wetly he spit out words that contained "s-t." He seemed not to notice but instead became more agitated as he went on.

"Drifters and bums—able-bodied men, many of them highly educated, just gallivanting about. They seem to think that all they need to do is float and be spectators to life, never doing anything useful, never staying anywhere long enough to build anything, to grow. They tell the world to go to hell. As though they don't have a part in it. Just like Nero, fiddling while Rome burned."

His cheeks had grown red as weathered brick and his accent had become more Germanic, adding a ponderous, dogmatic quality to his sentences. Janet looked on, fascinated and repelled. His lusterless sandy-gray hair hung limp and damp over his narrow long face, which was bisected horizontally by a bristly moustache and vertically by deep, sharp grooves alongside his mouth. All the while he spoke, he cracked the knuckles of his large red hands, first one hand, then the other.

He turned suddenly, suave and relaxed, as though the ranting had never existed. "I am sorry, I have not introduced myself." Even his color changed back to the doughy gray which seemed to go with his teeth. "My name is Rudolph von der Koll. They call me Rudy." He bent his tall frame over her outstretched hand as though to kiss it, "I know you are a friend of the Stones and your first name is Janet. May I join you?"

With a complete lack of enthusiasm, Janet gestured at the chair across from her. Rudy picked up his cup and saucer and camera from the next table. Janet recognized it as an old Leica, well maintained and lovingly polished. Rudy moved it as though hardly aware of his hands doing so. They settled down to serious coffee stirring and sipping.

"So. Are you here for vacation, some diving maybe?"

Janet shrugged. "Sort of." Then she sighed in resignation. "I'm down here to do research."

"Really? How interesting."

But Janet nodded toward the buffet and Rudy jumped up to pull her chair back as she rose. They both headed for the food table.

While Janet filled her plate with scones, plantains, taro with gravy, she explained about land grant systems and why, for a social historian, a small island was perfect for proving or testing theories. She noticed his glassy look, a reaction she knew well when talking about her work with non-colleagues. To change the subject she enquired about something that looked as though it had been scooped off a sidewalk but smelled inviting. Rudy said it was one of the house specialties called conch fry, assuring her it was worth trying.

Despite her uninvited table-mate, she enjoyed the food greatly and he, clearly, was happy to be off the topic of her research. They made small talk about issues of local importance. He informed her that he worked "in real estate" and that he believed strongly in the future importance of the Caribbean area. He remained the smooth, controlled man of the world except for one short moment when, again, spittle flew and his cheeks grew mottled. Janet had not been listening and missed the transition, her attention caught by the spectacle puffy white clouds racing over the reef and her visceral, gut-level realization that she was—really—in the tropics.

"S-t-andards. And all they want is handout-s. No honor any more. Vic-t-ims with excuses, bums, is all they are."

When he felt her eyes on him he coughed once, mumbled about the decay of the modern family in a lawless state, sipped coffee and then returned to the possibilities of real estate. Half an hour later they shook hands again outside the now full terrace.

On the path that led to the marina a woman was walking. Her silhouette against the light was so lithe and beautifully proportioned, Janet caught her breath. It was Michelle, the woman she had seen shortly after arriving on island. She wished she were a painter, a photographer, anyone who could capture such beauty and grace. Von der Koll seemed arrested by the same vision, but when Janet looked at him she saw an expression of such spite she turned away from him.

After she returned to her room she lay down on her unmade bed and recalled the vision of the walking woman outlined against the morning light, her hair like a halo, her blouse filmy. The ceiling fan rotated lazily and her eyes followed the blades, absorbing the rhythm while her mind relived the vision.

Then she remembered that she had not even looked at the letter Billy had delivered to her at the airport. She pulled the pink, perfumed envelope out from under the clutter on the table. It was addressed to Miss Janet McMillan, Professor, and the back flap was embossed in flowery script, Francine Stone.

After apologies for missing her arrival, Francine proceeded with general survival suggestions. *If you need anything ask Sophie. Don't go anywhere without insect repellent,* and *Be careful of the beach, it is full of sand fleas.*

The letter ended by addressing her reason for visiting:

We are glad we can help you with your research here though I, for the life of me, cannot see what could possibly be of interest to anyone in those dusty old papers. I do look forward to your explanations. While it is true that Hamilton House has been used to store the island's archives, that, in itself cannot possibly mean much. I do believe that my brother Thomas tends to exaggerate and I just hope you will not be disappointed by what you find. My husband, Sam Stone, is an amateur historian, and he can probably be of help to you. Please come Thursday around ten o'clock and we can get acquainted. Until then, enjoy the hospitality of our humble island.

Janet shook her head. She hadn't known people still wrote this way. Suddenly she felt out of her depth, as though she was much farther from her normal world than some thousands of miles. She experienced a flash of nostalgic longing for her office, her colleagues and the fevered departmental gossip that normally she professed to hate so much.

"Time to move, or you'll turn maudlin," she said to her image in the mirror, then twisted to see what her back looked like. "Ugh, what a whale," she said out loud. "A white whale with black dots." She shrugged off the urge to feel sorry for herself. "One chambered nautilus shell and everything will be fine. I will feel better as soon as I am on the beach. I know I will."

She lathered herself with Cutters and sunscreen wherever skin came close to being exposed. She outfitted herself with her hat, shades, a water bottle, snack, and her catch-all for shells, and set out. At the last minute she grabbed the snakebite kit and stuffed it into the pack too. She had a couple of hours before her sailing date with Johnny and the beach was long and mostly deserted. Better to be prepared.

She took the short path through the resort grounds to the grandly named marina, where she had been yesterday. A dilapidated wooden dock jammed with all sorts of shore boats, a shed which contained windsurfers and other water sports equipment, and a pebbly beach constituted the whole of the marina. The Old Turtle Resort, too, was seriously afflicted by naming inflation. Maybe it was something about the island.

"Hey, Billy. Glad I ran into you. So, where did you say is the best beach to find nautilus shells?"

He looked up from sanding the barnacled bottom of a rowboat and squinted against the sun.

"Head out on this trail and keep going east. About three miles on, there is a break in the reef and then a deep lagoon, sort of like a pond. Can't miss it. But remember, no promises! They're hard to find whole this time of year. Mostly I find bits."

"Sure. Thanks."

Janet turned away, then called over her shoulder, "Just remember, if you forget about my encounter with sea urchins, I'll forget about your afternoon break." Billy had the grace to blush and look embarrassed about being seen behind the shed smoking.

She headed along a narrow trail which led through the scrub and sea grape. The gray cloud of bugs hovering six inches above her head sounded angry, as though enraged at being deprived of a meal because of her smelly exterior. The kamikaze mosquitoes were bad, but the no-see-ums were worse. The bites of the black gnats didn't itch at first but their toxin raised painful welts, as Janet had found out to her chagrin. Now she walked in relative peace, careful to avoid the long thorns of the barrel shaped cactus called Turk's Head Cactus, with its red cylindrical flower the shape and color of a fez.

Kicking up sand she said to the brush, "I, Janet McMillan of Gaylord, Minnesota, survivor of Catholic schools and dusty libraries, am strolling in paradise." She giggled and shocked herself with the sound.

Looking around furtively, she then skipped a few steps in sheer uncontainable pleasure. Stopping, she assumed an authoritative stance, hands clasped behind her back and intoned sonorously, "Doctor McMillan, I presume." Nodding gracefully in acknowledgment, she continued in the same tone, "On behalf of the American Historical Society, I would like to present you with the Livingstone Prize for your work on the socio-economic history of the Caribbean Basin."

Janet walked on a few steps. "No. In the name of the President of the United States, and on behalf of the Caribbean nations, I would like to offer you the job of ambassador at large." She tasted the sound of that, then shook her head, "I think I'd rather teach. With tenure, of course! Mr

President, I love my field, I love the crispness of thesis, research, and conclusion. Modern life is too messy for me to work with. Nice to live in, though." Having resolved the issue of how she would answer the President, she continued on contentedly.

The trail ended at the beach, broad and white, strewn with sea fans, coral, and bright fragments of shells like a pirate's treasure trove. Just above the high-water mark a line of sea grapes grew, leading to low irregular sand dunes. A tall white shaft rose on top, a running mark for boats entering the reef.

Enveloped in beauty, Janet gratefully remembered Thomas Houston, her colleague at the history department in Minneapolis. She had him to thank for the inspiration as well as the introductions. Francine Stone, author of the pink perfumed letter she had read only this morning, was his sister and Hamilton House, the island archive where she was going to do her research, was Francine's home.

Archives made her think of what she had learned so far of the island's history. Providenciales, and the whole Turks and Caicos island chain, had been passed back and forth between the Bahamas, Bermuda, the Spanish, the French, and the British ever since their discovery, which was officially marked as having been achieved by Ponce de Leon in 1512. Invasions and evictions occurred with startling frequency until, finally, the islands became part of Great Britain's territories. According to the latest Chamber of Commerce data, the island chain counted twenty-one schools, several airports, and landing strips on all inhabited islands, ten-thousand plus inhabitants and a two million dollar deficit. Its major economic resources were tourism, banking, insurance and some seafood exports.

Statistics, trends and historical dates whirled in her head but she found herself sidetracked. Out to sea, the offshore reefs broke up the large Atlantic swells so that the waves touched the shore gently, invitingly. The beach stretched bone-white as far as the eye could see. In close, the water sparkled brilliant turquoise with brown splotches where coral heads came close to the surface. It became deeper blue until it turned almost gray-blue at the outer bank where the reef fell off. White fluffy clouds dashed across the sky dancing with the white caps on the open sea.

She walked along the waterline, her eyes out for shells, while the low steady rumble of the surf breaking over the reef filled the air. When two figures rose from the lagoon like marauders, she had just tried out the introductory phrase of the first chapter of her book. "Providenciales, land of myth and mystery, land of pirates and gold, a contradiction of salt rock and paradise in the middle of the Caribbean sea."

Right out there, where the two suited, masked individuals emerged with their spears and air tanks, lay one of the major passages for the Spanish Main. Pirates and other outlaws, discarded by civilization, had had their hide-outs on this island. This was their world—arid, beautiful, jealously guarded and peopled with men who lived for the fight. Watching the two divers come closer, she realized by the silhouette that one was a woman.

"Hm, and what about women in those days?" She realized with surprise that she had not considered the question of women in connection with piracy. As an economist she was used to the fact that women were generally invisible and had to be consciously added, in order to achieve a balanced picture of a society. Piracy and treasures were so male, so Robert Louis Stevenson, that she, too, had forgotten about the female gender.

The two people were now close enough to shore to begin taking off their masks and fins. When the woman pulled off her wet suit hood and shook her curls loose, Janet recognized her with a shock. "Michelle! How nice to see you again."

When Michelle looked at her questioningly, Janet realized that they had not, in fact, officially met. Somewhat hastily she explained who she was, and how she knew Michelle's name.

Michelle said, "Andre, my husband,"

He said, *"Enchanté,"* with a little bow during which his slate gray eyes assessed her coolly and completely. Andre was a compact, wiry man with the skin of someone who spent much time outdoors. His face was the color of light Dutch tobacco and his skin looked like cured leather.

"I was just thinking about pirates and wondering what the women did, back then," Janet said, inviting them to join her fantasy. "Other than be raped and murdered I mean."

Andre squinted out toward the reef and shrugged. "The same as women do now; marry and have children, non?"

"Yes, but, what if a woman wanted adventure, didn't want to raise children? What if she wanted to become a sailor, or be a pirate herself. Would she simply pass as a man? Probably easier than being a woman pirate."

A woman, among men who had been at sea for months and were spoiling for rape, would be in constant danger. But how to pass as a man in the tight quarters of those fast, narrow brigs pirates loved so much? Looking at Michelle she said, "How would you deal with personal hygiene without being discovered, I wonder?"

Michelle did not answer but shrugged, her face a study in conflicting emotions. Janet read into it horror at the thought of passing as a man, pity for the loneliness of the women and admiration for their courage, hardly bothered by the idea that she might be wildly projecting.

They all looked out to the reef for awhile. Michelle said, "Mostly they were raped and stolen." Peeling off her wet suit she asked, "Do you want to ride back with us?"

Janet accepted. Michelle seemed a different person today, her accent more British, less French, and she herself less withdrawn. Maybe it was the presence of her husband. Janet turned back to the reef once more. The lagoon lay under the hot sun like a sensuous promise and the sand glittered with fragments of shells exquisitely colored like mother of pearl. She would most certainly come back. But this way she could visit the settlement before it was time for her appointment with Johnny from South Africa and his *Rosinante*.

Land crabs with dark red backs and purple claws scuttled across the sandy bush path up from the beach. Green lizards with eyes like gold beads slithered off the blinding white coral rocks when they got too close. The air was full of whirring from grasshoppers with dry rattling wings, underscored by the continuous dull boom of the surf. The road, when they reached it, shimmered like a mirage in the heat and pointed straight as far as the eye could see, like the spine of a long slim animal whose body, the island, was rimmed with green water.

The thing parked just off the narrow road could, by quite a stretch of the imagination, be called a car, as it had four wheels. Maybe dune buggy would have fit it better. Along its side hung a wooden sign which read "The French Connection." The floor was made of boards, the steering wheel was off a boat, and all four seats looked like they had come from a sports fishing boat.

Andre loaded the diving gear in the back and climbed into the driver's seat, lighting a filterless Gauloise as he did so. "If you have finished admiring my vehicle"—only he called it a vehi-cool—"you may climb on. Or did you change your mind?"

Michelle smiled and gestured at the back seat, then climbed in herself. When he started the car Janet recognized the unmistakable high-pitch sputtering of a Deux Chevaux engine.

They took off with a speed that, Janet was sure, was largely beyond the safety limit for the car as well as any living creature in the vicinity. But maybe the dust clouds announced to all and sundry that something was on the road because nothing offered itself to instant annihilation. The trip took only some ten minutes, and suddenly, still in shock from the hazardous ride, Janet stood in the main street of the settlement.

"How about dinner tomorrow?" Andre said in farewell. "We'll pick you up at eight."

She nodded and waved goodbye as the car roared off toward the South End and turned to look at her surroundings. She was standing in front of a large Victorian house with a pillared porch and benches set along the front wall. Gilded letters over the central door announced "Sam's Grocery" underneath which the letters "Hamilton Dry Goods" still showed vaguely. So this was the Hamilton House, where Francine lived, and the attic she was planning to spend so much time in. A handsome Victorian, fiercely whitewashed and jealously shuttered, the three story building with high, steep roofs, pillars and gingerbread carvings, stood out heavily, like the proverbial white elephant among its diminutive neighbors.

Several of the adjoining houses shared the whitewashed walls and roofs of silver coral slate which reflected the light with such brilliance that it hurt to look at them. Narrow eaves, concave and graceful lintels also of coral stone, presented a picture of planned and conscious seduction. Farther down the road the buildings became smaller and boxier, and were mostly built of planks grayed by sun and salt air until they appeared like soft hide. In the other direction Janet could see the roundabout and its monument, now totally without people or a single parked car.

She headed away from the airport. Over the top of the ten foot hill, around which the town was built, she found a cafe where she was the only customer but where the conch fritters were hot, spicy and fresh. She wanted to talk to someone local, ask about what the islanders felt about being re-'discovered' by a rich American, find out what they knew about the island's own history, about land grants and salt manufacturing. But the waitress/cook did not give her a chance to ask and no one else seemed to be about. The street outside was deserted in the noon glare and all the doors were closed.

From her table she could see a real estate office which, she assumed, had to be Rudolph von Something's domain, the angry guy she had met over breakfast. Maybe she would visit him in his office some day. Or maybe not.

Chapter Four

Johnny was waiting for her at the dock with the dinghy. Janet could see that *Rosinante* had recently been rinsed down. Its sail covers were off and the diesel engine purred smoothly, spitting exhaust water. As soon as the dinghy was lashed to the stern Johnny released the anchor rope whose end was tied to a round red float. They puttered out of the anchorage through the channel in the reef and headed downwind. Janet could feel the roll of the boat remind her stomach of the french fries and fritters she wished she had not seen, let alone eaten. But ten minutes later, when the boat heeled a steady angle to the fresh breeze and the engine was off, she began to enjoy herself. Johnny was a quiet sailing partner. He seemed content to watch the waves and sails, though he answered her questions freely.

While he did not personally know Corinne's brother he had heard of his death. "Twenty-two he was. There is so little to do on the island, so few jobs it happens all the time. Work in tourism and drugs is all."

After a long silence he added, "If I didn't have *Rosinante*, I don't know. I might end the same way."

He told her of his singlehanded trip from Johannesburg, South Africa. *Rosinante* represented a lifelong ambition and, though her interior was stark and incomplete, she was strong, built of concrete with solid telephone poles as masts. Ever since he could remember he had dreamed of going to Australia, and now he was on his way.

"When I get there I will start a different life. I'll work as a carpenter and build beautiful things. Bugger all prisons. South Africa is a country in chains and we, her people, built the jail and locked ourselves in."

They dropped anchor in about ten feet of water off a sandy spit on the island's south coast and Johnny invited Janet to swim ashore with him. "I want to show you something here," he announced.

Behind the sand spit lay a landscape which most resembled a vision of hell as might have been conceived by Coleridge, Dante and Doris

Lessing in collaboration. Sculptures of solidified sulphurous yellow foam edged against slabs of white salt crystals, and small ponds of pink brine carried on a mocking travesty of life-supporting water. A long legged white bird stood unmoving on the crumbling remains of a former footpath between the ponds. Janet could find nowhere to rest her gaze. The brilliant white of coral rocks, the blinding salt slabs and the reflection off the water hurt her eyes.

"Salt reservoirs. All over the islands there are ponds like these, where salt water has thickened into brine. In many places you can still see the windmills they used to speed up the evaporation process. Doesn't this place give you the squits!"

Johnny almost whispered but he was so emphatic, Janet burst out laughing. "That's exactly what I would have said, only I didn't know it. And what are the squits, or dare I ask?"

Johnny turned away but she saw he had turned red. "Let's walk over to the lagoon for a spell and see the caves," and without checking to see if she was following he led the way.

They passed several arrangements of coral and shells, some with food offerings. Johnny nodded in passing, "Santería altars. Just don't touch."

Janet was less impressed with the small, empty caves themselves than the desolate world around them. But Johnny's tales of pirate hoardings and modern day drug deposits made them come alive in her mind and when they walked back she could almost imagine she had actually seen treasures stacked in them. She promised herself she would use them as part of her scene-setting for her book.

It was Johnny who found a treasure on the beach—a bale of marijuana. She helped Johnny load it on the boat. They were back on board before the sun had totally set. Johnny wanted her to see the green flash. He explained how she needed to keep looking very carefully or she would miss it in the blink of an eye, literally.

While they were staring in the direction of the sunset, not daring to take eyes off it, Janet mused on the square bale strapped securely on the foredeck. Helping Johnny she figured made her an accomplice. In the process she had learned the proper terminology so she now felt she could sound as though she handled such cargo regularly. "What are you going to do with that square grouper? Are you sure you're safe with this thing on board? It wouldn't be worth risking your boat for it, would it?"

Johnny answered without hesitation, "Of course not. But, really, beachcombing is quite legal, and it does in bring some badly needed extra cash. You know, it is similar to conch fishing for Carl's restaurant. That's illegal without a commercial fishing permit but no one minds. I won't have the bale on board for long. I'll pass it on by tomorrow for sure."

"How much do you think it'll bring?

"I don't really—look, there it is!" In the excitement of the famed green flash and their heated debate on whether it had really happened or only been imagined, Janet never found out how much cash one bale of soggy weed could net.

Back at the resort and exhausted from a very full first day, Janet decided to pass on dinner, brought some fruit to her room and locked the door. She could hear the incessant cricket conversations with that constant background, the surf. Together with the humming of her overhead fan, the tropical medley made her feel bohemian and pleasantly Hemingway-esque. She began writing the story of the Salt Rock, a tale which contained the Spanish Main, pirated treasures, and the abysmal situation of women trying to scratch food from its thin soil, but soon grew impatient with the self-conscious tone of her writing. There was a very good reason she was an economist not a fiction writer! She began reading Hecksher's study on landholding systems, and Arnold Toynbee on the history of the world.

When she rubbed her eyes much later, she had turned into a cauldron of conflicting emotions. Like a script for a repetitive, bloody, TV series, the history of these islands, seemingly quiet backwaters of modern politics, exemplified the horrors of European expansionism and its obsession with wealth.

Anger was there, and shame by association, as well as consternation at the boundless European greed and ruthlessness. Sadness was there, for the destruction, the pain, and blood spilled. But also, she recognized amazement at the indomitable human spirit. After a raid the island people rebuilt their houses, buried their dead, and continued on with life. After the next invasion they did it again, and each assault left some to pick up life and create a new generation. Buildings stood mute witness to the mixed history—the Victorian next to a shack, a French chalet rubbing roofs with a model of modern American suburban fantasies. And now, in 1984, a people struggling for independence, for a separate island culture, still bucked overwhelming odds. Working hard, enjoying the sunsets, loving and laughing, the islanders represented the life force, and a hope for the future she could not help but envy in the quiet seclusion of her dark room.

Chapter Five

When Janet walked through town Thursday morning, a door opened and Rudy von der Koll popped out, smiling. "Good morning Janet, and how are you this lovely day?"

Janet nodded and slowed down.

"Since you don't seem to be in a hurry, may I show you my office?"

"Sure, I'd love to see it. How is business going this morning?"

The low wooden building was pleasantly cool inside. Lightly paneled walls and metal desks imparted a sense of airy spaciousness.

"Oh, very well thank you. See this model here," Von der Koll pointed to a large table taking up most of the center of the room. "This is our island and here is where the future Paradise Club will be. It is my dream, modeled on Club Med, only nicer. And it will be primarily financed by local money, built by local builders. In fact, it is an enormous economic opportunity for the island. And we are about to break ground."

He gestured at the framed picture of a handsome, very dark black man. "The prime minister stands fully behind the plan." Then, as an aside, "Norman and I are very good friends."

From his picture Janet's eyes traveled over the rest of the walls. Prints of available properties, mostly largish estates photographed from the air, covered about half of the wall space. Between and around them, as though they were the permanent residents among temporary interlopers, hung exquisitely beautiful black and white photos, some studio portraits, some un-posed snapshots. In front of island scenery children played, men stood talking under great clouds, and an empty building hosted lush vegetation. Her eyes came to rest upon a shot of a beautiful black woman set against a darkly looming sky. In three-quarter profile the woman looked past the camera with an expression so soft and vulnerable that Janet was almost ashamed to look. Michelle! Janet could not pull herself away. The picture filled her with an unspecified longing and a wish to protect that vulnerability from hurt.

"These are absolutely brilliant. Who's the photographer?"

Von der Koll strutted exaggeratedly and said, while cracking the finger joints of his right hand, "Oh, that is my hobby. You see, back here I have a darkroom where I do my own developing. I do weddings and funerals too, as needed."

"Congratulations. You're quite an artist."

After one more quick round of the office, Janet said, "But I do have to go now or I'll be late. Thank you so much for showing me your office, or rather, art gallery."

He bowed his head minimally and suggested, "You need not beg for a portrait if you want one. You have a lovely bone structure." Not pausing long enough for Janet to find a response, he added, "And, any time you decide to live down here permanently, do remember, von der Koll makes your housing dreams come true."

On her way out the door Janet found herself passing under a large, heavy carving which read, "Buy land. They don't make the stuff any more—Fritz Luddington." Von der Koll saw her look and informed her, "Great man that. Great vision."

She decided not to comment but mentally indulged in a pithy comeback with some rude references to cultural megalomania. The rest of the way to Hamilton House she was haunted by the memory of Michelle's picture, the poignancy of her expression, wondering whom Michelle could be looking at with so much love.

At exactly ten, Janet stood in front of the three story building again. This time she entered through a screen door which announced her passage with the clanging of a ship's bell. Inside, cool and dark, a well stocked grocery took up the street level. A set of stairs led up to the living quarters which the young clerk pointed out before Janet had even introduced herself. She climbed up the stairs, going from the smell of salt fish, flour, and pickles, to a hint of lemon furniture polish and silent afternoons.

The door at the top of the stairs stood open and led into a dusky anteroom heavy with sideboards, chests, and even an umbrella stand, which could not be of much use unless someone was into parasols. As expected, it did not hold any umbrellas, only a highly decorated walking stick fashionable in alpine Europe. The stand was made of an elephant foot. Two feet tall and hollow, she had only seen its likes in a Christie's auction catalogue. Hoping it would turn out to be fake she could not resist the temptation to touch it. Just then Francine Stone herself burst out of a side room, wiping her well-tanned and floury hands on a red and white checkered apron.

Like a cartoon series, Janet's mind flashed a set of associations. Aprons with ruffles—Mrs. Brady, or the housekeeper at Tara? Are we playing 'plantation,' with slaves and elephant leg furniture?

But then she heard Francine speaking. "Hello and welcome. I hope you did not overexert yourself. This hill can be exhausting at midday."

Francine's tone of concerned fussing sort of went with the decor. Maybe it wasn't only Janet but Francine herself who was having a problem with reality, with pulling off a consistent role in this environment?

"Come in, come in. How about an iced tea while we get acquainted? I do hope you brought yourself some dust-clothes. It is very dirty up there."

During the somewhat stiff tea, which was laid out in the kitchen so Francine's baking would not have to be interrupted for too long, Janet took a closer look. Francine was darker than her older brother Thomas whose island heritage wasn't obvious, and although seven years younger, looked every one of her fifty-five years. Sharp creases alongside her nose down almost to her chin gave her a look of dissatisfaction. But her social form was impeccable and she confessed to being impatient to hear about 'the project' as Janet had begun to call it.

"My project could most easily be compared with a study of Social Darwinism. Land grant systems illustrate the structure of society. You see, when the war of independence in America came to an end, many Loyalists were rewarded for their faith by being given tracts of land in the British colonies. Many of those who came down-island in the 1790's had visions of plantation life like what they had been accustomed to on the American mainland. Within years one can see the beginning of the conflict between agriculture and mineral extraction."

Francine stirred her tea and her eyes began to stray to the mixing bowl. "Yes, yes, and why does brother Thomas think our attic can help with all this?"

"Is it true that Hamilton House holds the island archives for maybe the last hundred years?"

"Oh yes, dear. Ever since the original Salt Tax House burned down, those papers have been stored in the attic. But no one has needed them in donkey's years, and until a central museum or a library is built, it was decided to leave things alone. Dennis Hamilton, my great-grandfather, was a well respected man and he built Hamilton House practically before there was a settlement here, in the mid eighteen-sixties. So when Salt Tax House burned down in 1870, they moved the files into the attic." As though stuffing dusty documents into their proper container Francine's hands disappeared into the central pocket of her apron.

Janet, with barely contained excitement, said, "See, there we have it. For the socio-economic history of the Caribbean Basin and, in particular, the period between the War of Independence and the Civil War, a study of the land grants and transfers is just what I need. Having an entire island's archives available—in original documents—is like a dream."

"And to think that our dusty old attic would hold such treasures. Trust me, that place has seen more treasure hunts than the island as a whole. As children we spent many summers looking for gold and pirate chests up there and all we got for our troubles were spider bites."

Dusty it was and the spiderwebs were so thick in places they looked like cloth. It was also hot. The beams cooked in the midday heat and before Janet was all the way into the attic she was thoroughly drenched. The smell was of tar and hot wood, of mice droppings and herbs forgotten and mummified. Francine followed closely on her heels and Janet got an uncomfortable feeling of being herded.

"Most of the things up here concern family history. It would be so much more convenient if we could move those Salt House trunks somewhere for you to read but unfortunately, I…" Francine's voice trailed off dispiritedly and Janet began wondering whether she actually resented her presence more than she let on.

"The Salt Tax House boxes are somewhere over there, farthest from the door. No, these are business records from the store. You can tell because the crates usually have some import label on them. Sam's books and sports trophies as well as the things of value from his family home are somewhere too. I think his boxes are labeled."

Francine's voice died down as though in despair at the magnitude of the cleanup task. Janet herself felt a passing surge of resentment. What did Francine have to get discouraged about? After all, it was she, Janet, who would dig through the accumulated minutiae of multiple lives. This was not how she had envisioned her summer, either. She realized that, prior to coming here, her 'Hamilton House attic' had looked much more like library archives—cool, shelved and with rows of boxes. Not this kind of chaos!

In an attempt to reassure herself as well as Francine, Janet said, "I'll start by checking boxes and when I have a sense of which ones I need a closer look at, I'll consult with you. Would you mind if I shifted boxes around, and maybe created piles of related materials or something?"

"No, no, no. I will help, for a while."

Janet tripped over the remains of a rocking horse and almost fell, having spied a brighter dimness at the far end of the dusty room. The window promised light and air. It, however, had become warped with years of heat, dryness, and rainstorms and Janet could not budge it.

She wiped her hands on her shorts and the streaks they left were dark and quite wet. Determined now, she pushed aside an empty suitcase, a standing lamp with a light green glass lampshade, and squeezed her way past a lump of what seemed to be carpet material.

For a couple of hours she worked in silence and mostly forgot about Francine's presence. Her help seemed to consist of staying close by the door, watching. The house creaked in the heat, heavy lumbering flies droned and mosquitoes buzzed. Janet doggedly worked a swath down one side of the attic, opening boxes and trunks if they were not labeled, separating those containing papers into a lot worth looking at later. Once or twice she noticed Francine anxiously craning for a peek into a particular trunk or chest, but they did not speak.

She did not notice when Francine finally left. By the time she creaked down the stairs from the attic, the light had changed to soft yellow from the slanting sun. She had forgotten the heat, the mosquitoes, even lunch. Her head felt as though an air pump had blown it up to twice its size, and her tongue was stuck to the roof of the mouth. Hands, arms, and legs were gray-coated and streaked. Her shoulders ached, her knees were sore and her calves did not want to unlock.

But in the meantime she had travelled years and lifetimes. While she had not—yet—encountered any boxes which looked as though they held official documents, she had touched many lives. She had fingered faded school uniforms and glimpsed fragments of letters written home by frightened, lonely children in far off boarding schools. She had unearthed birth linens and christening dresses and traced strange carvings shrouded in monogrammed kerchiefs. She had felt like a voyeur, thrilled and guilty. Just like eating chocolates, she had been unable to stop and now she felt somewhat ill.

Reaching the bottom of the attic stairs, Janet hesitated. If she did not get to a bathroom soon she would wet herself, even though it seemed she should have sweated out all liquids. The first door she tried, to the left of the stairs, held a bathroom complete with a sink with shiny silver faucets.

Janet tugged down her shorts, sat on the cool porcelain seat and stared in fascination at the color of her thighs. Where the skin had been covered by the shorts she was pinkish, everywhere else a streaky gray.

The mysteries of lives lived long ago excited her. This attic held a micro-society waiting to be raised from the dead. It allowed her to become an archaeologist, excavating the pyramids. She became the eyes which validated love and hate, the hand which marked life and death. As she realized that during her research she had been completely happy, her muscles relaxed and she streamed into the bowl with the glorious noise of a tropical rainstorm. She drowned away everything, bruises, mosquito bites and sore muscles.

By the time she was done she felt as though even her head had drained back to its normal size. Looking for the flushing mechanism she came across a horror mask on the wall. A polished silvery chain with a carved wooden handle which went with attics and aprons turned out to drain the overhead water tank and when she checked on the mask again she realized it had been herself, framed in gilt curlicues. Looking closer in the mirror she saw a specter to frighten children, hair full of spider webs with sticky gray strings dangling off her ears, a visage generally gray with streaks of darker, sweatier black, and parts of mosquitoes and dried blood stuck to the skin. The eyes were red rimmed and bulging as though water had indeed backed up into the eyeballs, and the lips had dried and cracked into variously unhealthy colors.

Janet washed her hands with soap, scrubbed her face, drank as much as she could hold and then tried to rinse off hair and neck without making a total mess of a previously spotless bathroom. And finally, regretfully, she left the retreat. Armed to meet the world, or at least enough to deflect it.

And the world was waiting. Sam had returned from his trip and the couple were decoratively perched in Victorian chairs, balancing drinks. Francine had to have heard the commotion because as soon as Janet appeared in the doorway she jumped up from her perch with a large drink in her hand, saying, "I was getting worried about you. I've been down here for hours and told Sam maybe we should come up for a look-see. But he said to leave you alone."

Janet saw something like resentment flit across Francine's face but it was gone before she had a chance to make sense of it. For a second she thought Francine was offering her a drink but realized in time that Francine was not interested in letting go of it. Considering the state of her clothing, Janet decided that she, indeed, was not fit for a social moment in a civilized setting.

"I really appreciate your letting me work in your attic and, as you can see, I should probably get going so I can clean up. I have not found the archival section yet, but even so, to a historian, your attic is a treasure trove. May I come back tomorrow about the same time?"

A few minutes later, walking toward her room, she wondered why Francine was so intent on hovering. Was she afraid of something Janet might discover, or was it just possessiveness that made her stick so close? Francine's words had made it clear that she was intensely curious about what she might have missed upstairs after she had had to go see to her husband's needs.

Her mind drifted away from Francine to the documents she was looking for. The archival records stored in the attic covered most of the 19th century, which had been a highly volatile period. One hundred and fifty years ago social upheaval shook the Western world: slaves became free, there were civil wars in America, social upheaval in France, and the decay of the Caribbean triangle trade was in full swing.

The original land grant deeds, made to the Loyalists during the American War of Independence, were stored in the islands' capital seat in Grand Turk. Providenciales had not warranted any official representation until 1820 and then, as the name Salt Tax House suggested, it functioned primarily to ensure tax payments to the British Crown. At some point she would have to go over to the archives on Grand Turk to fill in those early years.

Maybe she would have time for a swim in the lagoon before getting ready for dinner. Andre's invitation had come so unexpectedly during the roaring drive across the island that she had agreed without thinking. She regretted her impetuousness but it was too late. They were coming to pick her up by eight.

Chapter Six

The ride up to Andre and Michelle's house in the French Connection was rough and several times Janet thought Andre was going to lose the other two guests who were hanging on for dear life in the back seats. Being in the front, she had the advantage of a board to brace herself against.

When they reached their destination she decided that the ride had been worth it. She could look over the whole island with North Caicos a shadow toward the northeast and West Caicos, uninhabited and mysterious, clearly visible against the setting sun, The whole island as far as the eye could see was scrub, cactus, sea grape and rocks, surrounded by a green lagoon. At this, the highest point, the low steady rumble of the surf breaking over the reef made itself felt rather than heard.

While they had been waiting at the bar for their ride, the three invited guests had exchanged personal information in the short-hand dictated by social convention. Janet learned that the couple's boat was named *Serenade*, and that it was a forty-eight foot, fully automated Gulf cruiser. She concluded from their tone that this was good, that it was something they were proud of. *Serenade* had been moored on the island for close to two years but this would be their first time at Andre's house, too.

Chester was a portly, white-haired man with a luxurious white beard who looked like he might often be asked to play Santa Claus. His eyes never smiled, however, and his deep, authoritative voice quickly disabused notions of cuddliness. He was an oil man with several producing wells back in Texas and a family which included a wife, four kids, dogs and a station wagon. He lived on the boat for nine months of the year while the wells and the family took care of themselves. Annabelle, his travelling companion of five years, used to be a secretary and was aware of his other life, but seemed not to mind. Decades younger than Chester, Annabelle had one of those large breasted bodies that feature in the fantasies of teenage males, and are a nightmare for the women who live in them.

Annabelle grew noticeably more lively when she began to enlighten Janet about their hosts. Andre, billed as a French chef, was in fact from Marseilles, but he was not really a chef. It helped the resort, to have him billed in this way, and the job paid quite well by island standards. "Of course being a chef in a restaurant here doesn't mean much. Tourists always want lobster, or conch. When you think about it, what can you do wrong with all that fresh seafood?"

Janet did not know whether the comment was aimed only at Andre or whether the smiling, soft-voiced put-down had been directed at Janet herself, intimating that she, too, was one of those tourists who would not know a chef if they came across one. Either way, the blow had been skillfully administered and she resolved to keep well-guarded.

Annabelle's comments concerning the mysterious Michelle, using a term she pronounced with visible quotation marks, were barbed but still delivered with a smile. Originally from Martinique, Michelle was known to despise the Turks and Caicos, inhabitants as well as the islands. She was sophisticated, well-educated and utterly francophile—and somewhat immoral. Chester had raised his eyebrows at the last assessment and the conversation had moved on to safer topics.

Having arrived at the house, Andre walked ahead of his guests and with a lithe, animal grace, he bowed and bade them enter his studio. An afterthought, the studio grew out from the original two room box house. An airy octagon with windows wherever they could be fitted, it housed a cello, an old, solid gramophone and an impressive record collection. A reading chair of cracking burgundy leather and studded silver together with a small square table loaded with books were clearly the heart of the room. The book table of dark mahogany, inlaid with mother of pearl mosaics, also held a cut glass decanter and a small crystal glass, engraved AFD.

"Andre Ferrand de Devilleux," he introduced himself with a flourish, bowing from the waist with one hand behind his back, as though he had once been trained to it. "Cognac, a smoke and good music—delicacies worth dying for; and all available at Andre's—your host and guide."

Chester looked slightly ill, as though he wished he had never agreed to this excursion. Annabelle advanced through the room with her breasts jutting out like bulwarks, and Janet found herself watching them, fascinated. They delivered messages only remotely related to their owner and, though Janet became the nominal end point in Annabelle's crossing, she realized that neither the message of Annabelle's breasts nor anything else of Annabelle's, was focused in her direction. Almost visibly, waves of sexual awareness seemed to flow toward the two men standing by the decanter. Janet smiled to herself and shook her head. She had known women like Annabelle all her life and, while she sometimes felt jealous, their antics also made her feel superior.

When Michelle came through the doorway with a tray of glasses, Janet surrendered all semblance of observational superiority. Michelle was dressed simply in a muted golden wrap-around which set off her perfectly proportioned legs. In the soft light she looked exotic and sophisticated, and her smile carried a promise of unknown delights.

"Ponche," she announced. Her low voice caressed the word, accenting it mysteriously, as something delicious rather than ordinary and alcoholic, the way "rum punch" would have been. And in fact, the mixture of cane sugar, water, and lemon with two kinds of rum, was very different from what Janet had tried so far. It went with the idea of French Caribbean *savoir faire*, of wondrous women and a romantic paradise. After everyone had toasted and returned to their conversations, Michelle, slender and graceful, disappeared again.

The talk, superficial and scarcely heeded, moved from the weather to the state of the roads to the weapons-and-drug bust at the old settlement. Janet remembered the people milling around the settlement when she drove by with Billy on her way from the airport. It appeared to be a small bust, not worth the energy of more than a couple of sentences.

She watched more than she participated and felt that a great deal was going on below the surface without her. She uncovered one obvious source of tension during the dinner, at which she found herself placed between Andre and Michelle. Andre announced to the company, seemingly playful and tolerant, that Michelle was not interested in reefs or diving, nor, principally in Andre himself. Still smiling, he added, raising his glass to her, "But I am a white man and we are married. As my dear wife's plans do not include penury or disgrace to the family—*alors, voila*."

Everyone toasted as though it were a joke and Michelle's face did not reveal her thoughts. Overall, she was an attentive hostess and mostly listened to the others. Once Andre began to relax he turned out to be an entertaining storyteller. As intrepid a diver as he was a constant Gauloise smoker, he acted out, with flair and panache, his tales of arrogant, foolish, rich tourists and his own daring exploits in diving.

When Michelle brought in the main course, a bouillabaisse à la Martinique, their equanimity failed once more. Andre explained that the dish was a culinary adaptation to exile, developed between the two of them after years of trial and error, a "fruitful intercultural melange of French memory and Caribbean know-how."

To which Michelle added, smiling sweetly, "Andre's part does not, however, include the hands-on. He says his job has spoiled for him the pleasure of inventive preparation."

Janet almost missed the quick flash of anger that blackened Andre's face like a storm cloud, but the grimace which distorted Annabelle's smile was unmistakable, and surprising. Only Chester missed the whole exchange as he was fully occupied with spreading lobster eggs onto a piece of toast.

Those two, Annabelle and Andre, are having an affair, Janet suddenly realized. And Michelle knows it. Does she mind? Does Chester know?

The food seemed to direct the conversation toward the sea and its economic potential. Soon the men's voices grew louder, but Andre held the floor, expounding on his favorite topic. "As part of the Bermuda triangle, our reefs are full of wrecks, sunken treasures and, even corpses. You all heard of the Molasses Reef wreck, *certainement*? It is the one they say might have been Columbus' ship Pinta? But wreck diving is not a sport."

Overriding both Michelle and Chester, Andre continued, stubbornly insisting on his point that there was no skill involved in wreck diving since the target did not try to escape. You found the wreck, dove on it and removed what could be taken.

Annabelle spoke up before Chester could grab the conversational gauntlet, and asked Michelle, "Isn't that a brother of yours, young Mark Sanders, the professional wreck diver?" Fluffing her hair as though indicating distress, she smiled sweetly.

Andre said loudly, with one of those Gallic shrugs as though that settled everything, "*Eh bien, voila.*" At which point Janet decided that she disliked Andre and that his conversational use of French terms was deliberate and unnecessary.

As Michelle did not rise to the bait the conversation drifted onto another topic. Janet, for a while, tried to watch for physical signs of the affair but finally she got bored and decided to just enjoy the food.

Once, when Michelle passed her chair on the way to the kitchen, Janet felt fingers caressing her exposed neck. The touch had been so delicate, she wasn't sure she hadn't made it up, and only the goosebumps that rose along her spine made her believe it. Janet had just brought up the name "Midway" and Sophie's complaint of the prevalence of drugs on the island.

She heard Andre answer, in the tone of a recital of a prepared piece, his accent slight for once. "The politicians' posture but everyone knows drugs are the main Caribbean economy. If Great Britain will not invest some real money, it will just get worse. We cannot pay our politicians enough to keep them from getting involved with the drug trade."

Glancing around the table Janet noticed that Andre was prepared to carry on speaking. Chester, his eyes unreadable, swirled the wine in his glass, while Annabelle placed watermelon seeds as though she planned to build a mosaic on her plate. Behind her she could hear Michelle rattle cups in the kitchen and, suddenly, she felt the need for movement. She pushed her chair back on the tiles with a screech, felt herself blush and followed the clinking of dishes into the kitchen.

"Can I help? You've done such a wonderful job and the food was absolutely delicious. How about you take a break and I clean up here?"

Janet began stacking dirty dishes on the counter to clear a space to work from, while wondering what topic would draw this mysterious creature into a conversation. She tried again. "Do you know Billy well? Remember he and I met you by the airport on Tuesday?"

Michelle, her back to Janet, shook her head and rattled the Italian coffee maker some more. When she finally turned around, her eyes seemed somewhat reddened but she was quite composed. "Ah, oui, I came to pick up painting material from the plane."

For what seemed like a long time, Janet rinsed dishes and thought of possible topics. After a while Michelle said, with a cold fury Janet had not imagined from her, "Drugs, weather and politics is all they talk!" Leaning against the stove as if forcing herself to relax, she then asked, "What do people speak of, where you live?"

"Weather and university politics?" Janet joked and was gratified to see a mocking smile acknowledge her attempt at lightening the atmosphere.

"Not drugs?"

"Well, not often. Here, I do get the sense that four hundred years of piracy has influenced what is considered acceptable table conversation. If you had your druthers, what would people discuss, instead?"

"Films, books, paintings?"

"Ouch! That's hard to find other than in Woody Allen movies. I rather think you wouldn't enjoy our faculty parties either. Being academics, we are supposed to be interested in those kinds of topics. But I think we talk more of food and sex than art."

"What do you teach?"

"Economics and history, in Minneapolis. You know Francine and Sam Stone?" When Michelle nodded, Janet continued, "Well, Francine's brother, Thomas Houston, is a colleague of mine and he put me on to the archives in Hamilton House."

"What is there?"

"I study land grant systems and Hamilton House holds original documents possibly as far back as several hundred years."

Michelle smiled incredulously, which made Janet add, "When the old Salt Tax House burned down in 1870 they are said to have moved all the files into Hamilton House. God knows what I'll find. I went there today and the attic is huge. I have my work cut out just to get to the material, let alone study it."

"Careful with Francine!" Michelle said with intensity. "She can be very mean to people." She seemed to want to add something but instead turned away. At that moment the light fell across her profile just as it had in the photo, and Janet found herself flooded by something like homesickness. She wanted Michelle to look at her the way she had in the photo. She wanted to have known her for years. The wish hit her with such force it made her knees buckle.

"Janet? Are you all right?"

Michelle's face was scant inches away, the large luminous eyes were full of reflected lights, her narrow long-fingered hand rested warm on Janet's arm.

"Sorry," Janet moved back against the sink instinctively. "I'm fine."

"You look faint. Here, drink some water."

The water was cold and Janet pressed the glass against her forehead. "Thank you. I'm really OK. Where were we? Oh, yes, Francine and Hamilton House. The theory of landholding systems. And economics, as it can be used as the fulcrum of society." She drank some more, wondering why she was babbling on about fulcra and system analysis.

"You sound like my brother Mark does sometimes. Only he says how a society works can be seen through drugs."

" Speaking of which, did you know the young man who died recently? He was related to Corinne who works at the Old Turtle Resort?"

"Yes, Corinne's brother. He was nice. He did not OD the way they— Oh, *merde*."

The coffee was boiling over and Michelle began wiping the mess before it dried all around the burner.

"Michelle, so tell me what do you do?"

But the rattling of dessert plates covered Janet's question and when Michelle turned to her with an armful of plates she said, "Let's speak of something else. Are you married?"

Here it was. The question that seemed to follow her ever since she had turned thirty. But Michelle did not have the pitying, solicitous look that went with the question when it came from her parents' friends.

"No. It just never seemed to be the time, or something. I was too busy studying, then writing and teaching. And—" Self-conscious, she picked apart an orange rind.

Michelle reached out to lift Janet's chin with one hand and smiled at her, nodding once as though to say, "It's OK." Out loud she said only, "Here, you take this. Time to go face the lions, eh?"

Janet took the tray full of cups, saucers and a fruit plate from Michelle and together they carried everything into the studio. Annabelle and the two men followed them out from the dining room without interrupting their conversation.

Chester, much more relaxed now that he had cigar, cognac and coffee, displayed his local knowledge. "Not quite two-hundred square miles, these here islands are a treasure of history. I am an oil man myself, and I can appreciate enterprise and resilience."

Addressing Janet as though he were about to impart a secret, Chester lectured on. "Did you know that for three hundred years these here islands have kept themselves going on salt exports, sisal fiber harvesting, and piracy? I have even heard of plans to sell bat guano from the caves. Nobody can tell me there isn't oil here, too—if anyone were to look. Caves, salt veins and the proximity of volcanoes down-island—it's ideal. As a rule, islanders are just too lazy," expansively gesturing with his fat square hands around the room, "present company, of course, excepted. I am talking history here."

Andre smoothly refilled Chester's glass and, while Chester's mouth was busy around his cigar, launched into a dramatic refutation, his French accent thickened by alcohol, or emotion. "Ah, non! For hundreds of years, killing, robbing and adventuring has gone on here and for me—*quel paradis*. I dive, I chase sharks, find treasures or explore underwater caves. I can be hundreds of years old before I have to dive one place a second time. I am glad entrepreneurs like Chester are not working here but only visiting."

Superficially relieved by laughter, the conversation idled and Janet used the time to try to make sense of this exchange. Andre had a job here, a house and a wife, and maybe a mistress. What about the others? Annabelle was, possibly, busy with her two men and, being a well-behaved female, she would go and live wherever Chester wanted to. But what was Chester doing here on his fancy yacht? Why would he settle in such an out-of-the way place instead of the Bahamas or Antigua, where the yachting action was? And Michelle, what did she do here, other than be married to Andre? Who were her friends, what kept her on this dry salty rock of an island? From the depth of her leather chair Janet glanced in Michelle's direction and caught a most brilliant private smile that warmed her down to her toes.

When she dialed back into the conversation it had snagged upon British colonialism. Andre emphatically dismissed the notion of "the white man's burden" as British imperialist romanticism.

"We never let go of Colonies. In France, we intermarry and make everyone *citoyens*, and we send the military when there is a decision to be made. The children in Martinique and Guadelupe learn more of France than of the Caribbean. But the British, *eh bien*. They pay for education and roads, pull up their socks and look the other way. As long as their club makes gin and tonics and keeps people out who don't belong, they just keep on."

Every so often Chester tried to interrupt but Andre was not to be stopped. What had set him off, it seemed, was that road taxes had been raised over the last several months. Next to the Prime Minister, the Minister of Public Works and utilities came in for the most vicious attack.

"They dare do that to us who work, while all they do is run the drugs. I do not say drugs are horrible. Piracy is a venerable tradition. But elected officials must be more private. Corruption needs finesse. *Le ministre* must not be caught with his hands in the jar. Until he retires, at least."

By the time Janet returned to The Old Turtle it was late and the reception area was deserted. On the way to her room her spine tingled and the hair of her neck stood up with the feeling that somebody was watching her. Even with the door locked and the curtains drawn tight she felt uneasy, but soon the long day and too many drinks won and she fell asleep.

Chapter Seven

Francine was wearing a kerchief around her hair when Janet showed up at ten the next morning. Its paisley pattern was repeated in an apron with puffy sleeves and white piping. "Things get so dusty here in no time at all, I am sometimes tempted to just let it all go." But the duster in her hands combined with the stalking glint of her eyes bespoke the lie.

"I'll just get myself upstairs then. Don't bother, I know the way." Janet smiled and edged around Francine.

"No, no, I'll come with you." The duster was abandoned, and the two women filed up the steep stairs. "By the way, dear, Sam wants to meet you, officially. So, what do you say you come for foursies?"

Looking down on Francine from several steps higher, Janet slowed and frowned.

"You know, four o'clock tea?"

Actually, Janet had not known. And she did not really want to. That would mean she would have to quit early, get to the hotel to change, and be back by four. But there was nothing to be done about it. Her hosts had beckoned.

She went to work. Francine stayed the whole time. A neutral witness or a quiet enforcer? Sometimes Janet felt as though she was suspected of lusting after family valuables and wished she knew what they were. For much of the time Francine kept up a light patter of conversation neither of them paid much attention to. Whenever Janet tried to engage her on the early history of the Hamilton family, Francine was rather vague. She seemed more at ease with the recent developments, the lives of her brothers and her children, Sam's family.

Finally, after hours of moving furniture, boxes, and old paintings, Janet encountered a set of wooden boxes bound with sisal rope and stamped with official looking numbers and a letter series. She had found part of the Salt Tax House records.

By four, cleaned up and dressed in a light frock, Janet found herself in the shadowy, immaculate living room sunk in the depths of an over-stuffed chair well protected with doilies.

"How has your visit to our island been, so far?" Sam was mixing drinks at the ornately outfitted house bar.

"Wonderful, thank you. Everyone is so friendly and welcoming. And, of course, the island is breathtaking."

Sam turned toward Janet with a beautifully cut crystal glass of gin and tonic and asked, his sweeping arm indicating the island, "What have you seen of it?"

"Oh, lots of beautiful underwater scenery as I swim everyday. I have walked some of the island, and I've sailed around to the south coast with a new friend who showed me salt ponds and some caves."

"Ah, salt, yes. The mysterious edible rock. Core ingredient to civilization, salt is the child of the sun and the sea."

Janet wondered for a minute whether he was joking. But Sam looked as drawn and wooden as an undertaker and she decided to play it safe. She nodded politely.

"Try some of these," Francine urged, "I've just finished making them."

Janet took two of the delicate mini-sandwiches and asked, "How on earth do you find cucumbers here?"

Francine almost preened. "On Grand Turk they have real stores, so whenever we go there I stock up."

Sam said, "Did you know that the original folk tale behind King Lear dealt with salt?" Janet looked over at him sitting on the sofa in story-telling pose. "The youngest daughter of the king tells him that her love is not like silver or gold but rather like salt. He throws her out of the palace in a rage."

At Janet's puzzled look, he explained, happily, "It was too base a comparison for a king, and he assumed she was ridiculing him. But at her wedding, to which the king is invited without recognizing her, he finds a feast which is utterly inedible, because it was prepared without a grain of salt! He begins to cry for his daughter, realizing, finally, that she had been right all along. Et cetera, et cetera. You can imagine the end. Without salt life would be tasteless, flat and dull."

Passing the serving plate around again, Francine smiled somewhat too brightly. "Yes, Sam is very interested in the history of salt and its procurement. He is practically an authority on it."

Rather than discouraging Sam, this seemed to inspire him to further elaboration. Janet was trying to draw Francine into a conversation on the house's history but Sam was not to be distracted. He began talking of the long history of salt harvesting in the Turks and Caicos Islands, of the uses to which salt had been put, and finally, when Francine began stacking the dishes in clear indication she felt a need for change, he pressed on with salt trivia. He solemnly stated that putting salt under a witch's cushion prevented her from sitting down.

Janet could not resist the comment, "This must come in handy at crowded parties. Sort of an invisible test. I suppose I can consider myself lucky I managed to sit. Talking of luck, what can you tell me about the history of Hamilton House?"

"Were you aware that road salting in the United States has become so widespread that it amounts to a redistribution of terrestrial salt? In 1974 they used thirty-three kilos of salt per person, on roads—"

Francine finally interrupted, telling Janet that the house cornerstone bore the date 1864 and if Janet wanted to see it she would be happy to show her.

"The basement has a sunken storage place for 30,000 bushels of salt and next to that a tank for about 25,000 gallons of rainwater from the roof, plus a storeroom for drying conch meat." Sam moved smoothly into the conversation.

For a while the topic was food preservation techniques, about which Francine knew a lot. "We have not had refrigeration for long. We used to dry everything. Fish, conch, octopus, even lobster meat. But that didn't work out as it did not reconstitute too well."

At that point Sam interjected a comment which showed he was still caught up with his pet topic which complicated the conversation considerably. "Men can live without gold but not without salt."

Janet was beginning to wear out. But Sam was still going strong. "Since you're a historian you might know that Humphry Day first separated the components of common salt in 1810. He could not possibly have foreseen the horrors he unleashed. Chlorine and sodium, as poisonous and corrosive as they were, represented only the beginning. The PCBs will kill us yet."

But even Francine seemed to gain a second wind. She began talking of the pleasures of living on a small island, of the safety and good air.

"Sam says that the values are clearer in a smaller society and I agree. It does get lonely, though. And I do miss my women friends sometimes."

A quick glance at Sam seemed to reassure Francine, as she continued, "Three of my friends live close to one another in Tallahassee. And they go on trips together, call each other up all the time. They are all widowed. And…" A wistful expression came over her face like a shadow, but then she focused on Sam, her eyes drawn like iron to a magnet. "Dear, would you mind refreshing our drinks? It has been such a dry day."

"Over seventy percent of our body mass is saline," Sam said as he collected everyone's glass. "Desiccating and water soluble, common salt attracts water and is changed by it. An eternal puzzle which preoccupied the alchemists greatly."

This contradiction caught Janet's attention and she missed Francine's next comment. "Excuse me, I was thinking about something else."

"And when you find the documents, what then?"

Janet stretched her legs and thought for a minute. "I will write a paper about my findings. I hope to turn it into a book on Caribbean Basin landholdings. I need to have one out pretty soon or I won't get tenure, you know?"

Francine looked polite and glazed, brightening at the sight of her drink. During bartending Sam had refound his energy and he held up his arm for attention and said, "You see my dears, salt is a highly dynamic substance. It both alters itself *and* causes change. It comes out of the sea, like Aphrodite. It is exciting, dangerous, and gives pleasure. Just like sex."

"Sam, please!"

Janet had not seen that side of Francine before, but Sam quietly sat back on the couch. Smiling tersely, Francine white-knuckled her glass and for a while no one spoke.

Luckily a knock interrupted and the young clerk from downstairs poked his head into the living room. "Mr. Chappell to see you, sir."

"Ladies, excuse me for a few minutes. I will be right back." Sam straightened his vest and disappeared through the door. Francine looked put out but tried to smile. "Ah, men. Always something that cannot wait, no matter that it is the end of the week and we are having a visitor. Now, where were we, dear?"

Janet could only remember having salt and sex paralleled and she did not wish to remind Francine of that. Then snapping her fingers in sudden recollection, she asked, "What is the meaning of flamingo feathers here on the island?"

"What flamingo feathers?" Francine suddenly looked alert and worried.

"I meant to ask you yesterday, and forgot all about it. I came across this trunk with a painted lid, with the monogram D. H. 1843. Smaller than a ship's trunk, more like a girl's hope chest, and in a pocket inside the lid it held this piece of ancient linen with five beautiful flamingo feathers."

Francine turned on her with sudden fury. "I really must ask you not to poke into our family's keepsakes. As my brother Thomas—to my dismay, I don't mind telling you—has encouraged you to come here, I will do my best to make the attic available so you can find your documents, but I would greatly appreciate if you confined your curiosity to the boxes you came here to inspect."

Janet felt as though she had been slapped. This was a very different voice, a person she had not seen before. "I'm sorry. I didn't know I was trespassing."

Just then Sam entered the room and returned to his seat on the sofa. He looked over at Francine, a worry line deepening in his mournful undertaker's face at the look of her stiff, still presence. "What is she talking about, dear?" Not getting any response he turned to Janet and, as though realizing his chance, he appealed to her. "You really should write a history of salt instead of people or land. Much more satisfactory."

Francine seemed to have recovered, and when Sam took a breath, she interrupted, saying, "In fact, dear, when you came in we were talking about flamingos."

Almost smiling in his desire to be of service, Sam filled in. "Flamingos used to stop here often on their voyage south. Throughout the nineteenth and early twentieth century they nested on Mayaguana. Their feathers were used in spirit ceremonies and came to represent the power of love and beauty. But the flamingos were easy prey, hunted close to extinction, and now they have not been seen on the island for many years."

Like a proud parent, Francine smiled at Sam, then looked at Janet as if to say, "You see how good he is?"

Sam, in the meantime took up where he had left off as though the encouragement he'd received permitted him to tell this final, essential story. "Really, a history of salt would be fascinating. Volatile and dangerous, it is a substance that makes life worth living. Did you know that, in old Europe, impotence used to be cured by having a rowdy bunch of women publicly salt the offending or, rather, disobliging member?"

When Sam began talking, Francine got up and went over to one of the windows to rearrange a house plant which seemed perfectly fine. Her face was grim and stiff as though carved of wood and two feverish round red spots had appeared on her cheeks. Sam glanced over at her and his voice lost volume in direct proportion to the intensity with which she tore off leaves.

The phone rang shrilly twice, then twice again, and Sam and Francine, who had both frozen to attention, relaxed. Sam explained to Janet as an aside, "We're on a common phone line and that is not our ring. But of course, if no one answers sometimes you end up taking messages anyway. Party lines are the one drawback of simple island living in the midst of modern technology."

Janet took advantage of the moment's lessened tension and got up quickly, thanked both of them and insisted on carrying the dirty dishes into the kitchen.

Francine, while seeing her out, said distractedly, "About your attic work in the near future, let me see." Her polite, eager tone was back as though the prior interchange had never happened. "The weekend does not work well for us, and Monday we are both to go to Middle Caicos. So, how about Tuesday?"

"Great. That will give me the chance to take a trip to the library down in Grand Turk, for a first check of what's there. And I really am sorry about the chest."

Francine did not respond to this, but made what felt like an insincere expression of her pleasure at meeting her and disappeared back inside the house.

Halfway down her dusty walk Janet grumbled about being treated like a child out of line. "What's Francine's beef about the attic? Why did she agree to have me do my research at all, if she feels this way about her family heirlooms?" For the rest of her walk she amused herself imagining what it would be like to live with a party line system. "It must cut down on gossip if you can never be sure who's listening in. But how would you ever keep a secret, or conduct a hot affair?"

Back at the resort, Corinne was on duty, looking regal with her head cloth and an ankle length dress of Dominican fabric setting off her glossy black skin. Janet, heading for the bar, found her staring out toward the sea, idly flipping a string of beads.

"I'm sorry about your brother," Janet said. Corinne nodded coolly but did not answer, waiting for Janet to go on. Janet gazed at the sea for a while, then said, "I need to get to Grand Turk as soon as possible. How do I go about it?"

Corinne looked at Janet speculatively. "There is the Thursday ferry. But it won't return until the following week."

"That's way too long. Where is one supposed to stay for all that time?"

Corinne shrugged. "Well, you stay with people, mon. And you stay there instead of here, probably cheaper. And if you don't like that, you go on the ferry, then come back by plane when it lands on Grand Turk. That one goes from Nassau, Grand Turk, Middle Caicos, then here, on Tuesday."

They were both quiet. Janet had found she learned more by waiting than by asking questions or begging.

"Or you can go with someone here. I ask some people and let you know." Corinne flipped her beads again, intent on the curve they formed flying through her fingers. "Maybe my cousin would take you. He is known as Fast Freddy. For his boat. And he will get you there and back."

Corinne inspected Janet as though weighing whether she could be relied upon not to damage Fast Freddy's boat, or his reputation. She shrugged, "If he decides to take you, you get yourself to the East End. He cannot pick people up in town."

They agreed on Sunday afternoon. If Freddy agreed to ferry her, Janet would be in charge of getting herself over to the East End. Corinne added, "Can't miss him, he's the tallest and the blackest, with the fastest speed-boat around."

The bar was buzzing and Janet took her rum punch out on the deck where, while not quiet, it was not quite as loud. She had brought one volume of Arnold Toynbee and a small treatise on Caribbean history. The light in the west changed to orange, then purple and finally pink and the gas cylinders began hissing, and still Janet read.

The voices had been loud for quite some time but, engrossed in her reading, Janet had blocked them out. Now they were coming closer and she looked up. A tall beefy, red faced man was backing out of the bar, his neck corded below the wet dark hair plastered to his skull. "I'll get you, you bastard, and you won't have a friend left in the islands when I get done with you. Shark bait will be too good for your sorry carcass."

A slender, handsome mulatto—the word came automatically to mind since she had just been reading about the variations of color distinctions—followed close on his heels.

"Look, Chappell, why don't you go home and sleep it off. Maybe if you paid a little more attention to your wife, she would not—"

Before he could finish his sentence, the redfaced man hauled out and punched the other fully in the face. A couple of other men got into shoving matches and for a while it was not clear who was trying to fight and who was trying to break it up. Glass broke, punches thudded on flesh, and chairs crashed and broke. Janet saw Chappell pinned by three men who stumbled toward the door with him in the middle. The slender man, whose name Janet found out was Mark, was bleeding all over his white shirt. One of the waiters brought him a towel with ice in it as calmly as though the brawl had not even happened.

The melee spread from the bar to the deck. Janet vaulted over the deck rail to avoid a launched chair flying perilously close to her head. In her haste she forgot she was still wearing her reading glasses and miscalculated the distance. Instead of jumping agilely she landed on her rump, the wind knocked out of her. She lay watching sparkling lights and listening to the fight while the night spread velvet dark and bright, innumerable stars above her.

Not far from her on the other side of the rail, Janet heard a woman's gasp, a thud, then a man's voice, "Oh, knock it off you idiot. Go get Rudy over there, he's the one you want to square off with."

While she was still on her back wheezing and trying to get her wind back, she heard an authoritative voice. "That is enough. Everybody break it up. Break it up. There, now. That's enough."

The scuffle calmed, the chairs creaked when they were put back on the floor. Janet fumbled for her glasses which had landed close by, wiped the sand off the back of her shorts and legs, and stood up as though she had just come in and surveyed the scene.

There was some broken glass, some unattached chair legs, some people bleeding and some holding their heads, elbows or knees. But no one was prostrate and handsome Mark still victoriously held the middle of the floor with his ice pack. Janet climbed back over the rail and reclaimed the table where her book still lay waiting. Many people did the same and within minutes the place looked like a normal mid-week island bar except that there were snatches of conversation about the fight.

She gathered that Mark's nose was not broken, that Chappell had gone home, that three local men and two tourists had been arrested and were now being led to the police station and that Rudy von der Koll had lent his Olds to transport the prisoners. But she did not hear anyone speculating on the meaning of Mark's comment concerning the other man's wife.

After one more rum punch accompanied by bar appetizers instead of dinner, Janet turned in. Her walk was uneventful and she did not feel like she was being watched. Relieved, and sore from her landing, she stripped off her shorts and shirt and climbed under the sheets. She soon dreamed of a romantic sail with an indeterminately gendered person, at whose side, she knew, she was going to spend eternity. Only, she never could see the person's face.

Chapter Eight

Saturday's sunrise found Janet awake. Her heart was light and fluttery when she thought of the day ahead. Momentarily the image of Tony flashed through her mind, how much he would love the idea of catching lobster, how he would look in his tight Speedo suit with well defined muscles tanned a dark glossy bronze. But, with a start, she realized she was glad he was not here. And not only because he had left her so long ago. She wanted to have Michelle to herself. Meaning what? Forcing herself to stay with the fluttery excitement, she remembered Michelle's caressing touch at the dinner party. It still made her body tingle, made her want to turn toward that hand like a sunflower toward the light. She had never felt that way about anyone before. Tony had accused her of being cold and castratingly ambitious. Though it had hurt, she'd known he was right in some way. Relationships simply had not taken that much space in her life. They were too messy, too volatile, and she had never totally committed herself. She used to say her heart was committed to her students, her career. And now?

The only thing she was sure of was her book, the basis for her tenure review. Pushing away the disturbing question of how Michelle could have become so central to her, or why, she decided to get to work. The list of subject areas she wanted to check out at the library focused her mind, and the excitement of being this close to source material that existed nowhere else made her feel tingly inside. She regretted having to leave for the bank, but by nine o'clock she stood in line at Barclay's to get cash for the trip to Grand Turk.

When the bank door opened, the people scattered chaotically and she found herself blocked by a solidly fleshed white man who smiled at her expectantly. She smiled back, absentmindedly, and started around him to find the tellers. But he was not to be deterred. He stuck out his red meaty hand and moved it up and down in a pantomime shake.

"Ah, sorry, yes. Good morning. I need to cash some travellers' checks."

"Good morning and welcome. I am Mr. Bob Chappell, Vice President of Barclay's Bank, Turks and Caicos Branch. Anything you need, just ask for me."

Now she remembered where she had seen him last. He was the one at the bar who had punched Mark in the nose. He did not seem to remember her and she did not wish to remind him. Now, as though satisfied with the present encounter, he looked around his domain and, spying something untoward, marched off to harass a hapless young teller. Even though he spoke barely above a whisper his neck and ears grew redder by the word, and the teller shrivelled correspondingly.

To Janet's surprise and delight Michelle stopped by in the morning honking the French Connection, and invited her to go diving for conch. Johnny was waiting for them to help him.

Michelle drove them to the eastern end of the island where she parked right by the pier and they waded from the beach to the whaler. Her driving was only marginally slower than Andre's and Janet was beginning to appreciate the feeling of adventure which accompanied every ride in the contraption called the French Connection.

The white sand glittered brilliantly through the light turquoise water and every time Janet set her foot down it set off a sugary cloud swirling around her calves. She kept her eyes carefully on her path, avoiding sting rays or coral patches, particularly those with sea urchins. When she climbed over the side of the squarish aluminum boat it hardly rocked, which made her feel light, agile and capable. Suddenly she was looking forward to the trip, no longer afraid about her lack of diving experience but convinced she'd do just fine.

Johnny was waiting in the whaler and greeted the two women with a wide grin, "Lucky me, out with the island's two most beautiful women."

Since the water was going to be shallow, mostly about twelve feet deep, they did not need scuba tanks. They carried snorkels and masks along with their fins and a view bucket through which to spot their prey before diving in. While they were puttering out into the bay Janet told them about the bar fight the night before. Johnny was distracted by his navigation, but Michelle encouraged her rendition of flying chairs.

Suddenly Michelle blanched as though just realizing what she had heard. "Who did Bob Chappell punch?"

Only when Janet began describing the handsome mulatto they had called Mark, did it dawn on her that he was Michelle's diver brother, Mark Sanders.

After being assured that Mark had not been seriously hurt, Michelle declared with great intensity, "*Le pauvre vieux*. He does not know what he is up against. What did he say about Charlotte, Mrs. Bob Chappell?"

Janet could not add much, other than to repeat the comment, "'If you paid more attention to your wife—'"

Michelle muttered, "*Salaud*." But whether she was talking of Mark, Bob Chappell, or maybe even Charlotte, the wife, Janet could not guess. Michelle did not answer when Janet asked what Mark's comment meant.

Some time later Michelle said, "He is my older brother but we are very different. We even have different last names. He grew up with Papa on the other side of Martinique and I only got to know him here on Provo, really."

Janet took the proffered chance and asked, "How did you learn English so well?"

"You are teasing me! I know I speak with a terrible accent and when I get excited I mix up words more."

"No, no, I mean it. I don't speak anything but English, and as the British say, not even that correctly."

Michelle smiled and waved away the compliment, then said, "I need people and words to understand myself."

When they were about five hundred yards into the bay Johnny began checking the ocean floor with the view bucket. He gave a signal and Michelle dropped the anchor. The water was completely clear, about two fathoms deep, the bottom mostly sandy or covered with eel grass. Janet could see fish dart and grasses weave through the view bucket. The anchor settled in a dusty cloud, bit, and held.

They all geared up and rolled over the side. Michelle showed Janet how to look for the winding, aimless trails at whose end a conch usually lay buried. Underwater Janet's reflection wobbled on the silvery undersurface, and from all around her rose the sound of thousands of shellfish feeding, like an army cracking nuts. She swam easily along the bottom and picked up the crusty cone-shaped shells in both hands.

In an hour they collected enough to supply the restaurant for a week.

Michelle and Johnny had also grabbed some twenty or more of the spiny, clawless lobsters which they called crawfish. They were numerous, walking underwater over the sand like families out for a Sunday stroll. The trick was to grab them from the back, behind the head, and keep away from their snapping tails. They looked and sounded quite fierce, and Janet contented herself with the comparatively motionless conch.

They unloaded their catch into the large concrete holding tank at the end of the pier. Janet was gazing across the tank toward the reef when a brightly colored piece of flotsam caught her eye. Something blue and yellow had lodged in the rough concrete at the seaward corner. Janet climbed out of the whaler and floated over to the spot which held what seemed to be a small doll. Michelle, having followed with her eyes asked, "What is it? Please bring it over so I can see."

Janet picked it off the wall and recoiled at the way it felt, soft and squishy, somehow repulsive. Without wasting any time she returned to the boat and handed the doll to Michelle who froze, then dashed it onto the deck with a wail.

Johnny straightened up and asked, "What the bleeding hell is going on?"

Michelle stammered, "*C'est*...it's horrible. It's too realistic! It's...Rudy von der Koll."

Still in the water and half leaning over the transom, Janet made herself look at the thing again. "But, what is it...? What does it mean?" She felt her stomach turn, partly because of the chewed up face of the doll staring at her from the bottom of the boat, partly in response to the tension coming off Michelle who answered, "Magic. Santerìa, Voodoo—*tu sais*?"

The gray painted eyes of the doll stared straight up into the sun which glinted off the fish hook that went into one pupil and exited the other. About six inches long, the doll was dressed in long pants and a white top and had lank blond hair. The cloth had the initials "VDK stitched on the left, like a monogrammed shirt pocket, and a camera was sketched hanging by a strap. What made the doll horrible was that it had been fashioned from bait, from something which crawfish liked. After having been in the holding tank for awhile, it's face and arms were now those of a deformed half-devoured monster with loose flesh dangling from its wounds. Between the doll's legs, where his penis would be, a single, detached, crab claw clutched the soft flesh. And sewed into its left arm stub was a single dark gray pebble.

Janet winced and held her breath until she heard Johnny say, "A von der Koll doll. A message to the budding real estate baron? I think we could safely say it was not a friendly one."

Janet asked, "Who would do such a thing, and why?" No one answered.

Finally, Johnny looked at both women in turn. "What do you think? Should we show it to him or do we consign it to the sea?"

Michelle shuddered with repulsion and jerked her head in the direction of the reef. Janet shrugged undecidedly and Johnny tossed the remains as far into the lagoon as he could. Thoughtfully, he said, "Rather nasty end this one. I might tread carefully if someone did one about me. But, then, that's partly why he's rich and I am not, wouldn't you say?"

They unloaded the rest of their catch without saying much but the rhythm of work seemed to settle everyone. They rinsed the whaler, pulled it out of the water and carried it above the high tide mark. Johnny accepted a ride back to the marina and after a short, silent drive they arrived back at the Old Turtle.

Johnny, with a final wave, headed toward the dock while Michelle offered to fix Janet lunch back at her house. "As long as it isn't seafood. I don't think I could stand any right now."

Michelle laughed, "*Ma cherie*, you are a woman of my heart. I was thinking of a lovely, greasy, fiery hot Cuban sausage with callaloo and allspice."

After lunch, the empty dishes sat forgotten on the ground by their chairs and music rolled out of the open windows as a cool breeze caressed them. They sat in companionable silence, underlined rather than broken by bits of conversation. The reality of violence seemed to have been left behind. Michelle spoke some more of her family, of her friends on the island and off, while Janet talked of letters home and flamingo feathers, as well as Francine's curious reaction to their mention.

Michelle idly said, "Well, there is a scandal in the past. She probably wants you not to revive it by accident."

"What scandal?"

"Many years ago, a generation or two back, there was something. I think no one knows the details but Francine is so proud of the family…" She fell silent. After a long cello piece she picked up the thread again. "I have wondered if it was about sex, or—what do you call *un batarde.*"

"An illegitimate baby?"

Michelle nodded, then shrugged. Having conveyed her ideas she seemed to lose interest in the Hamilton mystery.

Finally, while rousing themselves and getting ready return to their respective lives, Janet idly asked, "How well do you know Chester and Annabelle, and what are they doing on island?"

Michelle, with the all-encompassing French shrug, said, "Not well. Andre sees more of them in the restaurant. What do they do? Ah—a bit of this and that. *Tu sais, les riches…* What do rich people do?"

"Can I ask…do you think it's possible that he's involved with drugs?"

The phone rang shrilly, in a pattern reminiscent of Morse code. Janet observed Michelle who at first listened intently, then relaxed.

"Party line?" Janet asked and Michelle nodded, "This was for von der Koll. He's one of the four people on our line. Most calls are for him."

Janet persisted, "So, do you think Chester is involved with the drug business?"

Michelle just laughed, good naturedly. "You may ask and the answer is, yes, of course. Everybody is. Almost. Not Andre, he is against it because it brings police. Not Mark, either, he is a purist. You remember Corinne's brother who died a few days ago? He worked for Chester, supposedly as a local middleman. It looked, rather, as though he was a general gofer. Mark is convinced that Chester is setting up a drug pipeline to Texas, probably, and that's why he is living on that fancy boat, masterminding electronically."

She shaded her eyes and leaned back against the door post. "*On n'en parle pas*, as we say down-island. I do not like to speak of it as you know. Smuggling is island life, just like hurricanes." And for a while only the distant thunder of the reef was heard.

Back at the resort Janet went to find Sophie, the owner and mother of Billy. While she could understand Michelle's categorical refusal to talk about the thing they had found in the tank, it still bothered her. Sophie listened carefully to her description.

"It sounds like a voodoo doll of Rudy von der Koll, all right. Especially because of the pebble." To Janet's baffled look she answered, "You know, pebble—land—real estate? I'm not surprised. He has alienated many local people with his project, the Paradise Club. You must have heard about it? People call it Hell's Plan—an air conditioned Disneyland with imported staff aimed at jetloads of gamblers who would destroy the island life. He does not heed anyone's suggestions and maybe somebody was trying to even the odds a bit by invoking higher powers."

"What do you think about it? Don't be shy now."

They both smiled, acknowledging the strident tone that had crept into Sophie's voice. "Yes, you're right. I am against it. It is just too big and a resort like ours would surely go under. But Rudy has bought a lot of votes and I'm not sure anyone can stop it any longer."

Just then Rudy von der Koll himself, camera around his neck, appeared at the door of the dining room where they stood. Sophie excused herself and he advanced on Janet, insisting she have a drink with him. He looked somewhat fuzzy around the edges and she was sorely tempted to ask him about his effigy. Out on the open deck with their drinks she forgot about it, having gotten him involved in reminiscences of island life. It was not long until the talk turned to Hamilton house.

"I've been wondering about the history of that family. What do you know about them?" Janet asked.

"Well, they are the one of the oldest families on the island and have been well regarded. Things like that count on islands. Even if Francine hasn't lived here for long. She grew up on the American mainland, as far as I know. She and Sam only took over the grocery after her mother died a few years ago. A sudden cancer and pfffft..."

His gesture flicked the air as though to indicate the direction in which the soul had gone.

"Francine has been sort of hovering while I work in the attic. I am beginning to wonder if there are any skeletons she's wanting me not to find."

"I have heard of some history the family would rather keep buried, but I don't think anyone knows details anymore, it's so far back. Maybe not even Francine. There is an aunt who must be close to a hundred. She vegetates in some nursing home in Florida. God knows, she might remember. But why should you bother yourself with this kind of dusty excitement?"

And, to her surprise, he proceeded to court her, smoothly and really rather skillfully, she had to admit though she still found him repellent. He was a hard man to fathom! Seeing him now it was hard to connect him to the half-eaten thing with a crab claw attached to its privates.

The next morning, the first stirrings of consciousness brought back memories of the dive with Michelle. Vividly she recalled the giant brain coral sitting in the sand like mirages in a desert, the stands of stag-horn, and everywhere, like weeds, the stunning Gorgonias. Sea fans weaved and patches of eelgrass covered the sand like a neglected lawn. And among sea ferns floated the sun-speckled lithe figure of Michelle. Why would Andre claim she did not care for the ocean? She clearly was an accomplished diver. She was also, Janet realized fondly, a linguistic chameleon in that when she was with Johnny, Michelle's speech took on a South African tint. And then Janet began to wonder why the woman was so persistently in her thoughts. It had to be a fascination with perfection. Having solved that puzzle she went off for her morning swim, much relieved.

Chapter Nine

Janet swam while the island was still deceptively quiet. The water in the lagoon was as smooth as glass and she became entranced by the underwater activity, so much more lively than at midday. The rocky bottom was crowded with sea fans, coral fronds, orange sponges and anemones that shrank as she passed. And everywhere there were the brilliant parrot fish with buck teeth and garishly painted lips.

After a solid workout, which included a couple hundred yards of butterfly stroke, she collected her towel and snorkel from the beach and walked toward the marina. Mark caught up with her about halfway.

"I was wondering who was out so early just for sport. Oh, and by the way I am Mark Sanders. Pleased to meet you." His accent had barely a trace of French.

"Janet McMillan. Same here."

They walked side by side for awhile. Janet said, "Actually we met, in a fashion. I was at the bar Friday night."

Mark only winced and shrugged, but did not comment.

"And I have heard only good things about you from Michelle."

"Ah."

She was tempted to ask what "ah" was supposed to mean when he went on. "And how have you two become friends already, while I haven't even met you yet? Really met, I mean."

"Oh, I don't know—oh, yes, I ran into her and Andre at the beach, sort of like now. I think your sister is wonderful."

Mark smiled at Janet and she thought, With that smile he must be a danger to the entire female population. Those two. It's not fair, they have it all.

Meanwhile Mark said, "My sister and I are just getting to know each other. She grew up with our mother. I know she did not mean to end up with me on Provo. She had hoped, marrying Andre, she would go to

Europe, but he loves the tropics. And she needs him more than she cares to admit."

They walked quietly and Janet wondered how to ask him about the brawl. "So, I hear you are a diver."

"Yes, I just came from a sunrise dive."

"How long have you lived on island? You don't have nearly as much of an accent as Michelle. And, if you don't mind my asking, how do you make a living diving?"

He smiled at her again. "I work stand-by for a salvage outfit on South Caicos. I also take groups of archaeologists and underwater historians to wrecks, of which there are hundreds in the area. In my off time I write poetry." Forestalling her comment, he rapidly added, "That I don't want to talk about, but all else is open for conversation."

"I heard about your wreck diving the other night at Andre's."

Looking impish he said, "And Andre gave you his spiel about how we destroy the reefs and create legal messes?"

"Well, something like that," Janet admitted. "So, how do you do all of that singlehandedly?" They sat down in the sand, both facing the ocean.

"A salvage outfit on an island is a mixture between a wrecker, towing service, and touring company, all in one. A historical wreck—like *The Nia* they think they found off the Banks—creates much interest and suddenly you have swarms of people all over where before you had a quiet reef."

Sifting sand through his fingers he continued, "Not only divers like Andre are upset at us for that. The people who are in the business of running drugs hate it too. Too many officials, too many eyes."

"Which reminds me," Janet said, "I read this article which kept referring to Choke Point and I got the sense it was somewhere close. What and where exactly is it?"

Mark drew a picture in the sand and Cuba, Southern Florida, and the island chains appeared as if by magic. He pointed out the narrow passage between the islands, where Coast Guard ships, Navy destroyers and submarines tried to head off traffic into the southern United States. Troubled, he said, "The drug trade is destroying the etiquette of the sea. People no longer help vessels in distress for fear of a trap."

"Smugglers sit out there in open waters in leaky boats and pretend to be in trouble. When a civilian stops to help, they shoot the people and grab the boat. Grasshoppers we call those boats, stolen for one run to Colombia with delivery somewhere along the Florida coast and then they are scuttled. No one knows how many there are. In my business we know they are often claimed as having sunk on the Turks and Caicos Banks because insurance pays if you sink on a reef but they don't pay for capture and seizure of a vessel."

Slumping dispiritedly he added, "We spend many salvage hours and thousands of sea miles looking for boats that have never been anywhere near our reefs."

He shrugged, "Piracy. That's all it is. We don't deal in slaves and molasses any more but the results are just as deadly."

Standing, he reached down to help her up, his face drawn. "It's the island kids that worry me—getting pulled into an international war where they have absolutely no chance..."

When they reached the Old Turtle Resort grounds Mark smiled another of his daybreak smiles and said, "It is Sunday morning, and a beautiful one at that. Don't let my doom speech get to you. Not even High Church is as depressing, or so the Reverend has told me. Consider yourself purified for the day, skip services and enjoy the resort brunch. It is sinful, delicious and well worth the time."

She could not convince him to join her as he was due for work. She had hoped for a chance to talk about Michelle, or maybe Hamilton House. But watching his back disappear behind the casuarina tree she realized how skillfully he had detoured her—she thought she was questioning him and all along he had steered the conversation.

While she lingered over her final cup of coffee she witnessed what clearly was a Sunday morning ritual: the island's dignitaries convening. Dressed stiffly and displaying the self-satisfied look of officially blessed minds, they filed into the dining room where the large central table stood in pristine readiness, the waiter attentive with the silver coffee and milk pitchers.

Janet recognized several of the "important" people. Francine led the parade, her arm linked with Sam's. Rudolph von der Koll followed by himself and bowed old-fashionedly in her direction. Mr. Bob Chappell of banking fame held a chair for, what she assumed was Mrs. Bob Chappell, a bland, thin woman who did not seem to fill enough psychic space to cause a bloody bar brawl. Morris Cromwell, the Chief of Police and Immigration entered, his bearing that of a military man. Janet concluded she was also finally seeing the elusive Carl, father to Billy and proprietor of the resort, when a middle aged man led Sophie into the room, his hand possessively on her lower back. And, coming in somewhat hurriedly, a tall thin man in black with the white collar of the clergy.

She was glad she had finished eating because the portentous procedure of service according to rank seemed to weight the air in the dining area. She took her book back to her room and began packing an overnight bag.

By noon Janet left for the east end. Almost as soon as she stepped out on the road she got a ride with a taciturn white man whose truck smelled of fish. After he had deposited her about one mile from the end of the island, he continued on down a sandy track while she walked east until the road dead-ended on the short concrete dock. The huge tank at the end was still full of conch and lobster, covered with chicken wire and locked with a padlock. No colorful dolls. She looked all around, almost expecting Michelle to emerge from the lagoon by the pier. Only then did she notice the blindingly white speed boat which bobbed at the nearby dock.

As she headed toward it, the most spectacular human being Janet had seen in a long time stepped off its deck. He was over six feet tall, of a glossy obsidian color, with a muscle definition that put anatomy books to shame. His smooth skin made every move reflect light off a different, perfectly chiseled muscle. He wore bright red high tops, tight, bright red short shorts with slits up the side, and a cut off t-shirt, also bright red, which ended directly below his nipples. His smile, displaying perfect, glistening teeth, brightened the beach and the motion of his outstretched arms, with which he welcomed Janet, made the rings on his fingers reflect royally. She was entranced.

"Freddy at your service. Corinne told me you needed me."

"I am most pleased to meet you and, yes, I need to get to Grand Turk and would like to get back as quickly as possible." Janet hoped she didn't sound as clumsy as she felt.

"They don't call me Fast Freddy for nothing. I get you there in three and a half hours at this time of day. When do you want to return?"

"By tomorrow evening?"

His dazzling smile lit and he said, "Just say the word."

A short price negotiation followed which was, in truth, more like a one sided verbal ballet—he had a price, she would have said yes to anything, he felt bad for her obvious gullibility or maybe assumed Janet would tell cousin Corinne, so he lowered his price and they were ready to go.

Lithely Freddy jumped onto the deck of his boat, held out his hand and Janet took it. There was not much opportunity to talk, between the noise of the engine, the aluminum hull thudding on the tip of the waves, and the wind roaring by. Freddy, behind his dark wraparound shades, was steering with a single minded absorption and Janet was alternately lulled by the speed and excited by it. The Turks Island Passage was open water and the waves looked as though they had not encountered any obstacle since leaving the African coast. Until now. And they were taking out their anger on the little boat. But Freddy pushed on, unconcerned.

Just when she thought she could not stand the constant pounding of the boat against ten foot waves, the water smoothed out in the lee of Grand Turk Island. Tying off at the dock in Cockburn Town Freddy pointed her toward the hotel and, before he roared off again, they agreed to meet the following day around three, at the same place.

Janet sat for a while on the nearest bollard. She was as glad to be off the boat as to be out of his imperious aura. It was not that she lusted after him or that he intimidated her. It was the power of an absolutely beautiful physique which overwhelmed her. She thought again of Michelle. She wondered how it would be to feel spectacular, to *know* oneself to be so, to confirm it in every mirror. It baffled the mind.

The hotel was very British, understated and regal. She luxuriated in a claw-foot tub and well laundered, hand-stitched bed linen. There was even a telephone in the room and the luxury of such convenience seduced her into trying to call people—in Minneapolis, Los Angeles, it didn't matter. But despite it being the capital, international connections from Cockburn Harbor were difficult to achieve at best, and she fell asleep without having had any success.

She was waiting by the front steps of the library when the time came for it to open. A beautiful example of colonial architecture, Bascombe House served as the island archives as well as the court house. The large echoing rooms were cool and empty and Janet felt the peace of order envelop her.

The mustachioed young man in charge of the archives was, if not exactly resistant, not particularly helpful. He only consented to part with one set of files at a time and, each time, heaved himself out of his hard wooden chair with a momentous sigh, remaining away from his desk so long Janet feared he had left.

She had decided to begin with the Loyalists. When he brought the box containing the Government Decrees 1780 to 1800, it seemed so heavy, she offered to help carry it, but that suggestion, if anything, offended him more violently. He looked her up and down as though to suggest someone of her age and circumference should know better.

But deliver the box he did, all the way to the table where she had spread out her notebooks. Between 1789 and 1791 there had been nearly a hundred Imperial bounty land grants. Unfortunately, they were mixed in with secondary transfers and sales, so she needed to check each entry, but Janet was fired up like a hunter with its prey in sight.

Hours later, having waded through miles of paper, Janet had pages of notes. She had taken down all the information she could decipher, allowing for spelling alternatives where necessary. She had read court records, General Assembly rulings, migration lists and Will And Deed books, until she no longer understood one word of the convoluted language of officialdom.

Most plantation plots in those years had been given out in the Caicos group, but she had found four grants for Providenciales. Of those, on April 13 1790, a relatively small lot was granted to one Dennis Hamilton "in Recognition of Faithful Servitude" to the British Crown. Bingo! Here, certainly, was the beginning of the mystery of Hamilton House!

Janet had decided that she would need to create a master index for the body of records generated by different governments and pieces of legislation. But for now, she told herself, following one man's journey through the maze of governments and laws was a good way of getting a feel for the reality of island living. It also would, in the end, make her book more alive. Having convinced herself, she eagerly went back through the files in search of more traces of this particular title.

Hamilton, formerly of Boston, had arrived in the islands by way of the port of New York on the Dutch trading vessel *Mynheer van Graat.* He applied for himself and a transport of seven servants. Three years after being deeded this parcel of land, he appeared in the court records again.

In 1793, Hamilton bought one hundred acres from one William Boddie, who was compelled to sell because his Quaker tenets prevented him from using slaves to work his land and he did not have enough children. Then in 1798, Hamilton was involved in a dispute with one Michael Johnson who claimed to have bought the Hamilton land in what turned out to be a land swindle.

Once more he appeared before the magistrate, contending that Morton Cahill was illegally grazing his cattle on Hamilton land. This piece stumped Janet and she gazed out the window for a while. Cattle? How did they get cattle onto islands without any ports for deep draft vessels? Did cows swim? Maybe they unloaded them, with cranes, onto the small island lighters which were not much more than dinghies. But even if they got them ashore, how had they fed such large animals on islands that support-ed mostly lizards? With a contented sigh she returned to her documents. This was the part she loved about her job—the thrill of the chase, the uncovering of worlds unknown.

Ten years after the cattle dispute, Hamilton had freed all seven of his slaves (fifteen years before the general abolition of slavery on the islands, she noted with satisfaction, as though she had a personal investment in him) and was appealing to the court for larger water allocation as there were now several families on land originally meant to support one.

Checking through the court proceedings for those years gave a clear sense of what farmers like Hamilton had been up against. Many planta-tions, modeled after the American mainland (where most of the men came from) went under within years. Drought and boll weevils killed the cotton industry. Tobacco failed, and pineapples shrivelled on land that was arid and harsh. Salt and sisal fiber, which were the traditional exports, were harvested with backbreaking labor and offered small gain. And finally, in 1817, Hamilton too had given in and returned to the mainland, marked as an outgoing passenger on another Dutch trader bound for the Port of Boston.

Janet was intrigued. Did this mean she had been wrong? This Hamilton had packed up and gone home, back to America, and had noth-ing to do with building Hamilton House almost fifty years later? Maybe the name was just a coincidence?

Rather unlikely. Hamilton might be a common name, but two of the same settling on such a small island strained belief. She just had to keep looking. Maybe he returned, or one of his descendants did.

Reluctantly she turned her back on the stacks. She had not really planned to go into that much detail at this point but rather to establish the parameters of the source material. And now it was time to meet Fast Freddy.

"What do you mean we don't leave today?"

"The weather has been blowing up since yesterday. Have you not noticed? There is an early hurricane rolling in from Africa." Noticing her horrified expression, Freddy smiled, brilliant teeth flashing like treasures. "Just ragging. It's only a little blow. But it is a bad time to go out in the open. You would not like it and neither would my boat."

They stood facing the ocean which, Janet noticed, did indeed look foamy. White caps broke and whipped past in an angry spray.

"But I told Francine I would be back and I've checked out and everything." Janet heard the whine in her voice but could do nothing about it. Freddy looked as handsome as the day before, if somewhat more mellow. His eyes, which he proceeded to wrap in his shades, had a slight telling redness.

"Look island people is used to this. I tell you what. I will radio Provo so they know you will be in late." He slouched against the lamppost and even then he modeled torso muscles that Janet was convinced had been left out of her own body. His shades were on, his decision made and she decided to bow to fate.

"What time can we leave tomorrow?"

"Let's meet here at eight and I will have you back before noon."

Having suddenly gained a measure of time Janet returned to the library where for a while she wandered the aisles and picked up books at random. In the civil records section she was leafing through several volumes when, suddenly, her attention was caught. Under Marriages Performed, she found, listed on May 15, 1865, names which were quite familiar. One Dennis Hamilton and one Sarah Maynard had appeared on that date before the Governor of these islands planning residence on Providenciales.

Who could this be? A son? If so, when had he come back to the islands? She knelt down right there in the aisle and pulled out her notebook. A Hamilton had arrived in the Turks and Caicos Islands the first time in 1790. How old would he have been, sixteen? Maybe twenty? He left in 1817, which would make him more than forty by the time he returned to Boston. If the same Dennis Hamilton returned to get married in 1865, he would have been about ninety years old!

But, seeing that the newlyweds were planning to live on Provo too, this had to be the thread she had hoped for. Who was he, a son, a grandson? Or someone farther removed on the family tree?

Suddenly she could see the book taking shape. She could have the Hamiltons move from being individuals to becoming metaphors for an economic model. A gentleman farmer or plantation owner for twenty-seven years then frees his slaves and comes back home a failure. The new generation returns and takes up life where he left off. If she followed their lives, made understandable what had driven and what had defeated them, she would have the specifics to explain her thesis of systems. The Hamilton story would serve as a sort of prologue connecting each of the chapters.

Satisfied with her research, she meandered into the main room where she found copies of the local weekly, the *Conch News*. Skimming the last year's newsworthy items she found herself face to face with a black and white half-page photo of Chester Taggett, von der Koll, and, "my friend Norman," the Prime Minister. The caption read: *Movers and Shakers on Provo: these are men with a vision who will bring the islands into the modern age.*

Before she could read what else the movers and shakers were up to, the young man locked the files and began turning off the lights. It was all she could do to get him to make a copy of the article, and he politely but firmly escorted her out the door. She spent the evening wandering the streets of Grand Turk, watching daily life being carried out with color, grace and music. She dropped in on various bars listening to the expatriates and, slowly, began to think of how it would be to live on an island— living life instead of researching it. The peace and happiness she imagined included a shadowy husband and several happy, healthy children in a life of rural simplicity. Rather sternly she admonished herself not to fantasize merely because she was worried about the outcome of the tenure review. Besides, the vision of that rural life contained more than a trace of claustrophobia.

Chapter Ten

The morning glistened without even the faintest breeze, and they left on schedule. Freddy was in a talkative mood which necessitated their standing close together so he could yell into her ear. As soon as they had crossed the roughest part he began boasting of his successful beachcomber business. Collecting square groupers, the bales of marijuana smugglers threw overboard when the law chased them, he claimed, netted him a "lovely" income. He insisted Janet understand that he did not deal. He cured the stuff he found and sold it to someone who collected bales. He called his work a social service in the interest of cleaning the beaches and reducing waste. His conviction shone righteously and Janet found herself almost believing him.

He argued that beachcombing was much safer than dealing if not quite as lucrative. "I don't wish to cross the police or big dealers. Much too much trouble. Besides, everyone knows me."

Janet could well believe this. He would stand out in a business where invisibility was an asset. She asked him about some of the people she was curious about.

"Chester off *Serenade*? Sure. You understand—drugs is daily business, is life. Everyone participates, some by fighting it." Freddy's voice changed to island patois as though to underscore his connection with the other islanders against outsiders like herself or Chester the Texas oilman. "Chester—he big. But some don't like he come in from the continent. They want he leave."

"Is Rudolph von der Koll involved in drugs, too?"

"You want to stay away from that man. He bad news! You watch you around he!"

He clammed up after that and refused to be drawn out. As the blue-gray outline of Provo appeared on the horizon, Janet realized that listening to him had made the trip shorter and much less scary.

After they reached the East End he very politely shook Janet's hand, accepted the fare, and roared off with an impressive wake, back toward Grand Turk. He had not even stepped ashore but merely passed her up with one hand while holding the dockline.

The French Connection stood parked at the side of the road a few hundred yards inland, its engine off, its driver's seat empty. Janet's heart stopped, then beat on rapidly. It was possible, of course, that Andre had driven the car and gone diving or something. But Janet felt sure it had to be Michelle.

Standing next to the contraption she became aware of a woman's voice humming. Janet followed the sound along a small footpath into the scrub to a hollow where baked sand cracked into hot flagstones—an untouchable mosaic. She stopped to the sound of scuttling soldier crabs.

Michelle sat in the spare shade of leathery stunted sea grapes and withered bay-plums, a background of silver and gray. An easel was in front of her, a palette drooped off her left hand. She stopped her private song when Janet appeared.

Michelle looked like a religious icon with that silver frame setting off her glossy mahogany skin. Their eyes locked. A moment out of time. The hollow quivered with lizards and the hot still air was alive with the crackle of grasshoppers. Beyond was the pounding surf on the reef, more a feeling than a sound filling the cells of living bodies.

When Michelle rose, the dense spell broke and released Janet into movement. Inevitably they hugged and their lips touched. Janet helped collect the art supplies while babbling about being late, about not realizing that Michelle painted, about Freddy, until Michelle, staying the flood by linking her arm in Janet's, said lightly, "*Salut* and welcome. So nice to have you back. Did you find what you went for?"

Janet talked about land grants, marriage certificates, writs and deeds, feeling only the spot where Michelle's arm had lain, seeing nothing but her smile or frown. All too soon the car stopped by the cutoff to the resort. When Michelle refused a drink at the bar, Janet was aware of sharp disappointment.

But before she could escape to nurse her hurt, Michelle took her face in both hands, looked her deeply into the eyes and kissed her, once, solidly on the lips. "I want to show you my favorite place on the island. Can we take all day? Friday?"

Michelle did not let go of her face until Janet had answered affirmatively. Hurrying into her room, Janet shut the door and closed her eyes, leaving the world outside, and gave in to the internal uproar.

After a while, having firmly convinced herself that her dizziness was due to a delayed attack of seasickness, she got up and carefully marked the calendar for Friday. Then, ready to escape into work, she removed her notes from the overnight bag. Clearing the table, her eyes fell on a yellow manila envelope someone had placed there. Posted in Minneapolis, it was from Thomas Houston and was signed off by the postmistress as having come in on today's plane.

Dear Janet. The weather is very sticky and hot and Tucker misses you with his whole large dog heart. (He is sitting on my feet to make sure I write this to you and drooling copiously, to convey the intensity of his sentiment).

Your departure for Provo has made me think of my family, the island house, and other issues usually buried under the demands of everyday life. So I sacrificed my Saturday to go through the lovely steamer trunk in my foyer, the one we use mostly to set flowers on, you remember? Among many mementoes that don't particularly concern your research, there was an old Bible. Inside, stuck to the pages from age, I found a chit marking a departure on October 29, 1817 from South Caicos bound for Boston. It was made out by the East India Company and comes complete with a logo of a stately merchant ship in full sail.

I wager this chit represents Dennis Hamilton's departure from said island. I don't know when he originally arrived or why he left but I assume—and this is why I spend the time conveying this information to you—that it will hold with your research. If Dennis had not lived down there why would he return from the islands to begin with? It's not like they were the tourist attractions of the day.

Only: if this is so, Hamilton house must have been built at the turn of the century, not, as family tradition has it, around 1860. Just goes to show how memory adjusts fact.

Unless, of course, he later returned to the islands to stay. This remains for you to find out. Though I am a historian and though it is my family, I hold to my credo—which you have heard many times: The study of history should not include one's family and even forbears need to be subsumed under the rubric of psychoanalysis rather than history.

Janet put the letter face down. The timing of this piece of mail was almost coincidental. It made her think of ESP, synchronicity, or voodoo, concepts she professionally ridiculed. But separating logic and facts from coincidences she came up with the following list:

Fact: Her research and Thomas's family keepsakes supported each other.

Fact: She had long known about the old steamer trunk with its memorabilia which Thomas had often threatened to make her look at after too many drinks. Her not being particularly interested, the threat had remained just that. Now, with her the on island, he obviously had gone through it again for himself and thus had found tangible proof of great-great-grandfather Dennis's return from the islands to Boston in 1817.

Now came the piece of coincidence: She had, on Grand Turk, discovered the same fact at almost the same time. But was that really so surprising? True, she had not gone to the library with the intention of finding the Hamilton family roots. But the name was in her mind and considering their ongoing residence on the island, traces of Hamilton presence were bound to appear. And she had a new piece: there were two Dennis Hamiltons.

"All right, all right," she grumbled, "so what's supernatural about that?" There was old Dennis Hamilton's doings, from over a hundred and eighty years ago, which they both had found traces of, and young Dennis who had just popped up, so to speak, in the island library.

Extraordinary? Hardly.

Leaning against the headboard she thought of Thomas. Twenty-seven years her senior, he sometimes seemed more like a younger brother. His boundless energy and fascination with people and their motivations frequently made her feel old. He was the Grand Old Man of the history department and had taken her under his wing when she arrived. They had slowly become friends. Their most enduring argument was about Janet's preference for research topics which lent themselves to solitary study. "Your unregenerate denial of human need," he called it and labeled her chosen field the "emotional ostrich approach to history." She had long suspected that the source of his disapproval was much more parental than professional, particularly considering his stance on objectivity in his field. He wanted her "happy," married with—preferably—several children; or, if not that, at least busy being involved and in (or out of) love rather than solitarily ensconced in her study. Well, she thought, I want that too. But my recent forays into committed relationships were rather, let's say, dispiriting. Some people might just not be meant to be coupled.

In her head she began a response which included the comment, You should see me now! Talking of human need, there is so much intimate involvement on this island I am beginning to feel like a ping-pong ball.

As if to prove the point, she remembered Michelle's smile. Janet's master matrix of land transfers all at once seemed deadly boring. The attempt at the Senate chair's Brontë book made her shudder and she put it back down.

She could not go to the attic as Sam and Francine were off island and so, restless, she left her room. The bar was quiet in the afternoon sun and did not provide relief, and neither did the marina. Her mind jumped with disjointed thoughts and her blood raced.

OK—so, yes, she liked Michelle, a beautiful human being befriending her, Janet, alone in a new place. It was a mistake to think it meant anything more, though she couldn't remember being that excited about any of her lovers. Tony? Not really. Though she'd thought they had a great relationship, until he kept pushing for more commitment, and finally left her. But physical hunger? It was true, her knees had gone wobbly when she'd noticed Michelle's car. But she had just stepped off a boat, so that made sense. The skipping heartbeat had to be about the pleasure of coming home, of being expected by someone. She liked her own company and had trained herself away from the idea that unless she was in a couple she was somehow incomplete. But coming back from a trip was different; then it was nice to be welcomed back. That was all.

Not that she didn't know about women loving women or found the concept inconceivable! After all, this was the mid-eighties. It simply had nothing to do with her. Or Michelle, for that matter.

Besides, living in the tropics did strange things to one's perceptions. It was time to stop reading meaning into things—it was time for a long swim. She would go to the beach on the south coast she had heard so much about. That should keep her mind occupied.

She'd been walking only a few minutes when a highly dilapidated truck dating back at least twenty years and held together with wire and rusty patches, slowed for her. She felt it rude to refuse and got on.

The driver, who was of indeterminate age, introduced himself as Mohammed and his wife as Sarah. Lighter than her husband, Sarah was russet colored, of stocky build and looked about thirty.

"We looks after tourist houses," Mohammed said proudly to Janet's question. He explained that when the owners of the houses came to stay on the island Sarah became housekeeper and cook and Mohammed chauffeur, gardener and "all around houseman."

Sarah nodded. "Good job, this. It pay year round and more during the season. When them all gone we have time. We fish, garden and take care of the family."

"Do you have any children?" Janet was entranced by their accent with its traces of sixteenth century Elizabethan English, and she felt she would gladly listen to the recital of a grocery list if necessary.

"We have four. Two are Mohammed's family. His brother be working in Trinidad and so we looks after the babies. One from my sister who lives in Miami in a big house with many televisions and automatic cookers and washers. The baby, Maria, is my youngest sister. My mother now old and not wanting to look after her. Mother cannot stand up—always walks with her face to the ground. But the doctors say there is nothing they can do, not even in Miami. Or else we would send her. We think to try a hogan for her but she does not want to go."

At Janet's uncomprehending look she prompted, "You know, Santería priests, voodoo, spirit healings and all?" Satisfied at Janet's nod, she continued, "Mother say only '*Pa baille Paradi*' which means this don' get you to heaven but I say to her, how about it just get you upright? But she be afraid of the church and she want nothing to do with the healer."

Mohammed shook his head. "The church done wrong." Though a Baptist minister himself, he strongly condemned the tortures that had been traditionally used to rout out pockets of indigenous beliefs, and listed several of the punishments meted out to dissidents. Janet could handle the traditional forms of quartering, drowning, and death by fire or strangulation; mostly because she had heard of them before. But the locally favored torture which, Mohammed said, had originated with the pirates, raised goosebumps. Janet promised herself to include it in her letter to Thomas.

Woolding was as simple as it was horrific. A strap of cloth or rope, tied around someone's head, was tightened by means of a stick until the brains literally popped out through the crushed skull. Just thinking of the pain made Janet grimace. She could not resist asking, "But if you know those kinds of things about the church, how can you still be a part of it?"

Mohammed answered somberly. "I am a Baptist when I am in my church. But when the white man Baptist enters that church I am a black man first and I honor the Gods of my forefathers."

His sincerity made Janet almost wish to be one of his flock, to be safely led through all her life's storms. As she climbed from the truck she momentarily felt lonely and bereft.

A few minutes later she saw the beach, spread shamelessly under the blue sky. The crystal-white sand was littered with queen conch shells and tritons, bordered by turquoise water on one side and wild orchids on the other. It seemed unreal. The only thing that saved it from becoming a Disney scene was a large piece of driftwood far down the beach, interrupting with its irregular, black density the smooth perfection of the coral sand.

Janet removed her sandals and left them by the sea grapes where the path came down. She wandered along the tideline, watching the eel grass weave with the water, idly picking up a shell here and there. Her blood vibrated with the pounding reef, the smell of ocean sand and heat filled the air, her body was enveloped in light.

She scolded herself for being a romantic fool. This 'paradise' was drenched with the blood of thousands—this land held the graveyards of centuries. But the sea and sand continually swallowed the loud human miseries, restoring it to seemingly untouched, virgin beauty. The unreconcilable contrast of human hell to this paradise so preoccupied her that when she came upon the corpse she initially thought she had conjured it.

As though the sea had become tired of pushing the weight, the corpse's feet and calves remained in the water, gently swaying whenever a swell arrived. The body lay across the hightide line which was littered with broken shells, coconut husks and even some plastic refuse. He lay on his stomach, arms spread out in supplication, his head tilted toward her. She saw enough of his profile to recognize Mark Sanders, diver and poet, now corpse. Her first thought was, "Poor Michelle! Who will tell her?"

His cheek was tucked under his right armpit, as if for shade. Like a merman risen from the depths, he was entangled in a large black fishing net. His bright blue shirt with its garish frangipani blossom print looked foreign and aggressively cheerful despite the long tear down the left shoulder through which his skin shone a shade of tan marble in its bloodlessness. He looked so vulnerable, Janet felt protective, then scared for both of them.

Her stomach heaved and her mouth filled with liquid but she swallowed it down. Only now could she see that, while there was no blood anywhere, the left side of his head appeared oddly flattened and soft, like a squashed melon.

She backed away. Walked a few steps. Turned and looked back to the spot where he lay there still. A flash of anger surged through her, at him, at whatever fate had thrown him onto this beach, on this day. She returned to his side to check for a pulse, but couldn't get herself to touch him. He was clearly so very dead. She walked in the other direction.

"I need to get the police, get someone. But where?"

Hearing her own voice out loud, she turned from the body and finally began walking toward the road. She began to cry, in angry short sobs. Soon this changed to hopeless wails.

Suddenly she thought, what if it wasn't an accident? Maybe somebody bashed his head in? And before she had had time to rethink the idea, her feet acted. Moving along the beach as fast as she could she did not look back. As soon as she reached the side of the road she was violently sick.

She walked for an hour before she found signs of human life. For once, not a single car appeared and she had plenty of time to question her decision. Finally, a dark gray shack appeared. Surrounded by a bare dirt lot with chickens pecking for invisible edibles, its wide open door suggested human presence. Her approach woke several sleeping dogs into a barking frenzy, started the chickens cackling and enraged the scrawny but brilliantly feathered cockerel. Janet stopped and hoped that the inhabitants would know how to hold off all that roused animal aggression.

The young woman who appeared from the shadowy interior, a baby on her arm and a toddler wrapped around her leg, did not say a word but leaned up against the doorway looking at Janet.

"Sorry to disturb you but do you have a phone or a radio? Someone needs to send for the police."

Nothing changed except that the snarling dogs danced a few feet closer and the two in front bared their fangs. Janet considered talking louder, slower. Maybe it would be best to simply leave and try somewhere else? Just as she turned away another shadow appeared behind the woman. This one, a bare-chested man, moved past the woman with her children and sat down on the doorstep, rolling himself a cigarette.

"Excuse me, but I need to reach the police station."

"I heard you fine."

Silence again. The man smoked, the woman stood and observed Janet surrounded by the two children, the three of them an unmoving tableau of dark round eyes.

"You stay at the Old Turtle and Fast Freddy take you to Grand Turk."

At first Janet felt the voice had come from the tableau vivant as a sort of ventriloquist's prank, the whole scene was so surreal and static, but then she understood it was the man who had spoken.

"What do you want with the police?" he continued, in a lilting rhythm.

She could feel her mind unravelling. Why did Mark have to wash up on the very beach she was walking on? What was she doing getting involved in island politics, stuck with a man who sounded as though he had a gripe against the police?

She wanted to wake up and have it all be a bad dream. The islands, her project, the whole thing. Snap, she was back in Minneapolis and none of this had ever happened. She shook herself. "There is a dead man on the beach back toward the East End, the big crescent shaped one. I found him and…" She had run down and still nobody moved.

"Who is he?"

"Mark, the wreck diver. Mark Sanders. Do you know him?"

The man's minute movement, between a shrug and a shoulder twitch, could have meant yes or no. After a few more minutes of silent smoking the man got up and said, "Come."

Janet followed him and his entourage, which included wife, children, dogs and even a few of the fowl, around the far corner of the shack where a truck of indeterminate vintage stood. Only now did Janet notice that the shack lacked overhead wires. The shack was without electricity or phone! The only connection with the outside world was through the truck's CB radio.

Despite its looks, it started right off and the radio signal came in loud and clear. The man worked the dials with practiced skill and raised an answering voice after only a few calls. Whoever had answered agreed to pass the message on. That was it. The truck fell silent, the family trooped back to their front door and Janet, despondent, followed.

She felt utterly let down. It was all so anticlimactic, so matter-of-fact. Janet thanked them all, turned away, and found herself back on the dusty road headed for town.

About fifteen minutes later the noise of a motor intruded into her numbed mind and she turned to see a truck gaining on her. Its driver, whom she recognized as the taciturn young man of the scruffy shack, waved her on board. The truck sped up, the radio blared someone's ideas on how to kill stingrays and the driver looked fixedly out the front windshield. Only when Janet prepared to get out at the resort cutoff, he said,

"They will say drugs killed him. But Mark is an island man and has no truck with white man's poison."

"You knew him, then? Do you have any idea who might have done this?"

He squinted at her as though assessing her dependability, then said something that ended with "who Hell Plan," and roared off in a blinding cloud of dust before she could ask him more. Standing by the side of the road she heard another car approaching from the opposite direction. It was, as her ears told her before it emerged, the French Connection. Andre was at the wheel, cigarette dangling as usual. The way her heart dropped when she saw the car reminded her of her Friday date with Michelle. And then she thought of the brother who lay like flotsam on that white beach and all at once she was so angry at him for interfering with her date that she wanted to kill him. The absurdity of this started her laughing hysterically by the time she had reached her room.

Chapter Eleven

By evening everyone was talking about the body on the beach. customs had picked him up with their shore boat because it was easier than moving him by land. Someone claimed they were storing him in the freezer-locker down by the airport until the magistrate could come over from North Caicos. The general opinion was that he had been murdered in a drug connected retaliation. The voices of restraint who argued that he could have fallen and hurt his head in an accident were few and mostly female.

The older white men, a group that centered around Carl, the Old Turtle's proprietor, and Bob Chappell, the banker and self-elected spokesman, had settled on an opinion of Mark's being a drug middleman. Around the table they regaled each other with stories of "drug busts I have seen/been part of" while ostensibly speaking to Janet who, as the person who had discovered the body, rated special attention. Rudy von der Koll hovered at her elbow but did not succeed in creating a private conversation, as his low-voiced questions and appeals got lost in the general noise.

Once she managed to escape their attentions she found herself addressed by the bartender, a man who had never before spoken to her. "A brain stone did him. You mark my word."

Before she could ask for an explanation of this particular phenomenon someone touched her shoulder and she saw Billy, looking blurry around the edges. "How did he look?"

"Oh, Billy, I'm so sorry. I know you were friends."

Red-faced and diminished, Billy looked too young to learn firsthand of death and pain. "We weren't really friends but he sometimes let me go with him on a dive. He was such a great diver. I don't see how they can say he drowned diving."

"What else are they saying?"

"They claim he was dealing drugs and crossed the wrong guy. That's a lie and the police know it."

Just then Sam was at her elbow and steered her outside, away from the crowded bar. On the deck Francine sat at a table with an extra drink and Janet let them fuss over her for a while. She was beginning to wonder why no one in authority had come to talk to her about finding a dead body. In the murder mysteries, the first thing police always did was to interview all and sundry. Maybe Sam counted as a police representative, and he was charged with finding out the details from her. Or maybe they already knew via bush telephone everything she could tell them.

They ordered a second round of gin and tonics, and Janet let her mind wander. Clearly Mark did not drown in a diving accident. He would never go swimming in a shirt and shorts, being a professional diver. Could he have fallen onto, or off, something and knocked himself out? But how would that lead to drowning unless the something was on or in the ocean, such as a boat? Was there a captainless boat somewhere? And where was Michelle and had anyone told her yet?

Maybe he had gone out on someone else's boat. That person could have pushed him off or killed him outright. But who? Maybe his death had, indeed, been connected to drugs, but not in the way the men at the round table claimed. What if one of those operators Mark had talked about, those whose business was disturbed by the divers and archaeologists he ferried, had decided to remove an irritating obstacle?

On her way to the bathroom she came across Corinne who seemed more shaken than the day after her brother had died. Her eyes were red-rimmed and her crisp turban drooped slightly around the edges. While she did not invite personal comforting she clearly wanted to talk of Mark. "I cannot believe he is dead. He was here just yesterday. Come in around noon, he was mad to spit nails."

"Yesterday? God, to think—Did he tell you what he was mad about?"

"Oh, yes. He told everyone. The bank had rejected his loan application, again. Mr. Bob Chappell, he don' believe in giving money to black people."

Of course, Chappell and the knockout fight! How could she have forgotten? The brawl that started because Mark had commented something about, "If you didn't leave your wife alone so much?" How did Mrs. Chappell fit in? Janet remembered her as the rather vague blondish woman who had about as much charisma as a fading Polaroid.

"Why didn't Mark try for a loan somewhere else?"

Corinne just shrugged and looked down her nose as though such a question did not deserve consideration.

"Do you know what he wanted the money for?"

"What else! He be wanting his diving boat so bad he can taste it."

"Right, I remember." Janet said. "He called *Dorothea* his five ton love who sings to him on high seas. What a mess."

Annabelle emerged from one of the stalls just as Janet entered the ladies' room. She fussed at Janet for "The shock you must have had! I can't imagine how you can stand it…" After which she proceeded to speculate on what had happened to Mark. Her conclusion, not surprisingly, coincided primarily with that of Chester and the other dignitaries of the round table, having to do with not staying in one's place and thus inviting a type of existentially deserved accident. However, her opinion culminated with a surprise bomb. "And you know, that's what comes of playing both sides of the street!" Adding, when Janet didn't seem to understand, "He was AC/DC. Didn't you know?"

Francine and Sam were waiting for her when she returned to the table, and she apologized for having been so long. Francine suggested she postpone attic work for a while, but Janet insisted. "I need to keep busy or I'll drive myself buggy."

They agreed she would show up whenever she was ready and Francine departed with several admonitions to take it easy and rest. After she had seen them off at the parking lot, Janet checked the bar and deck once more, not really looking for Michelle, just restless and kind of hoping. But neither she nor Andre were part of the crowd. Janet wished she could just call, say hi, how are you doing. And to hear Michelle's voice. But probably she was busy making arrangements, or something.

Rudy von der Koll snagged her arm and she let herself join the round table, which had grown more crowded as well as louder. Deploring the morals of the younger generation and ridiculing politicians, always excepting present company, they advocated stiffer penalties, bigger prisons and other palliatives of the status quo. Chester, face flushed and arm possessively around Annabelle, competed in punitive rhetoric with Bob Chappell, both seemingly more intent on air time than content.

By the time she returned to her room, once again chaperoned by Rudy von der Koll, who held tightly to her elbow, she had heard so many versions of Mark the drug dealer or distributor, that her head reeled. She realized, however, no one had the slightest details of Mark's alleged dealings. Considering the size of the island, this seemed rather unusual.

In the quiet of her room she kept seeing his feet swaying with the tide, his chin tucked under his arm and she wanted him to tell her where he'd been, what had happened. She hoped it had been quick and he had not seen death coming.

Before she could even consider sleep, she needed to clear her head. She filed the photocopies of documents she had made at the library, referenced the accumulated background material first chronologically, then by topic and finally by originating source location. Finally, facing a restless night, she listed possible sub-categories for organizing the originals writs, deeds and grants. The whole time she resolutely kept thoughts of Michelle and her loss beyond the range of conscious thought.

The next day Janet stepped inside the grocery store just as Michelle emerged from one of its gloomy aisles. She opened her arms and they stepped into an embrace as the most natural thing in the world. Sinking into the hug made Janet realize how exhausted she was and she let out the breath she had not known she was holding.

"I'm so sorry about your brother," she said and Michelle's arms tightened around her. When she stepped back, Janet noticed the black circles, the red-rimmed eyes. "When did you hear about it?"

"Oh, you know—the island drums. I went to meet the boat when they came in with him."

"Do you have time for a drink? Can we talk for a bit?"

Michelle took her basket to the clerk. After a mumbled interchange she turned to Janet and said, *"Allons-y."*

They walked side by side to the cafe where Janet had eaten lunch several life times ago. They did not speak until they were settled in a booth, Coke bottles in front of them dripping cold beads of condensation.

"Will you tell me about your brother?"

Michelle confirmed what Mark had told Janet. They didn't know each other well, they had grown up on opposite ends of Martinique. They had not planned to end up in the same place, but she had been pleased to find him here when she and Andre moved to Provo.

"I finally find a brother only to lose him forever."

Janet reached across the table and took Michelle's limp hand which she surrendered as though it belonged to someone else.

"He did not use illegal drugs or deal in them. But this is what they will say, just another island boy seduced by big money." Michelle shuddered. "If only I had told him how much he meant to me. I wanted him to be proud of me. He was so disappointed when he found out."

"Found out what?"

But Michelle shook her head. "Why did they have to kill him?"

"You don't think it could have been an accident?" Janet still held out hope. "Maybe he fell, hit his head and became unconscious."

"*Non*. Impossible. He was a natural around boats. And if he had been hurt, why was he not on his boat but on a beach?" Michelle charged on, "They will claim he was a drug dealer. There are not enough police and those are paid badly. Of course they pick up money from people who pay more, like Chester on his fancy boat. So they will bury Mark like they did Corinne's brother and not do anything about it."

"Michelle…"

"Who did this to him? Why kill him?"

"Michelle?"

"Mark loved the water, he does not fall in and drown. Chester killed him because he could not bribe him. Or because Mark did not want to have sex with Annabelle."

"Michelle, listen."

"Yes, *ma cherie,* what are you saying?"

"I am not, because you keep interrupting."

"It is that I am thinking through the problem. So?" Michelle's face suddenly changed to an expression of such exaggerated wide-eyed innocence, it made Janet laugh in spite of all the sadness. They both let go of the moment of lightness with reluctance.

"Remember the fight Mark had with Bob Chappell at the bar about a week ago?"

Michelle's lips tightened and her eyes became hard. She shook her head, playing with some spilt sugar crystals on the table and did not look up.

"There's more. Corinne told me last night that Mark had gone to see Bob Chappell on Monday for a loan and had been rejected. He was furious. Maybe he confronted Chappell later and they got into another fight? Couldn't we find out from Mrs. Chappell what the fight was about, what Mark could have meant with that comment?"

"*Non!*" Michelle's comment was sharp, her face suddenly fierce. She dropped some bills on the table and walked out of the cafe without looking back. Once outside she slowed down and turned to Janet who had followed her. "You must promise not to do anything without talking to me."

More astonished than offended, Janet nodded. By the time they re-entered Sam's store, it seemed Michelle had managed to relegate the events of the last twenty-four hours to a distant past and let only the present be real for now. Noticing Janet's quizzical gaze Michelle linked her arm through Janet's and said, "You are good for me. You make me laugh and want to be happy. I am glad you came here for your research."

Janet felt a shiver course down her spine as though something dangerous had just been put into words but she could not make sense of it. "Michelle, are you OK? Anything I can do?"

"Just be with me. Trust me, please?"

And Michelle launched into a long and intricate story about sailing through the southern Bahamas with Mark who had decided he was a more reliable navigator than she and had proceeded to get them utterly lost.

Watching her body language, Janet said, before she could stop herself, "You know, you are an extraordinarily lovely mixture of Frenchness and island savvy. I could watch you for hours."

"*Eh bien*, do," Michelle said with an impish grin. "And we do still have a date for the day after tomorrow, right? More than ever we need a beautiful place."

While she walked Janet felt a hollow spot below her heart. It felt like the onset of desire. What is going on? I swear, if I didn't know better, I'd say I was flirting with a married woman—one who, no less, seems to be flirting right back! I must be making this up. Just as I said, it is a tropical distortion kind of thing.

Francine was fluffing the window valances when Janet came down from the attic in midafternoon. She had been hovering most of the day but finally, as it seemed Janet was solidly ensconced in a box full of official-looking papers, she had excused herself.

"How are you feeling, dear?"

Groaning, Janet lowered herself onto the polished wood floor, the one spot which was not covered by a carpet or runner. "Fine. But tired and stiff and I forgot my glasses so I couldn't even read. Only there's so much sorting yet to be done I didn't have an excuse not to work." Janet crossed her legs. "Do you like living on the island?"

"It's a beautiful spot but..." her voice turned wistful, "...it does get lonely sometimes."

"Is your father still alive?"

"No, he died when we were young. He disappeared in Europe just before V-E day and was never found."

"I'm sorry."

"Yes, well, I don't really remember him much. I was so young when he left."

"Are there any relatives alive, back from your parents' generation?" Though Rudy had told her about the aunt she felt it more polite to find out directly.

Francine attacked something Janet could not see. She thought, only suicidal dust motes would dare hang on in this house. And she realized Francine would not answer the question. She thought, I wonder why?

After some time Francine turned back to Janet and said, "I gather those are some of the document files and you're planning to do more work tonight, in your room?"

"Yes, and thank you." Janet responded, patting the files in her lap. "I'll return them by tomorrow. I suppose I'd better get going." But she stayed on her spot on the floor. "What do you think happened to Mark?"

Francine did not seem surprised at the change of topic. "Oh it's just tragic. But I don't understand why everyone is saying he was murdered. Accidents do happen around boats all the time."

"Did you hear about the bar fight between Mark and Bob Chappell?"

"Well, yes. So did the whole island. But I don't believe that the fight was about an affair, though many have said so. Mrs. Chappell would not have an affair with young Mark, it would be so inappropriate. People always gossip too much. Just like they did after Rudy von der Koll's wife disappeared. Tsk, tsk," she clacked in disapproval. "Loose tongues! And talking of which, I better get on with my work, too."

Thus dismissed, Janet took herself to the bar near the airport for a late lunch. This was where the flight crews usually hung out. The food was predictably horrible, the burger dried and overcooked, the fries soggy and lukewarm, but the beer was cold. A few pilots hung out and their conversations moved sluggishly through the dank smoky air. They traded some gossip concerning a young islander who was said to have run afoul of a drug cartel, but in terms so vague they could have been talking about either Mark or Corinne's brother.

Only when she was waiting by the cash register to pay her bill did a quick, heated debate catch her attention. She strained to hear, as much because its intensity represented a welcome change, as because she thought it might have to do with Mark's death.

"Brain stone punishes familiar sins," an older man's voice insisted.

But a younger, higher male voice insisted that this was only true if both parties were thus publicly chastised. "If this be a traditional punishment, the woman be publicly stripped. Nobody even says he done any."

Done any what, exactly, Janet wondered. Adulterous sex and buggery? Or, is a 'familiar sin' something to do with the family? Something people in a particular family do? Where is my religious education when I need it?

Though hesitant to ask the cashier about the points of the debate she did find out that a 'brain stone' was the local term for the coral of the same name. With its ridged appearance and round shape the coral looked very much like a human brain and its texture, sharp as a file, made it a versatile and frequently used tool. Janet thought, What a concept—to have a particular rock to punish a specific deed. Kind of tidy. But, being honest she had to add, kind of weird.

Just as she turned to exit, someone bumped into her rather rudely from behind. Before she could turn, a voice rumbled near her ear, "Don't think we're not watching." She whirled but all she saw were the broad backs of men huddled around their beers. It could have been any of the three closest to her, and, clearly, none would step forward to confront her directly.

Out in the hot sun she repeated the phrase and tried to recall the incident exactly, to figure the size of the man, his age, race or any other useful information, until it all became so blurry she began to think she maybe had made it up. In an effort to distract herself she made up variations on the brain stone. A mandrake root, to beat child molesters with? Fools gold, to kill cheaters? Once inside her room she could not settle down. And though the thought of the beach brought bile into her mouth, she nonetheless pulled on her swimsuit and went for a long, exhausting swim.

Twilight had set in by the time she began working on the papers she had brought from the attic. Stuck in between thick files of governmental reports there were a few beribboned packets of personal letters. Janet felt a small twinge of guilt but told herself, I would not have to resort to such tactics if she weren't so petty. In the service of historical discovery a bit of pilfering is acceptable; just think of the British in Greece.

Not quite convinced, in penance she made herself work through the official papers first. Pages and pages of handwritten lists, names, dates and geographical descriptions of plots granted or transferred, they looked like a secret language. Mysterious to many, the code contained a world of meaning for her.

When she finally got to the letters, she just held them in her hands for awhile. She had found them in the drawers of an old sideboard which stood, swaddled in blankets, near the Salt Tax House record boxes. To get to those, she had to pass the old steamer trunk with the monogram D.H. 1843. And, as always, the mystery pulled at her. But she forced herself not to go against Francine's direct interdiction, arguing that, she did not say I was not to look into anything at all. She said to leave the steamer trunk alone. So she let herself open 'available drawers' and told herself, it's not idle curiosity, this is about authentic ambiance. Besides, there could be some documents I need that I might otherwise miss.

Most of the letters turned out to be from homesick school children writing home dutiful missives, thanking parents for birthday and Christmas presents, as well as parental responses. However, they some-times had yellowed newspaper clippings enclosed which talked of the hor-rific after-effects of the War, or stories of discoveries of wrecks and tales of aerial daring. She was about to give up when she came across a small bundle written in the precise script of a schoolgirl in the early part of the century.

The letters, from one girl to another, followed the two through a year of painful separation. Janet gathered that they had been in the same board-ing school and had been separated by parental decree. The loneliness and despair was so palpable, Janet felt her eyes mist. The last of those letters announced brazenly that without Reah life was becoming utterly intolera-ble. The writer had signed the letter "Your Aurelia, with Love forever."

Just then, a knock startled her into the present. Rudy von der Koll, camera around his neck, stood outside bowing, inviting her to join him for a drink. He had brought a gin and tonic for her from the bar. "I took the liberty of deciding for you," he said. "I could not find you so I came to look for you. You should not be alone tonight, it's not good to work so hard. Francine tells me you have worked all day."

Janet accepted the drink. They toasted, drank, and suddenly Janet heard herself say, "Yes, it was horrible finding that body. Do you have any idea why someone would have wanted to kill him?"

"Well, with these people, who knows what feuds they're carrying on."

"Who?"

"Down islanders. They are so volatile, just like children. And you don't want to become too involved with them, believe me." His voice turned chilly. "They are very different from us, and though some of them can seem very polished they nurse a deep hatred. They have for hundreds of years."

After he left, Janet remained standing in the doorway. I think I just figured out what Lot's wife felt like, turned into a pillar of salt. Stuck and baffled is mostly it. What was all that about? Shaking her head she re-locked the door and finished her drink alone.

Chapter Twelve

"Janet, wait, let's have some tea before you start. I want to talk to you about something."

Guiltily Janet stopped right inside the door, watching as Francine appeared from the shadowy regions of the large house, panting slightly. Today she wore gingham and, again, her head-covering matched the apron. Janet wondered if, indeed, she did it on purpose—trying to stay in character as the mistress of the plantation in a charade of nineteenth century civility.

Just in case it were the latter, Janet stuffed fists into her shorts pockets, slouched so her stomach stuck out, and slapped her sandals loudly on the shining parquet floor. Back in the sparkling kitchen, behind a tall glass of iced tea and a plate of freshly baked cookies, she sat up straight, hoping Francine had missed her childish act.

In fact, her defiance probably had less to do with a feeling of inferiority because she did not have a husband to look after than her unease about the pilfered letters, buried deeply among the files next to her chair. She was sure she would relax once she had returned them to their rightful place. What if Francine had discovered them missing?

But Francine, preoccupied, twisted a handkerchief, worried her hair-do, and crumbled cookies before she had composed herself enough to speak. "Last night the council convened." Janet's obvious incomprehension made her add, "You know, the men who really govern the island, Carl of the Old Turtle, Mr. Chappell the banker, Morris the Chief of Police, and, of course, my husband. Anyway, in this meeting, your name came up."

She stopped as though that was all she would say. Janet, baffled, asked, "Why on earth? And in what context?"

"They were discussing what to do about young Mark Sanders' death." Her voice deepened, as though she felt herself an official representative.

"The council feels that, without a doubt, he fell afoul of a drug dealer. That the murderer will not be found because he is no longer on island and that the job of the council and the police is to prevent further deaths."

"Yes?"

Francine got to her feet, went over to the sink and began vigorously scrubbing an already shiny faucet while spitting out the next sentence. "It has been noticed you spend time with that Froment woman."

It took Janet a while to realize that Francine was talking about Michelle. In the meantime Francine had continued, "She is spreading rumors and implicating respectable citizens, insisting that Mark was killed by someone who lives on the island. Now, in moments such as this, when a death is violent and premature, there are always malcontents, family members in particular. That is to be expected. But, as you are a writer, and not from here, it was felt you should be informed."

"Informed of what? What does this all have to do with me?" After a period of silence she began again, "Is this a threat? Am I being warned off, warned to stay away, or what?"

Irritably, Francine slapped the towel against the faucet. "Of course not. See what happens? You're already infected by her suspicions! We were trying to suggest you not listen too much to her rambling. She is not a balanced woman, you should know. If you wish, you could meet with some of the council members. And, really, all I can say is, it would be much better if you stayed away from her. It is not good to stir up people unnecessarily."

"I don't understand. What are you saying? What does my writing have to do with my spending time with Michelle?"

"All I'm saying is that it was decided to inform you that people are worried about your listening to her and forming a one-sided view of things. As you're not an islander, you might get taken in. Young Mark's death was an unfortunate accident, that's all. The island cannot afford unpleasant publicity. We are a small community, dependent on tourism."

She returned to the table, patted her head cloth into order and, once more composed, sat down. She shook her head regretfully, her words sliding unconvincingly over the table top, "I really cannot tell you more about her but believe me, you'd agree with me if you knew about her what I know."

Janet could discover nothing more specific and, soon thereafter, they headed for the attic, mutual dissatisfaction hanging around them like a cloud.

As though to make up for her strictness, Francine left the attic before noon because, as she announced, she had to prepare for a dinner party. Suddenly free of supervision, and still smarting from being treated like a recalcitrant third-grader, Janet thought of the Salt Rock Mystery, as she had begun to call the Hamilton's shadowy past. Moving one of the document boxes off the stack, her attention was caught by a small wicker suitcase wedged behind the Salt Tax House crates.

She pulled it out carefully so she would be able to put it back exactly as it had been. Always with an ear to the possible reappearance of Francine, she began to inspect its contents. Inside there were several oblong packages, each wrapped in soft tan chamois leather. The top one contained a small photo album bound in purple buckram with a brass clasp. She was unable to read the spidery inscriptions on the faded brittle pages. Stiffly collared men and corseted women stared out at her individually or in groups. Nobody smiled and, though many features revealed African blood ties, they were as Old World European as comportment and fashion could make them.

The next package contained a small, well-worn Bible, and another a child's reader. Then she unwrapped a pocket-size journal, the importance of which took her a while to comprehend. Its flyleaf was painstakingly and proudly inscribed:

This Book Belongs to
Squire Dennis Hamilton the Younger
The Bight, Providenciales
The Turks and Caicos Islands, the West Indies

Here was the man himself! He who was married in 1865 in South Caicos to one Sarah Maynard. He who had the Hamilton House built. Only a few days ago he'd just been a cipher in a government record. And here he was, himself. Or, at least, his earthly traces.

Heart pounding, Janet opened at the first page. It contained an inventory of possessions or maybe, young Dennis' fantasy of what a proper house would look like. Tidily lined up, page after page, the book listed kitchen chairs, reading chairs, footstools, highchairs and poufs, then dining room tables, kitchen tables, reading tables, end tables and card tables. Janet had never thought of how many ways there were of naming pieces of furniture with or without legs that were used to sit on, or at.

Why would anyone do that? What was Dennis thinking while he made those lists? Michelle said something about a bastard. Her mind raced to understand how this man could have caused a scandal big enough to frighten generations into silence more than a hundred and fifty years later.

She read on. After several blank pages, the book held a list of men's names with numbers and money symbols following each. The columns were labeled gin, poker, twenty-one. Dennis had kept a running gambling tab! He had to have been the scorekeeper, and Wilton, Samuel, Abraham and the others on the list were his gambling buddies.

Looking for the years during which these gambling parties had occurred, she began counting backward. Dennis Hamilton the Younger had married Sarah Maynard on May 15th, 1865. The tabs of gains and losses ran from 1878 to 1885, with some new names added and some of the old ones crossed out. For thirteen years Dennis and Sarah were married before he began gambling. What had made him start and what had happened in 1885 to make him stop?

She needed to return to the library in Grand Turk to see if the dates would correspond to events in the court records. A pity Provo had never had a resident member of the Legislative Board. Because if they had, the court would have sat right here, and the documents could be at her disposal in this very attic. Of course, it might just as well be something completely personal that had made him gamble, something no government source recorded.

She would also ask Thomas. After all, he got her started on this adventure. Funny, she hadn't thought to ask him about the family scandal. Somehow, having Francine watch her every move like a guard dog, had made the secret something large and frightening, something even Thomas would not want her to discover. All you can do is ask, she told herself, while she put the wicker basket carefully back into its former resting place.

Suddenly she smacked her forehead with her open palm: the trunk with the flamingo feathers and the monogram D.H. 1843! It had to stand for Dennis Hamilton and his birth year which, if he got married in 1865, would be just about right! While she straightened up and dusted herself off she said to herself thoughtfully, "Funny. I could have sworn it was a girl's hope chest rather than the steamer trunk of a young man. Hmm." She shook her head. She would have to get Francine out of the attic again so she could have another go at that chest. Prohibition be damned.

Chapter Thirteen

The next morning, she waited in the reception area for an hour until her call went through to Minneapolis.

"Of course," Thomas said. "I'd completely forgotten about that scandal, but now that you mention it… Oh, my god, I can't believe people still talk of it, it was so long ago. And you're telling me Francine is in a tizzy about that old story?" Without waiting for a response, he mused, "Well, I suppose, living on island would make old secrets more real than here where no one knows about my family's alleged disgrace."

Janet hardly let him finish before she interrupted, "So, what was it?"

Thomas stayed quiet so long she thought they'd gotten disconnected. Finally he spoke. "I'm sorry, and, believe me, I am telling the truth, I don't know!"

"Oh, come on, Thomas. You sent me on island, into that attic. You can tell me! I mean, how bad could it be? It all must have happened years ago, long before your time?"

"You got that part right. It was long before my time, or Francine's. But in truth, I don't know what the scandal was." Over her accusations of lies and obfuscations he finally shouted, "Listen to me, I don't know the scandal but I know it was bad and I think Francine might know some details. Only because she is the girl in our generation. The women kept the secret. I remember them whispering and my mother telling me it was not for me to hear."

"If, in fact, Francine knows anything it's because of that. Not because she was there. It all happened around the turn of the century and it disgraced the family so badly, they almost packed up and left the island completely. But instead, a few in each generation stayed on and took care of the business."

"What on earth could be that bad? Murder? Pedophilia or illegitimacy? And why would being a girl make a difference?"

"Look, all I know is, it was something *female!* Something one did not talk about between the sexes. And, anyway, it had happened years before we were born."

Janet was surprised at the intensity of her frustration. She felt like crying. Here she was, having discovered not only the first Hamilton to farm the island, but also his descendant. She learned whom he'd married, she was near to finding out how he lived, and all the Hamilton family suddenly turned deaf, dumb and resistant. She tried to appeal to his academic side. "Look, this whole history of the loyalist gentleman farmer and his descendants who take over land that had been granted to the family by the Crown itself, fits so perfectly into my project—you must understand, I *can't* let this go."

Thomas was apologetic and understanding. He apologized several more times for having dumped her into the wasp nest of Francine's intolerance until Janet wanted to scream at him, but he could not tell her the secret. He even tried to help her think of some way to get past the hurdle of Hamilton interdiction. Janet suggested that he should intercede on her behalf with Francine since, after all he was a member of the family.

All he said to that was, "Have you ever tried to make Francine do something she does not wish to do?"

Trying for compromise, Thomas said something about another female family member who might help. And suddenly they were talking of Aunt Reah, she of the nursing home in Florida, the last living member of their parents' generation.

"But I asked Francine about your family, and she did not mention any Aunt Reah," Janet said.

"Well, that doesn't mean much. Reah was a sort of black sheep and I can well imagine Francine blanking her from the family tree."

They hung up after Thomas promised to talk to Aunt Reah and see if she remembered anything about a family scandal. He'd call her back as soon as he knew anything.

Back in her room, Janet pulled on her shorts, clipped on her fanny pack, and went into whirlwind action. She stuffed loose papers under her mattress to keep them from getting blown about, tugged the comforter flat and straightened the files on the table. Giving the room one more glance, she ran out the door.

Michelle was dressed in white shorts, a tight white tee and a floppy hat. The air was charged with static as before a thunderstorm and Janet suddenly had a hard time finding her breath even though it was only a short run up the path. "Bonjour and sorry I'm late. I've been on the phone."

After exchanging the required three pecks on alternating cheeks they settled into the molded plastic chairs that served as car seats, and rattled off. Janet relaxed into being chauffeured and found herself watching the way Michelle's earlobe curved delicately back on itself. They drove east, parked by the side of the road, and sat in the welcome stillness.

"How are you?"

Michelle looked drawn but determined. "Five days ago my brother was killed and no one is doing anything. I will find who was responsible. They will not get away with it. Even if he was disappointed in me, I will finally make him proud." She looked at Janet with an intensity which bordered on a plea. "But, please, for today it will be just us! Promise?"

Janet was happy to comply. They got out of the car and she fell in behind Michelle. After turning off the road Janet joked, "How can you find this place? You count the seventeenth Turks Head cactus, or do you smell the cutoff?"

Michelle only smiled mysteriously. As though she had suddenly switched to another self, there was something about her, or maybe about the air, an expectancy that almost sparked and that made the hair on Janet's arms stand up whenever she came near Michelle.

They walked along the sandy track littered with empty shells of land snails that looked like rifle bullets, accompanied by the eternal crashing of the surf and the scritching of dry cricket wings. The tradewind dried the sweat off their skin and neither spoke. On top of a low hill, hundreds of yards from the seashore lay seashells, where storms had blown them, long flat skeletons with mother of pearl rainbows on them.

When they reached the beach Michelle still did not talk. She took Janet by the hand and pulled her impatiently along toward a castle of rocks at the western end of the white sandy expanse. Once there, she took her hand back and disappeared around a large boulder. Soon Janet found herself in a wide, tall tunnel leading away into the shadows. Michelle's lithe white-clad form moved on unhesitatingly and Janet plunged after her. The only sounds were the slap of their sandals and the echoes of their footsteps. Even the reef crashed no longer. Time stopped and Janet could only follow Michelle as though drawn by a thread.

The tunnel widened into a room shaped like a giant's bath. Water covered almost the whole cave floor and left only a narrow path alongside the wall. The room was softly lit from the reflection of sunlight which entered below water level via an underwater cave opening to the outside lagoon.

Janet wanted to stop and take in the enchanted scene but, ahead of her, Michelle still walked rapidly, entering another narrow tunnel at the other end of the room.

Around the next bend Janet began hearing a new sound to accompany their feet. The flapping of wings and the high squeaks of bats made her duck and when she straightened up Michelle had disappeared.

Hurrying to catch up, she entered a cathedral-sized room all aflutter and ended up staring about her with mouth open, knees weak. Soft daylight filtering through cracks in the rocks reflected off a round pool and made it shimmer brilliant metallic blue and silver. The smooth walls came down into the water on three sides and Janet understood this had to be a fresh water pool, not like the one in the ante-room. High above, stalactites had formed fantastic shapes like upside down turrets, and the mineral deposits glittered in unearthly iridescent shades. The air was cool and fresh and smelled of moss.

Framed by the brightly colored rocks Michelle stood, her unwieldy tote bag and large straw hat by her feet next to the water, which looked like glass on the velvety white sand. Large black bats flitted like shadows across the implausibly colored rocks.

Again, as on Tuesday in the clearing by the beach, Michelle broke the spell. "You like it?"

Since no answer was possible, she turned and pointed to an area behind her. "There is the dining room where we will have lunch. But first we swim?"

She pulled her t-shirt over her head and stepped smoothly out of her shorts. Janet was struck anew with Michelle's grace of movement, her delicate build. She envied her the freedom with which she moved outside of the protection of clothes. Copying her and dropping her bathing suit on the sand, Janet felt herself ponderous and she moved self-consciously. Once submerged in the warm silvery water, she began to expand to the limits of her skin and feel content.

They dove, splashed and played underwater cat and mouse. A few times Janet observed Michelle looking so sad and lonely it made her tease and yell for an echo even harder. After a phase of quiet Michelle said, "Being with you makes me want to start my life over again."

Janet did not know what to say and so she pretended not to have heard.

Several minutes later Michelle said, "You began telling me the life of Dennis Hamilton. Tell me again."

Without looking at Michelle, Janet began weaving her story. "In 1790, a young man named Dennis Hamilton landed on South Caicos, then the island's government seat. It was a time when British subjects fled the newly independent America and, for their pains, were given land by the King. Dennis was one of them and soon, his deed safely pocketed, he proudly sailed for his new home on the island of Providenciales. How old was he? Not old enough for a wife, but old enough to make a living among pirates and outlaws."

Michelle said quietly as if to herself, "I could never do this. I need people around me, even if I don't always agree with them. I do not know how else to understand myself."

Janet took up the thread of the story again when Michelle said nothing more. "He, like his fellow emigres tried growing pineapples, coffee, and then cotton, but one after the other his crops failed. For almost twenty years he labored and finally he gave up like so many others before him. Distributing everything he had among his former slaves, he took the next galleon off island. He only carried with him a set of clothes, a few papers such as the land grant and some letters, a Bible and someone's picture.

"After long and arduous sea voyages he returned to his homeland, which by now was part of the United States. But he'd given up on politics after so many years of island life and so he settled quietly, solitarily, along the upper Charles River. She of the letters he had been carrying had married and gone west years before, and so he could continue to dream of her as she was when they were both young. He lived for a few years with a widow and then died quietly in his sleep."

Michelle sputtered in protest and moved into the shallows where, in water up to her navel, she settled. "What a horrible story. I will give you his life now the way it really was." Her finger raised like a school teacher, Michelle spoke with the utter conviction of one being in the right, her accent just exaggerated enough to suggest she spoofed her own happy ending. "Dennis came to Provo and started his farm, yes. But he and his amour are writing all the time, waiting for her to join him. Her father is a believer of Yankee Doodle and she cannot marry Dennis the Loyalist. When it is definitely clear she will not be allowed to come south, he gives away his possessions to his slaves and friends and travels back to claim her. They marry, have lots of children and Dennis and his father-in-law spend Sundays arguing politics, while the wife and children live their lives around them." Suddenly she broke from the role, adding, "which is what Mark wanted, *le pauvre*."

After a small pause, Janet could not resist asking, "What do you want?"

"I don't believe in the ever-after, marriage and children like he did. But I do believe in love, in the one person who will make me complete."

"You haven't found him?"

Michelle's eyes narrowed and she looked sharply at Janet but seemed to decide against speaking. Instead she smacked both hands flat on the water dowsing Janet, jumped up and ran toward her bag. "And now is time for lunch."

The small cove near the water was indeed formed like a dining room with a natural table and bench. Michelle set out fish marinated in coconut sauce, vegetable rolls, fresh bread, fruit and cheese, and a light, young red wine. The only sounds were the sleepy squeaks of bats and isolated drops of water from the ceiling until Michelle, leaning dreamily against the cool rock, eyes closed, began softly singing a tale of lost love and yearning, or at least that was what Janet guessed with her limited high school French.

When Michelle opened her eyes, Janet felt caught looking. "Now for a siesta. Only, we do not really sleep," Michelle said. Janet had a momentary feeling of vertigo that was dispelled immediately with Michelle's next words. "I want to paint your portrait. So you sit and rest. Oui?"

"But I want to talk. I need someone to talk things over with, or I'll burst."

"OK then, you talk. But you still can sit, *non?*"

Deftly she pulled out a sketch pad and several pencils, and Janet, cowed by her victory, lounged on the stone seat as directed. For a long time after that Michelle sketched and Janet thought out loud. Talking made her aware how little she really knew about the Hamilton history, or whether knowing the secret Francine was trying so hard to keep had anything at all to do with her own research.

"Francine's brother Thomas, the man I just talked to on the phone, only knows that the scandal happened many years ago and almost drove the family off island," Janet said, then added, "But let's talk about something else. What did you ever do to Francine? She only talks of you as 'that woman,' and yesterday, she warned me against being seen with you."

Michelle did not stop sketching and Janet might have missed the slight hesitation had she not been watching so closely. Michelle said, "I have not done anything. She has decided I am immoral and dangerous, I think. I warned you from her, *non?*"

"How are you immoral?" Janet asked.

But Michelle was not paying attention. She had begun to lay out her paints, brushes and rags. Observing her, Janet asked, "Michelle, why do you want to paint me?" Tensely she waited for an answer she was not sure she wanted.

"Why not?"

"I'm serious. Why, really? Why are you showing me this private place, why are you spending so much time with me?"

This time Michelle put down her brushes. She turned and said, "Oh, Janet. Why why why! I am a painter. I am lonely, I like you, I like spending time with you. Is that not enough?"

They stayed immobile for a long while, looking at each other. Janet could feel the tension shift, saw it rise in a wave between their eyes, and finally settle in her stomach.

Michelle turned back to her painting supplies and the connection was broken. She said, "Sometimes words make things all wrong. Please. Just let it be for a while?"

Janet exhaled—the tightness dissipated and she said, "Sure. I'm sorry. It's an academic thing, you know, wanting everything explained at all times. Explain it to me in color and I'll try to see."

Michelle went to fill a cup with the spring water, then cocked her head and inspected Janet. Coming over to where she sat, Michelle adjusted her until the shadow play was just so. Janet's shoulder, hand, and cheek burned where Michelle had touched them long after Michelle had returned to her sketchbook.

After settling in front of her drawing Michelle said, "I am going to Mark's apartment to pack his things. Maybe I find what he knew—why someone wanted him dead."

Following Michelle's cue to move things to a less personal level, Janet said, "What did the postmistress ever do to make Francine so angry? When I mentioned her to Francine yesterday she could hardly restrain herself from saying horrible things."

"Ah, *l'amour!* Francine's husband Sam had an affair with her and Francine thinks she seduced him and is angry. Maybe the postmistress was sorry for him. He is such a sad looking man."

Michelle fell silent and became intent on her work. For a long time nobody spoke. Then Janet began to think out loud again, telling Michelle of Rudy's visit, of Francine's pronouncement concerning Mark's murder. She found it easy to talk in the space created by the sitting.

"Sam and the postmistress?" Janet felt as though she had only just understood what Michelle had said. "But how?"

Michelle, arrested in her mid brushstroke, looked incredulous. "What do you mean, how? You know—*l'amour,* sex—men and women, bumping?"

Janet laughed, "Bumping? That's not a word for sex! Of course I know sex. I meant, how did they do it without everyone knowing about it?"

"Ah that! There is not much to do on an island. Almost everybody had a 'petite affair' with someone. Only Katrin von der Koll was serious. She wanted to leave Rudy and she disappeared. Some think she was killed, some that she went back to Germany. *Voila,"* she finished triumphantly and dropped the brush into the water cup.

Leaning over Michelle's shoulder to peek at the painting Janet saw, at first glance, an abstract study in colors. Then she recognized the cave, the cool walls, the sparkling water and off to one side, she could see herself, a body exploding into space, drawing in its surroundings with violent blues and fiery reds.

The heat rising off Michelle's shoulder made Janet dizzy. When Michelle turned her head and their cheeks touched Janet wanted never to move again, so exquisite was the feel of that velvety skin. A minuscule shift and their lips touched, melted into each other, and she felt she had come home. When she finally straightened up they were both breathing hard.

This time Janet moved first. Awkwardly patting Michelle's shoulder she moved away and started repacking the leftover food. Michelle followed her lead and they were ready to leave within minutes. Janet's mind had gone blank. Unable to consider what had just happened she concentrated on moving one foot in front of the other.

Back on the beach the world they had left only hours ago enveloped them with sea scent and noise. The sunlight and heat were painful as well as exhilarating. When Janet felt she could trust her voice, she asked, "You said there was nothing else to do on an island but have affairs. Do you?"

Michelle grinned at her, impishly. "*Moi,* what?"

"Did you have a little affair too?"

"What will you do if I tell you?"

Janet felt her face flush. She shrugged and put her stuff down. "Let's bake in the sun, just for a little while," she said, her voice light.

After a while Michelle spoke up. "I have loved women." The photo on the wall of the real estate office flashed into Janet's mind, So that's why

I feel this way around her!

Michelle continued, "This is what Mark detested about me." The far-away look was back and it was clear she would not elaborate. Her voice became strained. "But we said we would not talk about sad things."

Janet wanted to protest that Michelle was wrong about Mark. Annabelle had told her he was like that, too—that he loved men! Only it seemed unnecessarily cruel at the moment to insist on talking about him. Neither of them spoke.

Sitting next to Michelle who was singing in that private, humming voice that nonetheless rose above the crashing waves, Janet found herself wishing fervently she might get another chance at kissing before having to think about what it might mean.

Back at the resort that evening, Janet asked, "Sophie, do you know about Katrin von der Koll and Mark Sanders?"

"That old yarn? Sure, everybody knows. The love story of the century! The young, penniless island boy, the cold, blue-eyed Germanic older woman. And suddenly off she goes, leaving husband, lover, and everything she owns behind. Why?"

"Do you think it had anything to do with Mark's death?"

Sophie looked down at the rings her beer bottle had left on the marble table. They were sitting outside the reception area, a space of flattened earth and a few tables, with a magnificent view to the harbor and beyond it, to the reef.

Finally Sophie sighed. "Believe me, I've wondered. Only I can't make out why he would be killed now. Katrin has been gone for, oh, six years or so. Mind you, I am not saying that von der Koll had nothing to do with Mark's death. But it would be rather about real estate than about love. This other story is too long ago. Their animosity continued on another level, when Mark got involved with the anti-Paradise group."

Seeing Janet's questioning look, she added, "I've told you about its proposed location on top of a former slave cemetery, right? Well, there's a group of people trying to organize against the development. I always go to their meetings, though I am not really a member. Which reminds me, there will be a public forum concerning the plans at the old school on Friday evening, two weeks from now, if you're interested." She fell silent and began drawing in the wetness the bottle had left. Soon her doodles began resembling rows of crosses.

Janet pushed on. "Then what about Chester? Could he have something to do with the two recent deaths?"

Tiredly, Sophie flicked her hair from her face. "Oh yes he could. But who's to prove it? Chester's got loads of money. Why does he need to come here? What does he want? Maybe it's just that once you're very rich, there's never enough money. Or it might have to do with oil. There's always talk about the immense potential here and if the government can be persuaded… Maybe Mark knew too much? But if Chester was involved, we'll never find out for sure. I believe what people say about his having bought the chief of police. For as long as he's been here he's gotten away with too much—just little stuff, you know. But still," she sighed, "as far as impartial justice goes island living is disillusioning."

"You're saying he killed Mark?"

"It's possible. If not he, one of his henchmen. Corinne's brother certainly died because of Chester—whoever killed him gave the little addict a bit too much of what he longed for… With Mark's death though, there are other things… Like Bob Chappell rejecting his loan application for the umpteenth time. Maybe Mark threatened him and Chappell killed him in self defense?" She shrugged as though rejecting the sad truth her mouth spoke. "Everyone knows Chappell never loans money to black people if he can help it! And there's not much one can do with Barclay's being the only bank on island."

She hesitated for so long Janet thought she had done talking but then Sophie continued, "And then there's this other thing. A couple of years ago Charlotte Chappell, Bob Chappell's wife, had an affair, a serious one. She never told who with, no matter how mad her husband got. Many people believed she was in love with Mark. So maybe he did die for love, after all. Only it was Chappell who killed, rather than von der Koll, as you suggested. Maybe Chappell found out for sure about the affair, lost it and killed him."

Janet was reeling. Whenever people thought about tropical paradise, this kind of festering cesspool of jealousies and power struggles was not usually part of the picture.

"So that was what the fight was about the other day? Was Mark the lover? Was that why he made that comment about Chappell having to pay more attention to her, or something?"

Sophie shrugged and said, "Yes, I heard about that. I think Mark meant it more generally. Like 'Don't just sit around being jealous, do something positive instead.'"

Corinne appeared around the corner from the reception area and announced that the police commissioner was here to see Janet "…in the dining room." They rose. Sophie took the empty bottles and disappeared into her lodgings, a set of rooms off the reception area.

Janet set off, all the while berating herself for meddling. None of these complications are any of my business. I would do better concentrating on my career. After all it's only months until the tenure committee meets. Not to mention getting in over my head with a woman! Wouldn't Tony love to hear this. One kiss and I'm unglued. What is wrong with me?

Behind her eyes a vision rose of her and Michelle next to each other washing the dishes of a meal they just had shared. So she is supposed to leave her husband and follow me? To my apartment in Minneapolis, where I would hide her from colleagues and students? This is insane. I haven't wanted to live with any of my last three lovers. Why this? What happened to my pledge of independence and casual affairs? She could feel an internal howl rise in her throat. What is happening to me?

Janet was glad to cross the threshold to the dining room. The waiter led her to a table against the back wall where a lone middle-aged white man sat, a reminder of the recent colonial past. When he noticed her coming, he got up, pulled the chair back for Janet and introduced himself in the pommy accent of the English public school as the police commissioner. He was affable and cordial, asking about her travels and, like the good father-figure he was, urged her to come visit North Caicos, from where he governed all of his small kingdom.

When Janet asked what they had found out about Mark's death, he was offended, possibly as much at her lack of subtle transition as at the question itself and became vaguely threatening. "Look here young lady, this man Sanders was a bad apple and you are better off not knowing about him. We have a large file on him and his ilk, and I am here to make sure the affair is handled properly, so you may rest your pretty head."

The Commissioner patted her hand with his own pudgy, liver-spotted one and Janet wondered if his accent and his role had, in fact, been acquired at a ham acting school. This close up she could see the broken veins of an alcoholic decorating his fleshy nose like lace and, somehow, this made her feel better. When he laid an impeccably typed report before her she found to her surprise that it was a detailed—and accurate—report of her finding Mark's body. She signed the document where indicated and returned it to him.

"May I ask a question?"

"Anything, my dear, anything."

"Do you know what time he was killed?"

"Tsk, tsk. Why would a nice young lady want to know such things? I myself have not seen the body and until I take him to the coroner's over on North Caicos, we cannot know how long he was in the water. But, let me assure you the time scarcely matters. We know who killed him."

Janet's head shot up and her mouth dropped open.

"Oh, yes. It has hardly been a mystery and even our decidedly under-staffed and under-financed police have been able to quickly close the investigation."

Basking in her full attention, he paused as though collecting his thoughts. "It is not classified information when I tell you that we have evidence that he was involved in drug dealings."

"But who killed him?"

"Well, we do not know the identity of the individual who struck the blow but we can deduce the circumstances of the victim's demise. What remains now is to find his underworld link. We will, most probably, not apprehend the murderer per se but we can and will find out who the victim was working with. Never fear. May I get you another drink?"

Sorely tempted to toss the present one in his face, Janet smiled and nodded instead. She needed to remain on his good side even if his assurance that, of course, the murder had been committed by the 'underworld' was self-serving and smug. Though she continued to listen politely to all of his paternal assurances, she could not find out anything new.

Finally she excused herself and, once outside, went stomping and grumbling down to the marina. "Sorry excuse of a chief commissioner. We know who killed him, my ass!"

Just when she was launching into a new line of insults, this time concentrating on his physical rather than mental shortcomings, she came upon a couple tightly entwined and vigorously engaged, no more than twenty feet away on the sand. Even the thin beam of the ground lamps was enough to illuminate the sheepishness in Billy's beet-red face. Janet turned immediately and headed back uphill, shaking her head as much at herself as at the two teenagers. Because just for a moment, she had imagined grappling with Michelle in this fashion, right there on the sand, in public.

Chapter Fourteen

Saturday morning Janet was at Sam's grocery just as the clerk opened up for the day. He grinned cheerfully and pointed with his head to the stairs.

Janet felt furtive but determined not to let Francine thwart her. Her plan was to become immersed in the archival files and to lull Francine into leaving the attic, then check out the monogrammed hope chest. She had convinced herself that the answer waited for her there.

Having greeted Francine cheerfully, the two filed into the attic. Without looking left or right, she headed for the serially marked wooden boxes, untied the sisal string on one yet unopened, and buried herself quickly in ledgers, cross-checking and making notes. To reassure Francine, she said, "This is so exciting. I think I have the complete records for the years 1900 to 1920. See here, this set seems to be arranged chronologically which is so much more useful than some of the others who tried to do it alphabetically, or by locations."

Francine was moving around a few feet away, listlessly shifting boxes and chairs and did not respond. Suddenly she resolutely wiped her palms against a handkerchief which, Janet noted was again of ironed linen. "OK. Well. You seem to be all set. I really need to go take care of things downstairs. Just come down when you're done with this," an arm waved warily in the direction of the wooden boxes, "and we'll have some tea."

Gratefully Janet concurred and soon she heard Francine bang pans in the kitchen below. That was all the signal she needed before she tiptoed over to the part of the attic where the trunk was stored.

Her heart stopped, and she frantically pulled piles of drapes and blankets away. It was gone! The hope chest was no longer there.

After an eternity of scrambling she found it, pushed farther back, hidden under stacks of folded cardboard. Did Francine do this so Janet would not be tempted to act against her dictum? Now she was even more determined to discover the contents of the mysterious chest.

She held her breath as she lifted the lid. It squeaked and Janet found herself listening to Francine's footsteps, but the banging downstairs continued undisturbed. This time she did not bother unwrapping the linen. She already knew there were feathers in there and silently she made herself a promise to research more on the local importance of flamingo feathers as soon as she got a chance.

Underneath a layer of tissue paper Janet found a black velvet beret, followed by a soft well-worn white linen shirt. A pair of small tan leather breeches lay carefully folded between waxed paper.

Having laid them out carefully next to the chest she came upon a sepia toned picture book for beginning readers, well thumbed and worn at the edges. There were some charcoal pencils and a half full drawing pad of landscape sketches. Janet easily recognized Providenciales in the lonely beaches and gnarled trees. One drawing was of a nautilus shell, so minutely executed and observed, Janet wished she could frame it and take it home with her. Almost regretfully she laid the pad aside. A slate board with chalk pieces in a chamois string-tied bag also showed hard use.

Next came a locket with a portrait of a curly haired young woman with a sad smile. Sarah Hamilton, born Maynard? Janet wondered. Where had she come from and why was she so sad? Had she not been happy with Dennis, or had she smiled like this before she had been married to him? Janet touched the filigreed silver softly, rubbing her finger along its curlicues.

Here, laid out before her eyes was the residue of a life, a part of history hidden away for maybe more than a century! But she shook herself from her reverie. Though fascinating and evocative, this was not getting her anywhere nearer the mystery.

She reached for the bundle of letters tied with a pink ribbon on the bottom of the trunk. Before untying the ribbon, she once more took up the musty, grubby reader, and flipped quickly through its pages. And there, as though jammed in hastily, she came across a thick-papered document, torn lengthwise down the middle but with both halves folded tightly together.

Flattening the creases carefully, she discovered a certificate of death filled out for March 21, 1912 in the name of DI Hamilton. The empty space where the deceased's Christian name should be assaulted the eyes. And the violence with which the death certificate had been torn spoke of more than mourning for an untimely death. This had to be Dennis Hamilton, who, if this chest belonged to him, was born in 1843, and who had married a woman named Sarah. He had died in 1912 and someone had been very angry at him, or something connected with his death.

"What on God's earth do you think you're doing?" Francine's voice screeched in a range Janet had not thought possible except for an operatic soprano.

She dropped the reader, scrambled to stuff everything back into the chest, and guiltily subsided once she realized the magnitude of her task.

"I had made it absolutely clear that you were to stay away from the family mementoes and you went directly against my wishes. I can't believe my eyes." Francine's face was mottled with red splotches." I must ask you to leave the attic immediately. And not come back!"

There was nothing Janet could say. Francine looked as though she would combust any minute, and causing apoplexy did not seem an improvement over the present mess.

Meekly Janet got to her feet and, pursued by Francine's voice, she headed down the stairs. Alternately screeching and hissing, the angry fury seemed to follow her out into the streets.

Janet emerged into the blinding light of a hot early afternoon. Now what? Idiot, why didn't you listen, to make sure she did not sneak up? Why couldn't you have left it alone? You're a disgrace. For a while she let her devils go at it with full fervor. Some days she could almost enjoy the torture those inner voices caused for their intensity made her feel alive, but this time she felt herself slip into self-hatred. She unearthed every shameful memory she could think of, until she concluded she was in fact an utter failure as a human being.

Now what am I going to do? Wandering aimlessly, she found herself heading for the hill west of town toward Michelle's. The thought of a supportive face made her step quicken.

Michelle was in the yard out back. When she saw Janet her face lit up, then creased in concern. "What is wrong?"

Janet blurted out the story in a rush of words in which facts, fears, shame, and discoveries all mixed together. "And now she kicked me out of the attic. She's so mad, she's fit to be tied." Finally, she slowed.

"What does it mean?"

"What do you mean, what does it mean? My research is over which means I will not write this book, which means I won't get tenure. And, oh my God," Janet began to wail, "her brother Thomas, the chair of the department, will be mad too. So I'll certainly lose my job. They won't even keep me as a lecturer." She buried her head in her hands.

Michelle began rubbing her back rhythmically, as though she were a small child. *"Doucement.* You are not fired yet." When Janet did not respond, she asked, "What does the discovery mean?"

Slowly, rubbing her face, Janet straightened. "That's the worst part. I don't know what was so horribly secret about that chest."

They sat in the lawn chairs where they had spent a leisurely afternoon what seemed like ages ago, and Janet went through the facts once again. "We know that Hamilton House was built in 1864. A year later, one Dennis Hamilton married a Sarah Maynard and they listed their residence as Providenciales. Now we find in the attic of Hamilton House a chest, with the monogram D H and the date 1843. If we assume that the initials refer to Dennis Hamilton, then he was born in 1843. That would make him a married man by the time he's twenty-two. So far so good.

"That same chest holds a set of clothes, books and other personal items. You know, like a drawing pad, a pipe, locket, and such things. And a death certificate. For one D. Hamilton who died in 1912. This could have been the same Dennis Hamilton who, thus, would have died at sixty-nine.

"The only odd thing about this is the fact that the death certificate was torn across the middle. And then it was sort of jammed into this old reader. But I can't imagine why, nor what makes Francine so uptight about it all."

By now Janet was feeling less desperate, enough so that she noticed that Michelle was not really paying attention but was looking preoccupied. "Sorry. I've been babbling. What's going on with you. You seem worried, and I can't believe it would be about my impending joblessness."

"Do you want a drink?" Michelle did not wait for an answer but disappeared inside the house. A few minutes later she appeared with a tray and said, "ponche," just the way Janet remembered it from the dinner party so long ago. And hearing the slight huskiness in her tone, Janet all of a sudden was struck again with Michelle's beauty, and passion welled up like a tidal surge.

She got up, removed the tray from Michelle's hands and set it on the outdoor table. Then she reached for Michelle's face, cupped it and lifted it toward her own.

Michelle pulled away and said, slightly breathy, "Not here. We go to the cave one more time, where we can be alone. Tomorrow I have to be with Andre. Monday, then?"

Weak-kneed, Janet sat down on her lounge chair and took a large gulp of the sweet rum concoction. Her body ached with desire and nothing else mattered. For the moment her professional future and Francine's rage had retreated into a distant discomfort, and not even mention of Michelle's husband could cool her need. There was the promise of Monday!

Michelle sat in the chair next to her and said, "Yes, there is something… In Mark's apartment I found some letters… Remember, I talked to you of Katrin von der Koll, Rudy's wife who disappeared? There were these letter she wrote after arriving in Germany."

"She talks of love, for Mark. And of her husband Rudy, of how dangerous he was. The details are old. But she tells Mark about some of the people her husband has blackmailed."

She sat in silence for a while. Then she added, "It is as if she gives Mark ammunition against her husband, in case one day he might need it."

Janet's mind was racing. She wished she could read the letters but she did not feel she could push. So, what did this mean? Von der Koll a blackmailer? She thought of him with his lank hair, his ever-present camera dangling, and a chill crept up her spine. Yes, he was creepy. Spying on people with his camera? And suddenly she recalled the feeling of being observed while in her room. Could that have been him?

"What do you think? Did Mark try to confront him about his blackmailing and Rudy killed him?"

"I don't know! But it is possible, *non?*"

The unmistakable chug-chug of the French Connection's two horsepower engine announced Andre's arrival. Michelle got off her chair, collected the tray and the glasses, made as if to go inside, then stopped. "Don't mention this to Andre, please?" Her voice was tight, anxious.

"No, of course not," Janet said, baffled.

When Andre entered the house, Michelle called out to him, announced that Janet was just leaving and had stopped by to say hello, and minutes later Janet was on her way down the slight hill.

What had just happened? Why had Michelle been so cold, so distant? Maybe she, Janet, had made up the importance of the kiss, her lust blinding her to the fact that Michelle did not feel the same way about it. Between the shame at having been caught, the ache of desire for Michelle, and the need to confront the imminent possibility of an empty future back on the mainland, concentrating on von der Koll's illegal acts was a welcome relief.

Back at the Old Turtle resort she ran into Johnny and they shared a drink at the bar. The need to talk about Michelle overcame any worry about what he might think, and she told him about the day they had spent at the cave. Johnny said merely, "That's nice. I like her."

While she was still casting about for a way to speak more of Michelle, to find out what he thought about her, Johnny changed the subject.

"Do you remember the square grouper we found?" When she looked lost he prompted, "You know, the bale of pot you helped me load onto *Rosinante*?"

"Oh, sure. What about it?"

"It turned out to be particularly high quality so I got a good price for it. How about you come out sailing with me again? I think you bring me luck."

Flattered, Janet agreed but then remembered that he had been with her and Michelle when they'd found the voodoo doll. "Talk about remembering, what about that horrible fish bait thing we found?"

"Of course I remember. But why think of it?"

"What do you know about Rudolph von der Koll?"

"Speak of the devil! He's headed for you I think. Just be careful. He lurks. And I have heard—" But by now von der Koll was standing by their table and Johnny took himself off with a smile and a promise to get in touch soon.

Chapter Fifteen

Sophie was sitting astride the deck railing at the Old Turtle with a cup of coffee when Janet came up from the lagoon after her swim.

"Oh, hello, Sophie! I've never seen you out this early. And at leisure no less."

Sophie did not twitch even the corner of an eye. Clearly she was in no mood for jokes. Janet toweled her hair and said, "What is it? Bad news?" Her movement arrested, she stared at Sophie. Suddenly she was sure that Francine had told about her disgrace and now Sophie was going to kick her out of her room. She would be homeless, jobless and publicly disgraced. And how was she going to be able to meet Michelle in the cave on Monday?

"Have you heard?" Sophie said, finally. "They found seventy tons of marijuana bales down by the customs dock at daybreak. They have commandeered all the pickup trucks on the island to transport the stuff up to the police station. That's where Billy is right now."

"Oh, my God. Why would anybody leave it there? And no one picked it up? That's a lot of money to lose." Sophie did not react but continued to look out over the reef, a troubled expression in her eyes. "It is rather ironic, leaving a whole load of illegal stuff for the customs man to find."

Even then, Sophie did not respond to her attempt to lighten the atmosphere. Instead she said as if to herself, "Oh, I don't imagine they'll let it go. So what will it be? A shootout? Sometimes I wonder if this isn't becoming too big for all of us…" Her voice drifted off.

"But why would whoever it was unload at the customs dock?"

Sophie answered, not looking at her. "It's the only dock with deep enough water on the island. And all that's required is to ferry the stuff up to the airport and load it onto one of the cargo planes. That's done rather frequently. You'll find there's lots of traffic at night here. But seventy tons is a bit much, even for this island!"

Then she turned to Janet. "You know, our police are not armed, really. Or, trained. Any serious adversary and they would just be slaughtered." She shook her head, slid off the railing and said, "I'll be glad when Billy's back with the truck. I don't like him involved at all!"

"Wait Sophie, I still don't get it. So they unload by the dock and then what?"

"Cart it to the airport and get it off island before morning. I'm sure we'll soon find out what happened to the plane." Noticing Janet's baffled expression, Sophie raised her eyebrows and shrugged resignedly.

The very air seemed charged that day. Everyone moved in a cloud of anticipation and dread. Janet felt slightly ashamed at her lack of compassion but she was preoccupied with her own problems.

She had been kicked out of the attic. What was she to do? Even admitting that she hadn't lost her job yet, things were difficult. Sure, she could go back to the library on Grand Turk for a while and leave for Minneapolis from there. There was much background material she could collect from those files. What about her three month sabbatical? Well, no one said it had to be spent in Provo! But how would she explain to her friends why she was back so early? The memory of being ordered out of the house, pursued by Francine's furious voice, nagged at her. But her desire to remain on the island was stronger than the need to escape the scene of her shame.

I need to stay and help Michelle find who killed Mark. Only she might not need me, or want me, to help her. Yes, she does! She needs a friend and I can be that. That's all. No hidden agendas, no extraneous expectations.

Having convinced herself for the moment, she let her mind focus on mystery. What was the connection between the Chappells, Mark and Michelle? Why had Michelle so vehemently rejected the idea of talking to Mrs. Chappell about the reason for the brawl? It didn't make any sense. If, as she said, she was trying to find the murderer of her brother, she needed to eliminate that possibility. Unless there was something so scandalous that, if discovered, would be worse than not catching a murderer. Which brought her back to her present predicament and yesterday's debacle.

Having cleaned up her room and tidied her files, there was nothing else she could think of doing and claustrophobia was beginning to set in. She slammed the door behind her and was on her way up the hill before she could talk herself out of the idea. It was Sunday morning when Francine and Sam would be at church and later at the resort brunch. This was her one chance to get back into the attic and pick up her note pads which she had left behind in her haste to get away from Francine.

There were days of work in those notes. For now, at least, she could be working on her land grant project until she figured out what to do next. About everything. No one ever locked the doors on the island, and she would just slip in and out, no harm done.

The main street was predictably deserted and Janet charged around the side of Hamilton House without slowing down. The back door was unlocked and she eased it open slowly, listening all the while to any sounds from upstairs. But all she could hear was the beating of her heart. She tiptoed up the stairs, across the landing, and up the attic steps, only hearing herself. The door to the attic creaked loudly enough to get Francine out of her church pew across town, but Janet figured it was too late to back out.

The attic was as hot and dark as ever. But today the silence seemed oppressive and the shadows threatening. Janet tiptoed over to the Salt Tax House boxes where her notepads lay, right where she'd left them. Clamping them under one arm she was half-way out the door when her eyes strayed over to the place where she had been discovered. Nothing had been moved. And before she had thought it through, she found herself out of the attic, the beribboned packet of letters stuck down inside her shorts. She felt as though the first breath she took was after she had closed the outside door behind her.

She could see people milling around the police station for some time before she reached them. Small groups formed and dissolved like a surging tide, while several men moved rhythmically and steadily back and forth. The drug bust! In her guilt she had forgotten about it. The police and its impromptu posse unloaded trucks full of marijuana into the police station. The audience was appreciative and applauded often. Room after room filled up with bales and when they were done, not only the jail and the office, but also the police living quarters were piled shoulder high.

The chief of police slapped locks on all the windows and finally the door of his now bursting police station to the accompaniment of good-natured laughter and helpful suggestion from the cheering locals. After he had dismissed the temporary help, only two uniformed police remained, sitting stiffly on wooden chairs out front, their newly issued rifles across their laps.

Janet could not help but laugh, too. This was the most amazing drug case she had ever witnessed. Not that there had been that many, she corrected herself. In fact, not a one. She wished she had a camera. No one who hadn't seen it would ever believe it.

She recognized Mohammed and Sarah who had given her the ride to that fateful beach of Mark's death. She even glimpsed the glowering face of the young man with the radio and the pickuptruck, the one they called Homer. Then she noticed Andre, which made her think of Michelle, which made her think of the attic, and with that, she was reminded of the sticky packet of papers against her belly.

The Purloined Letters! She could hardly wait until she would have the opportunity to use this line in public. Some time later, when all this had become a party narrative.

Back at the resort, hailed by Rudy von der Koll, she only had time to drop the notepad off in her room and stick the letters under her mattress, before returning to the bar. Sunday brunch was in full swing and speculation abounded. Francine and Sam sat at the far end of the table and Francine's gaze never strayed in Janet's direction. Janet on the other hand, had decided to act neutral. Her shame had become balanced by the power of knowing she potentially had the clue to the mystery sitting underneath the mattress in her room.

Taking a breather from the noise, Janet had been lingering in the ladies' room when Annabelle came in to refresh her makeup. Scrunching up her face while applying a sponge dipped in tan powder, Annabelle said, "I hear you've been spending much time with the lovely Michelle. Be careful people don't begin to talk."

To Janet's indignant question she answered merely, "Remember what I said to you about her brother? Well—" A few forceful swipes at her eyebrows served to supply the end of that sentence. After intense scrutiny in the mirror Annabelle drew a faultless line around the periphery of her lips with a lip pencil and, before filling in the field, lipstick hovering, she delivered her final blow. "Trust me, his death was due to a lovers' quarrel. You know how those homosexuals are!"

When Janet said furiously, "I don't know how they are. Please enlighten me."

Annabelle tsk'ed and sashayed from the lounge, leaving Janet weak-kneed with rage. How could Annabelle be so prejudiced and stereotype a whole subset of people? How dare she—And slowly she became aware of an underlying sense of dread or terror. Could Annabelle possibly know about her and Michelle's afternoon at the cave? And what would she do if that were to become public? Was she now one of "those homosexuals" because she had liked kissing Michelle? What about her six previous lovers who had all been male? Didn't that count?

Janet dashed some cool water onto her face and breathed deeply a few times. What was Annabelle really saying? Who was supposed to be the lover who killed Mark and what did it all have to do with Michelle? Or with their spending time with each other?

She was trying to decide how to proceed with life when Corinne announced a phone call.

"Janet? I'm glad I caught you."

"Oh, hi, Thomas. You won't believe what's been happening here." Janet blurted out the whole unlikely customs house story, insisting over his incredulous laughter that it was the unvarnished truth. She finally gave up trying, and said, "OK, so what's up?"

"I promised I would talk to Aunt Reah about the family history for you?"

"Right. What did you find out?"

"Well, she refuses to talk to me about the issue which still seems sensitive and is definitely gender-restricted. It's clear she knows about the scandal and I think she would talk to you, as a woman. So, are you still interested?"

"Ah, well, yes. But there's something I better tell you." And Janet confessed about the hope chest, and about getting caught. "Francine did ask me to leave the personal stuff alone but—I don't know—I was just— And now she's very angry and has kicked me out of the attic. So maybe it would be better if I simply dropped the whole thing."

"Come on! What could possibly be so bad that we would need to hide it, all these years later? By now I am curious, too. Must have been one hell of a mess."

"So you're not mad?"

"I'll think about it and let you know. Look, I know you're nosy. And intractable. But I also think Francine might have overreacted." He fell silent. Only static flowed through the ether.

"Francine has not had it easy." His voice sounded hesitant as though he were trying to find his way to the right expression. "She's the darkest of us and, as a girl, she suffered because of it. She so wanted to be accepted but, in this world…" He finished in a rush, "Ever since she was ten years old she was in love with this boy and they planned to get married. Finally his father forbid it because of her 'tainted' background and he went out and killed himself. They were both seventeen."

"Sam came much later. He's white, as far back as anyone can check.

There was not much romance but he represented security, I think. She's been afraid of opinions ever since."

Janet didn't know how to respond so she stayed quiet. After a long pause he said, "I don't know that I agree with Francine! Now, she doesn't know you as well as I do, and so her reaction is understandable. She doesn't want publicity about whatever it is. I fully trust your discretion. I think I'm tempted to let you go ahead and find out what you can!"

Having solved the dilemma, his voice became more businesslike. "So, if you are interested, I think Reah would talk to you. I think it would be good for her to have a bit of distraction. And, as I said, I think she knows what went on, and you're a woman."

"Thanks for your vote of confidence."

"Sarcasm doesn't become you. Do you want to hear, or not?" Without waiting for her answer, he proceeded. "Here's the hitch: Reah is scheduled for a hip replacement surgery in July. If you want to interview her it would be better to do it right now. You know how long old people take to rehabilitate, and also she might change her mind. Besides, it sounds as though you might as well be off island for a while."

"Look, I'll let you know tomorrow, OK? I don't even know if they have a space on the plane." And maybe after spending another day with Michelle I might never leave the island. But she didn't say that out loud, or even think it very loudly to herself. "Also, what if Francine gets ahold of her and asks her not to talk to me?"

"Well, that's another reason to get yourself to Miami PDQ isn't it?" Thomas cleared his throat and asked, "Have you met the real estate guy, von der Something? Francine tells me he is dangerous."

Janet was sorely tempted to tease him about being jealous but she caught herself in time. "Do you know why she thinks so? I've had dinner with him and he seems harmless, if pushy."

"So has be been making passes at you?" Into the sudden silence he hurriedly said, "Don't mistake me. I am not asking out of displaced possessiveness. Only, mind you, I've never met him but heard of him. He is rumored to have killed his wife which, of course, doesn't mean he is dangerous to anyone as long as he's not married to them."

He was talking unusually fast and Janet realized he was flustered. After a few wrong starts he seemed to catch himself and went on, "What Francine said is that he is "rabid," her word, about homosexuals. The kind who suspects any woman who rejects him for whatever reason of being a man-hater. Do you see why I'm asking?"

"Oh God." Janet barely caught herself before telling Thomas about kissing Michelle, their next date, and Annabelle's veiled allusion (or threat) in the ladies' room.

"I'm sorry if I scared you. I mean I know you can take care of yourself. But, look, let's just talk about something else. You say Francine has kicked you out? So where's your project at?"

Before hanging up, Janet told him about the state of her research, engaging him in a collegial debate, which made her heart ache with the potential pain of loss. Her academic world assumed the poignancy of a mirage now that its future was threatened. She also realized that, despite a vague sense of having neglected her book project, she had in fact progressed well, despite her other preoccupations.

On her way back to her room and the letters, Sophie brought word that Johnny had been arrested. He had been taken directly to North Caicos, in part because of the severity of the crime, and in part because jail space on Provo was seriously compromised, being full of precisely the drugs he was accused of having helped smuggle.

"Their evidence is that he's been selling square groupers," Sophie informed Janet. "But everyone's doing it. There must be something they're not saying."

Sophie seemed as worried as Janet felt. They soon separated to avoid seeing the helplessness mirrored in each other's face. There were not enough facts, no power to affect events, not even ideas of how to change the balance of things.

It was almost midnight by the time Janet actually began reading the letters she had smuggled from the attic. Soon she was lost in another world of more than a hundred years ago.

They were love letters, dated between the years 1859 and 1865, chronicling the years before Dennis and Sarah's marriage. Dennis, barely literate and seemingly uncomfortable with words, had run away from home during the winter of 1859, after some unspecified but implied offense. Reporting events from the islands and the successes and failures of his frontier life, Dennis revealed his loneliness and longings for the beloved Sarah mostly in his questions to her, his demands to tell him everything from "back home."

Sarah, more expressive, poured out her sadness and desire for Dennis and her letters read like the daily, private conversations of a lonely young woman with no one in her world to talk to. Her descriptions of life on a

New England farm were exquisite, detailed, and infused with a pervasive despair. Janet found herself wondering who the other members of Sarah's family were and what had finally driven the young woman to leave the life she knew, to set out for places riddled with piracy, hurricanes, and droughts.

When Dennis wrote "Where e'er I go my Heart travels back to you," or Sarah, in an unusually explicit moment declared that she was parched and life was dead until she could "refresh myself between your Lips," Janet felt tears in her eyes, along with the fleeting thought that she, too, now could write such thoughts about someone.

She forced herself to imagine the reality of what she was reading. Young Dennis had left home at sixteen, an adolescent, to brave an unknown world. For what crime? What unmentionable deed had caused the shame Sarah sometimes alluded to? Was this the Hamilton family shame? But it happened even before they came to the island. Did his crime pursue him, catch up with him here in the year of his death?

Even more interesting was why, six years after he'd left the mainland, Sarah abruptly followed him. Sure, they were in love. But until the very end they contented themselves with declarations of undying devotion. They wrote of their lives, their work, but neither spoke of a future together. Then something happened, and by May 1865 Sarah landed in Grand Turk where she and Dennis were married. What had suddenly driven Sarah so far away from her former life? The last few letters they exchanged were full of travel plans and a few, scattered references to "the hardship" which, Janet ascertained, referred to the event in early 1865.

Either a crucial letter had gotten lost or else it had been left out deliberately. Janet's curiosity was visceral. But, unless Reah knew about the "hardship" and, in addition, was willing to talk about it to a stranger, she had no clues left to search.

Chapter Sixteen

This time when Michelle came roaring down the slope from the settlement Janet was ready. Her daypack by her feet, her thumb out and a frangipani blossom for Michelle in her other hand, she stood by the side of the road.

She clambered on board, they exchanged the customary three kisses, and Michelle took off. The day was harshly brilliant but large black clouds were amassing against the eastern horizon. Before Janet could think of an appropriately imaginative comment, they had arrived at the cutoff. In unison, as though they had practiced for years, they unloaded, set the rocks behind the wheels to prevent the car from rolling, and single-filed down to the beach. Michelle still had not said anything by the time they entered the cathedral room. Janet stepped directly into Michelle's path and said, "Is anything wrong? Why don't you talk to me?"

Michelle looked up and for a moment the air was so static it seemed it might self-combust. Janet felt fear. Michelle moved a step closer and, with a groan, grabbed Janet's head and pulled it down to her own.

Hot feverish lips, cooled and made salty by tears, blindly covered Janet's face. Hands were everywhere—searching, touching, stroking. Michelle's sighs like signals of distress or passion, filled the air and Janet heard her own voice echo Michelle's. They sank to the cool ground and their bodies melded. Michelle's kisses became more demanding, her lips carnivorous and her tongue teased out nerves Janet never knew she had.

Fired far beyond her usual cautionary nature, Janet gave in to passion. Her whole being craved to get closer, to merge, and the need to know the taste of Michelle's skin was as intense as pain. But it was not to be. When Michelle felt hands urgently tugging at her shirt, she pulled back. She grabbed both of Janet's hands and held the wrists together above her head. Looking into Janet's eyes, Michelle lifted herself on an elbow, and slowly, almost imperceptibly, moved away. Without taking her eyes off, without letting go of Janet's wrists, Michelle began teasing her mercilessly.

Brushing the back of her free hand against Janet's puckered nipples under the shirt, arching her own back and rubbing her breasts down Janet's torso, she remained always just out of reach. She ran her tongue along Janet's throat, and tantalized the edge of her ear. The only sound now was Janet's moans.

This was not like anything she had known, no pleasurable exercise aiming for an orgasm. Janet felt like a starving person, as though she was engulfed in voracious need awakened and all-consuming—not in her genitals, not her breasts or lips but enveloping her body and taking over her muscles, her brain, her hearing and even her voice. She heard herself beg, moan and plead.

She promised not to move if only Michelle would take her shirt off. And then she thought she had never seen anything so beautiful as Michelle's warm caramel brown body with its plum colored nipples, tight and hard but so gentle against her own, much whiter skin.

Michelle bent over her, taking Janet's own shirt off slowly, tortuously, kissing every inch as it was revealed. Involuntarily, Janet's pelvis arched up, her body convulsing in its desire to be taken. Michelle stopped all movement, pressed down on Janet's wrists and bent over her again. *"Non.* Do not move or I will stop."

"Please, don't stop, please touch me." Janet heard the urgency in her own voice.

But Michelle was not to be deterred. "Take your shorts off and let me look at you," she whispered.

Michelle helped, otherwise Janet could not have managed the feat. Obediently she lay back down, open to Michelle, open in her need. Closing her eyes Janet felt Michelle's warm touch and heard only her heart pound, Michelle's fast breathing and occasional sigh of pleasure, and knew herself to be reaching with every nerve, every cell, for Michelle.

Just when she thought she couldn't stand the waiting any more, she felt a feather-light touch pass her clitoris and all sensation rushed into the area between her legs. Her clitoris was suddenly in command, signalling heat and a pleasure so immense it bordered on pain. The feathering touch came again and Janet forgot all promises. She opened her eyes, enveloped Michelle with her arms and pulled her down on top of her, imprisoning the teasing hand with her thighs. "Please, no more. Touch me. Touch me."

It was as though her vagina were sucking up Michelle's hand. She could not get enough; her legs opened of their own accord and her hips rose allowing her to take in more. Their rhythm sped up and Michelle kept rubbing fast circles around the clitoris, filling her, riding out the waves. Just when it seemed to Janet she could not take any more and her body collected itself for the final explosion, Michelle stopped.

Crying from frustration, begging and pushing harder against the hand that still filled her, she pulled Michelle's limp body closer in an unsuccessful attempt at forcing the magic to resume. Janet finally surrendered, feeling her will power float away. Relinquishing her hold she let Michelle steer her desire to whatever limit she might find.

Gradually Michelle resumed touching her. Janet's toes became instruments of delightful torture, the insides of her elbows turned into exquisite erogenous zones, and the back of her legs tingled with singular sexual energy. Every one of the myriad body areas Michelle touched, kissed and stroked, could have been the one that set her orgasm off. But ultimately, Michelle's tongue so skillfully danced with her clitoris and vulva, and her fingers teased her vagina so mercilessly, Janet was willing to give up her life, her sex, her future to the exquisite pleasure of Michelle's touch.

The orgasm, when it finally came, racked her body like a storm. It left both of them slick with sweat, shaken and utterly wrung out. Michelle had reached Janet in places no one had ever touched and her grunts, screams and pleadings had filled the cave.

"Mm, quel surprise." Michelle grinned good-naturedly, unabashedly pleased with herself. Returning into her own body, Janet began to feel raw, self-conscious and shy. But Michelle stroked and patted her like a kitten until her vulnerability retreated and they started a wrestling match that brought them into cool metal-blue water. Floating, Janet felt as though her awareness had expanded. Revisiting Michelle's touch she became a singularly tuned instrument of pleasure and she knew, without hesitation, just how to make love to Michelle, It was completely different than she had expected, and utterly satisfying.

When they emerged from the cave the sun lay low and flat over the lagoon. Up toward the eastern end of the beach Janet saw the sunlight reflecting sharply, blinding her momentarily, but in her state of bliss, she forgot about it immediately. The dark clouds had moved directly overhead and, with the sun illuminating their undersides, the sky looked like it was on fire.

Silly from the long hours of love-making the two women laughed at everything. They ran races with the tidal surge, they conversed with hermit crabs and they built a sand woman. Janet alternated between marvelling that she had let thirty five years pass without the ecstasy of making love to a woman, and being convinced that the magic was exclusive to Michelle.

They were almost back where the beach joined the path which would lead them to their car when a bolt of lightning flashed across the horizon, followed by almost instant thunder. In the sharp bluish light, Janet saw Rudy von der Koll sitting beside a scrub brush near the path, seemingly watching the beach, his camera around his neck. She turned to Michelle and heard the sharply indrawn breath and a whispered *"Oh, mon Dieu."* Janet felt Michelle's fear coming in waves. As sudden as the lightning, the rain broke.

Rudy sat without moving. It was as if he were not aware of them, though they walked a few yards from him. The roaring of the rain, dense as a waterfall, drowned the sound of their steps. He looked out at the ocean like a blind statue. Janet shivered. It was eery.

They got to the car, removed the rocks from under the wheels and climbed in, dripping wet and not caring. Michelle started the motor with shaking fingers and drove off, all in silence.

They were halfway across the island when the rain stopped, just as suddenly as it had started. Into the relative silence Janet asked, "What is going on, Michelle? Why was von der Koll so weird, and why are you shaking?" But Michelle remained mute, her face white and pinched, her eyes staring at the road and, finally, her terror infected Janet.

When the car stopped at the resort turn-off, they both sat unmoving in the silence. Michelle roused herself visibly and she said, "You go now. I cannot see you any more, we must not speak or anything."

No matter how hard Janet pleaded with her, Michelle did not explain more. She just repeated, "We cannot spend time or speak. We have to stay apart. Go now!" Finally furious, Janet got out, grabbed her pack and stomped away. The car's noise died in the distance before she reached her room.

Janet crawled into bed where she cried until she had no more tears. By the time the day broke, she had made up her mind. She would fly out on today's plane. There was nothing left for her on the island.

Chapter Seventeen

Shortly after sunrise Janet put on her swimsuit and quietly opened the door of her room. Only swimming might help her head. There, in the shadow of the building leaned Rudy. When he stepped in front of her Janet almost screamed. In the sudden change of light he looked green and she experienced a sudden, unexpected, surge of concern.

"I need to speak with you," he said.

"What's wrong with you? Are you ill?" On an impulse Janet opened the door to her room and stepped in after him. She offered him the only chair and sat down on the bed.

He said, "You want to know where I have been? Developing pictures in my darkroom all night. And guess what the pictures were?"

His eyes were glassy and his greenish color had not changed much. But now, instead of concern, Janet felt terribly afraid.

Hypnotically staring, he reached into his pocket and handed her a folded print. Janet took it from his hand, unfolded it and gasped. There she was naked, laying on a green and red towel with her eyes closed, her head turned toward the camera and resting against one of Michelle's thighs, her fingers disappearing inside Michelle's vagina. Michelle, on her side, one leg flung over Janet, had her head buried in between Janet's thighs. The picture was so clear and alive the bodies seemed to be moving and she could feel the pressure of Michelle's lips against her clitoris which, despite the fear and shock, became alive and pulsing.

"Does that answer your question? Now, about agreements. I thought you were better than that slutty half-breed Froment and refused to believe my eyes when I noticed her going for you. I gave you several chances and watched you for a while. But no! Rutting the first opportunity you had. And just in case you're fooling yourself about her—you're nothing special. That pervert has been through every cunt in this place. Maybe I should be grateful she's making me such an easy pile of cash. All these proper wives paying to keep their lurid rutting a secret. And their husbands, looking down on me because they still have a wife. Ha!"

He'd begun to lose his icy composure, his lank hair fell over his forehead and spittle flew. His breath, sour and stale, hit her in waves and nausea rose. Just when she thought she was going to throw up, he fell silent. He breathed in heavy short gasps and his body became completely still.

He began again, his tone monotonous. "As I said we have business. You might not be any better than that twat you suck off but hopefully you're smarter. I want those letters she has. Stupid cow to think she could simply waltz into my life and threaten me…"

"What are you talking about?"

"Don't tell me she didn't gloat about what she found at Mark's apartment?"

"I don't understand. What did Michelle threaten you with? What did she want from you, and now what do you want from me?"

"I'm not as stupid as you all seem to think. Just tell her from me, I want those papers. And those letters she says she has. And then we'll see."

"But why come to me? I don't know about the apartment."

"I tell you why you'll make sure I get the stuff from her—I know where you live, where you teach. How do you think a candid shot on the front page of the school newspaper, of dear Professor Janet McMillan sucking cunt, would go over?"

She could hardly get the words out but she had to try to conceal how scared she was. "And how would I know you'd keep your word?"

"You'll just have to trust me, won't you? Maybe that will teach you to keep your pants on in the future." He was not gloating, not even sarcastic. His tone was merely righteous.

"I might even give you something else in return for the letters. I know who killed Mark Sanders and why." Von der Koll got up from the chair and said, over his shoulder, "Let me know when you have them. In the meantime enjoy yourself." He dropped several additional photos onto the bed and left, slamming the door behind him. Janet got up, locked it and returned to the bed.

They were more shots of her and Michelle in the throes of passion. They were clear, unambiguous, and utterly undeniable. There was no question that if they got published, she would lose her job, and be hounded out of her profession. In fact, she would never again be allowed inside a classroom. She had to destroy them! She tore the prints into thousands of tiny pieces and stuffed them into the trash can, then realized she should have burned them. In her panicky need for action she picked them back out of the trash and flushed them down the toilet in small handfuls.

She needed to get out of this room! Still in her bathing suit with a towel wrapped around her, she unlocked the door, peered outside, slipped through the opening and quietly locked it again. When she came around the corner by the kitchen building she could hear a woman's voice. "Look, I was angry and acted on impulse. I was wrong. Please, give it back to me before Chester misses it. I'm afraid what he'll do if he finds out."

A male voice murmured soothingly, too low for Janet to understand. The woman had to be Annabelle. But who was she talking to? The woman wailed now, "But you don't understand. He's been edgy ever since this deal went down. Please? I'll come by your house later tonight, OK?"

Rapid female steps clicked away in the direction of the road while Janet ran down the path toward the beach. Though the lagoon was as calm as a sheet of glass and the water brilliantly turquoise, her fear did not dissipate.

What do I do? Michelle doesn't want to see me again and this guy will ruin me! What letters!? Michelle only mentioned one. And what 'threat' was he talking about? Why didn't she tell me anything? Would Michelle have gone to threaten him with her evidence? How could she do that when he might have killed Mark for the same reason?

The faster she thought, the faster she swam, the more scared she got. Finally she exhausted herself. At the moment of stepping back onto the beach, her decision was made. She would proceed as she had planned. She would leave the island today. That would get her away from von der Koll and his demands. Maybe by the time she came back she would know what to do. That way at least her book would get worked on. But first, she would go see Mrs. Bob Chappell.

Back at the marina she saw the silhouette of Johnny's boat *Rosinante*, and thought, Only a few weeks on this rock and what looked like a summer in paradise has turned into absolute hell. What did I do to deserve this? Straightening her shoulders she added, OK, Janet, what's the worst that can happen? Going through the scenarios she came up with, You lose your job, your lover, and get locked up for the rest of your life for drug dealing, having helped load one soggy square grouper onto Johnny's boat. Suddenly it did not look at all funny, not even as a mental game.

By ten, Janet was packed. Hoping Francine had not told people about their falling-out she counted on island hospitality to get her into Bob Chappell's house.

She stood before the dark, heavy wooden door without having formulated a plan. Her knock echoed deeply and, she thought superstitiously, portentously. When the door opened Janet squinted into the entrance hall black and impenetrable against the bright morning light. Instead of Charlotte's face she discerned only a white moonscape which gleamed expressionless. "Mrs. Chappell, I am Janet McMillan."

"Yes, what can I do for you?"

"I wondered if I could see you for a few minutes."

"Come on in. Though I am having some guests from off-island visiting with me right now. But if you don't mind, you're welcome to join us. We're just having morning tea. Call me Charlotte, by the way."

Not having considered the possibility that Mrs. Chappell might have guests, Janet could not think of anything to do other than proceed and hope she'd get her in private at some point.

Somewhat woodenly, Charlotte moved away from the door and closed it after Janet had stepped inside. They walked down a long corridor into a room furnished with heavy dark pieces. Charlotte stepped aside and introduced Janet to four people, clearly coupled, sitting with delicate china cups in their hands. Janet sank into an overstuffed chair with brocade covers and copper studding, an identical cup and saucer balanced on her knee.

The room began to emerge from its dimness to display heavy brocade curtains, old oil paintings on all the walls, and an antique refectory table with eight stiff chairs taking up half of the space. Muted noises came from behind a swinging door at the far end of the table. This had to be the kitchen.

Janet looked closely at the woman next to her. Charlotte was not faded, as she had first appeared, but was wasting away like a person being eaten up by some invisible cancer. Was she pining for love, or had she used up her energies withstanding her husband's demands? Whom had she loved so strongly she could not betray? Charlotte had to know that her husband thought the affair had been with Mark Sanders. Maybe she worried that Bob might have been the one to kill him.

If von der Koll was blackmailing her too, she might help bring him down. Wouldn't she turn on him if she had a chance to get her husband off the hook? Unless—Janet was getting dizzy. What if Charlotte hated her husband more than she wanted to get von der Koll and, thus, would do nothing to get him cleared of suspicion? Or what if, after all, she, Janet, was wrong and the killer was indeed Bob Chappell? She shook her head to clear it. No, the killer had to be von der Koll! He went after Mark because he was afraid Mark would expose his blackmailing. Von der Koll was vicious and he was violent. If he was threatening to destroy her he was probably out to destroy others as well.

She dialed into the conversation at a point where the visitors were talking about art exhibits in places like New York, Paris and Zurich. It was as though the art was less important than the far off places in which they had seen it exhibited.

Suddenly Janet realized her opportunity. "Actually there's a photographer on island who should really have his own exhibit."

Encouraged by the momentary silence in the room, and Charlotte's raised eyebrow, Janet charged on, now looking directly at Charlotte. "I've seen photos by Rudy von der Koll—photos that are easily as good as anything I've seen on exhibit in New York."

The transformation was dramatic, if brief. Charlotte's skin turned a mottled pink, her thin narrow fingers curled, and she bit her lower lip so hard she drew a drop of blood. Immediately, the faded whitish color returned, the hands lay motionless once again, and the bland, guarded face was back.

Charlotte finally spoke. "I'm sorry, I don't know his work." To the rest of the group she added, "He is our local real estate agent." Then to Janet she said, a shadow of fear in her eyes, "Has he told you he is considering a public showing?"

Before Janet could think up an answer Charlotte continued, "What am I saying? I am sure he has other things to think about right now."

"What do you mean?"

"Didn't you hear? Last night his house was targeted in a voodoo ceremony?"

The off-island guests, though not acquainted with the protagonist, were enthralled. A secret religious ritual was just the kind of spice to make traveling exciting. Charlotte became the focus of the gathering while she told the story.

Early that morning the von der Koll house had been found splattered with sticky blood and surrounded by chicken feathers, guts and innards. Several small animal heads had been impaled on a variety of cactus thorns and surrounded with bones. Von der Koll himself had not been home and, according to Charlotte, had possibly disappeared.

Janet decided to plunge in and asked, "Do you think whoever did von der Koll's house thought he had something to do with Mark's death?"

This time there was no mistaking Charlotte's reaction. The cup and saucer clattered loudly onto the small table next to her chair, and she hurried from the room. To the row of astonished and reproachful eyes Janet offered a shrug of baffled innocence. Since the two other women followed Charlotte, to "see whether she needs anything," Janet decided to take her leave.

She was several blocks down the road when she heard her name being called. Charlotte ran down the center of the street with an odd pigeon-toed trot which made her look so vulnerable Janet automatically reversed her own steps. They met by a freshly painted picket fence decorated with shells of all shapes and hues.

"Look, I couldn't talk in front of my friends, but you seem to know about the photos."

Janet nodded. "You're not the only one, you know."

Charlotte looked quizzically at Janet. "You know about the blackmail, don't you?"

"I do. He's threatening me, too. If all of us stick together I think we can stop him." Janet wasn't sure about that but just saying it made her feel better.

Charlotte took a deep breath. "Well, I've been so afraid that everything that happened was all my fault because you see—" she fell silent again. Janet hardly dared to breathe for fear Charlotte would change her mind.

"Well, you know. I'd been paying Rudy von der Koll this money for two years, but I was getting desperate. So I talked to Mark about it and asked him what to do—whether he thought telling my husband would help. And he said, 'I know just what to do. Leave it to me.' And then he was dead. And I could never ask Michelle because I was so afraid that—"

Charlotte covered her face with her hands and her body shook. Then she became very still and dropped her arms to her side. "If only I knew—"

As it seemed that she would, again, leave off the end of the sentence, Janet finished, "—Whether it really was von der Koll who killed him?"

Charlotte barely shrugged as though she'd gone over this so many times she had worn herself out.

Very gently Janet asked, "Do you have any reason to think that it could have been your husband who killed him?"

The bleak look in Charlotte's eyes told of that fear, while her words countered it. "He had no cause. We've done so well lately." Hopelessly she added, "No, it had to be about the blackmail and so I'm as guilty as von der Koll. I practically sent Mark to his death."

They stood in the hot sun for a time while Janet tried and dismissed all manner of comforting statements. Finally Charlotte sighed long and heavy, then said, "I really need to get back. It's horrible but I keep hoping Mark had something to do with drugs, as they all say. Only it doesn't make sense. Just tell Michelle I am so sorry." With that she turned back toward home and soon disappeared behind the dark heavy door. Janet began her walk toward the resort.

Billy was ready with the truck when she arrived at the entrance. Still flushed with the excitement of the drug bust, he delighted in a new audience to his ordeal. "And can you believe it, they came and got me at six in the morning. It wasn't like they asked us to help either. They practically said they'd lock us up as accomplices if we did not help move the loot. Just think: seventy tons! Why would anyone leave this stuff? If it were mine, I would certainly not let the cops find it."

Billy mimed a raking submachine gun out the side window and explained expansively, "Hey, you know I think it's the Mafia and if they decide to come down here and claim what's theirs, the two stoned clowns with their old rifles are not going to stop them."

"Billy, why did they lock up Johnny the South African?"

Suddenly young and serious, Billy said, "I'm not really sure. You know, I think they're shitting us on that one."

"Johnny told me you knew where to sell his bale. Who is the contact person?"

But Billy was on a tangent of his own. "You know what my friend Jason says? He thinks it's not the Mafia because they don't deal just in pot. There should have been other stuff—H', and metamphetamines, quaaludes. He might be right."

"Billy!"

At the sound of his mother's voice he sighed the world-weary sigh of the perpetually hounded. "The person who bought Johnny's bale is Ed, a guy who works at the airport. But he's small potatoes. On big stuff you want to talk to Chester."

With that he jumped from the truck and disappeared inside the building, soon to re-emerge with Janet's bag and a brown package, both of which he dumped into the truck bed.

"I don't think they got Johnny for selling the bale. That wouldn't make any sense. I think they figured he had to be the middleman, or something."

Janet did not answer. She was trying to make sense of the last twenty-four hours. Her head felt like a rollercoaster on which thoughts and pictures raced. Michelle, Johnny, von der Koll and his letters. Mark, Charlotte Chappell, Michelle—drugs, blackmail, arrests, death, voodoo.

So Charlotte had been blackmailed, too. Though Janet had blindly tossed out the comment about von der Koll's photographs, she had been lucky and Charlotte had bitten. Blackmailed for what? It had to have been the mystery affair. Why had she gone to talk to Mark, if not because he was the mystery lover? Charlotte was right to feel responsible. Mark had gone to use some of his information against von der Koll in order to get him to lay off Charlotte. Instead he had gotten killed. And now she felt guilty and wanted Michelle's forgiveness. This seemed pretty straightforward.

Only if that was how it had happened, what was Michelle's problem? Why was she procrastinating, refusing to go to the police with the evidence? Why had she refused to talk to Charlotte about Mark's death? Didn't she want to find the murderer?

Thinking of von der Koll made her think of the previous day. For the space of a breath her body filled with happiness—the feel of Michelle's body against her own. Then emptiness set in. What was Michelle so afraid of that would make her never want to talk to Janet again? The pain of that thought made her mind go blank.

She found herself wishing von der Koll had been at his house as the Santería practitioners came. And where had he been, anyway? "You want to know where I've been? Developing pictures, that's where." She heard his mocking voice. Of course, he'd spent the night at his office in the darkroom. She had the answer to at least one question others did not and the thought filled her with nauseating fear. She knew where von der Koll had so mysteriously spent the night. And why.

Chapter Eighteen

At the airport Janet joined the waiting tourists and attended with one ear to their listless exchanges, whiny complaints, and indifferent boastings. She recognized the after-effects of indulgence. It did not mean they had not had a great time nor that they did not look forward to their real lives again. It was more like the whining of children after an emotionally exhausting outing.

The plane, a battered-looking DC3 workhorse, stood on the runway where the pilot was loading the mail bags and various boxes of cargo with the help of two uniformed workers. The airport official leaned up against the wing smoking a cigarette, talking idly and sporadically with the pilot. Morris Cromwell, the dark, handsome, freshly starched and ironed chief of police, came out of the airport control trailer and signalled to the passengers. Like a well-trained herd, Janet and the tourists went to him, were checked off his list, handed up baggage and, finally, strapped themselves into their seats. The last thing Janet saw before the plane took off was the row of private planes at the end of the runway, and then they were above the reef.

Janet tried to write down facts and speculations she had picked up, as far as she could remember them. No one disputed that local businesses were involved with drugs. There was Carl with his resort, ideally placed to oversee a local operation. There was the smiling triad from the newspaper she'd found at the library—the Prime Minister, von der Koll and Chester.

She began looking through her notes to find the copy of that newspaper. She had stuck it somewhere and not looked at it since that day at the Cockburn Town library. There they were, the men who were to make the Turks and Caicos prosperous. It didn't make sense. What did someone like Chester want on this remote island? Money or power—find the source for either and you have the motivation. It's called the rules of the economics game! Which was it to be and how could she apply that here?

Maybe his oil business wasn't going well. His wells were running dry and he needed cash, thus he came up with the drug pipeline scam? Didn't make sense! There were other ways to get cash, safer ways. He wanted a political appointment in the Prime Minister's government and for that he needed to build a network to offer the Prime Minister? Too complicated. He liked the excitement and with his love for electronics he had decided to play a game that delivered serious cash return? Maybe the money from this enterprise was for Annabelle—he kept his lives completely separate and in one he was a respectable family and business man, in the other an adulterer and criminal.

Frustrated, Janet bit the end of her pencil. Her eyes strayed to the society news which filled the right hand column of the page. There was news of the annual High Tea Mrs. Hutchins of Cockburn Harbor provided which was reported in detail including the dresses the ladies wore. Someone had received a scholarship. Someone had gotten married. And a partnership for the improvement of local underwater research had been formed, of which the founding members were the men pictured above. How had she missed this? She made herself a note: Check what is the partnership's proposed joint venture?

Opening a new page in her notebook she carefully headed it: Mark's murder. She had to try a more scientific approach.

She remembered coming across Chester at the bar, the night of Mark's murder. She had had several drinks already and was feeling fuzzy and somewhat belligerent. She had planted herself in front of him and said, "If everyone is as involved with drugs as you all say, why would anybody care if someone like Mark refused to join in?" He had looked at her with complete incomprehension, so she had added, "Why kill him for being an outsider?"

Chester, chasing his cigar around his lips with his tongue, had finally said, "Get this. I don't buy this he-was-not-into-drugs shit. Assume just for a moment it was possible—here's a scenario. See, young Sanders was ideally situated to keep track of the Choke Point movements, the American surveillance, and so on. Maybe someone tried to help him make up his mind. And things kind of got out of hand." Luxuriously he blew out a plume of gray smoke. "Not me, though. Not my style. Primitive, those methods. These days you need to work with technology, that's what we invented it for."

Now she wrote:

A) Chester killed Mark:

1—Because Mark knew too much. (About drugs, oil, what other business dealings could he be into?)

2—It was an accident; Mark was merely meant to be frightened but things got out of hand.

3—Because Mark had an affair (or didn't, as Michelle suggested) with Annabelle.

B) von der Koll killed Mark:

1—because Mark confronted him about the blackmailing.

2—Because Mark found out something damaging about the Paradise Club project.

3—Because Mark was a homosexual and homophobia overcame Koll. (But why now and not earlier?)

C) Chappell killed Mark:

1—Because Mark threatened him about the loan.

2—Because they got into another fight. (About the Charlotte Chappell? Did he, in fact, have an affair with her?—Same question: why now and not earlier?)

D) Someone else killed him:

1—by accident. He hit his head, fell in the water, and person unknown did not want to get in trouble, thus did not report it (Why did he hit his head to begin with?)

2—Because he did or did not deal drugs.

3—Because he knew too much, about drugs or some other business.

Frustrated she tore out the page and crumpled it up. "This is stupid. Sex, drugs or money. Or all of the above." It certainly seemed as though drugs (and thus, money) were a central part of any interaction on the island.

She remembered Sophie telling her, "It's not really surprising that everyone's into the drugs, when you look at the islands' GNP or, even simpler, a government official's income. Our police make four hundred a month but about ten thousand with one planeload of illegal drugs they let pass. How can you blame them?"

Whatever happened to the accident idea? Michelle did not believe it and neither, if she were honest, did Janet. She looked out the small window and watched the shadow of the plane skim over the blue expanse below her for some time. Then she picked up her notebook again.

Trying for a different approach, she started with cause of death. That was relatively simple: a blow to the head had either killed him or rendered him unconscious, after which he drowned.

Then suspects. She began with the police commissioner's "unknown drug deale's henchman," and still ended up with the same list of four. Listing possible motives, it occurred to her that too many people seemed too ready to dismiss the death as drug connected. For von der Koll it meant no one was looking at a possible Paradise Club connection. With Chester it seemed the best way to keep suspicion away from himself or any other shady project he might be into. Carl and his men, along with the chief of police, simply blamed "those drug dealers from the outside," while Bob Chappell could divert attention away from Mark's connection with his wife. Just because it seemed such a convenient cause, for now she crossed out the drug connection as a reason. Then what was left? Money? Which left von der Koll for blackmail and Chappell because of the rejected loan. Sex? Von der Koll, again. But also Chappell, because of his wife, and Chester, because of Annabelle. Could Mark really have had an affair with her? Unlikely, considering what Annabelle had said about him!

Stowing her notebook she mused on the question which had been bothering her for some time. The lovers' quarrel. A homosexual lovers' quarrel. Had Annabelle simply shot off her mouth or had she actually known something? Did that mean she had to add another unknown to her suspect's list? But why would Annabelle know, and no one else? It was much more likely that she was speculating.

Janet sighed. She had to admit her favorite murderer was von der Koll. She wanted it to be him, objectivity be damned. Admitting momentary defeat, she drew several documents from her bag and immersed herself in the soothing, archaic language of century-old legal transactions for the remainder of the flight.

After checking into her motel near the Miami airport, Janet indulged in the conveniences of modern life. She ordered room service, had a bath while the television blared some giddy game show and, most of all, talked by phone to anyone she could think of. She even called a friend in San Francisco whom she hadn't heard from for a year, just because she could.

Stretched out on the bed with no one left to call, Janet began feeling like Alice in Wonderland. Only twenty-four hours ago she had sweated in her small box of a maid's room on Provo, and now she was covered in giant goosebumps somewhere in south Miami. The silence that choked the room despite the television made her long for Michelle with an overwhelming need. But Michelle was not home and the woman who picked up the call on the party line promised to pass on the request for a return call.

Aunt Reah looked more than anything like a dried walnut when Janet saw her across the large cold expanse of the Manor House Retirement Home's living room. Her face appeared leathery, with dark shrivelled skin and purple lips, her sparse hair was white and tightly curled, the dark brown eyes slightly filmy. Her gnarled hands lay entwined in her lap like wooden roots grown there long ago. She was wearing disgustingly pink fuzzy slippers and was covered by a blanket and woolen wrapper.

Taking stock of her environment, Janet realized that the incessant noise of air conditioners and TVs turned up high created a din that could almost pass for life. But nobody moved or talked in the large room. It was almost as though the TVs were alive and the residents wax dummies, part of the background. Reah's chair was placed so she could look outside, but the view was as static and unreal as the interior of the room. A row of spindly palm trees in painted-pebble gardens fronted square, brightly colored houses, many of them demonstratively hung with American flags, which reminded Janet that today was Independence Day.

When the nurse had wheeled the chair around and announced Janet, Reah's unfocused eyes stayed vacant and she did not react at all. Janet waved the nurse away and began to talk anyway, of Thomas, the island, of the attic, and the weather. Almost imperceptibly, Reah's eyes began to soften. When Reah's mouth moved suddenly, Janet said, flustered, "Excuse me?"

In a reedy voice Reah said, "I can't hear myself think, you talk so much."

Both of them fell silent for a long while.

"So Thomas sent you here on the double before I had surgery? Anyway, the question was not whether I could see you, the question was whether I would, and why."

Another spell of silence, while Janet was trying to figure out what the correct answer would be.

"Cat got your tongue, suddenly? You talked much more a few minutes ago. So tell me, who are you? Thomas is a good boy but he is too easily fooled."

For what seemed an eternity but, by the wall clock was no more than a half hour, Reah kept Janet off-balance by asking questions which did not seem to have anything to do with anything. She asked about siblings, of which Janet had none, about boarding school experiences, which she did not have either, about food preferences, travels, favorite writers, and weekend hobbies. Only later, thinking back on it, could Janet see the pattern and realize, with growing respect, that Reah had amassed a thorough profile of her during those thirty minutes.

"But do tell me about Thomas. He sent you to Francine and now he sent you to me, right?"

"Well, not exactly. He didn't send me anywhere, though the chronology is correct. I am in his department so he knew this was my field and told me about island documents that hadn't been studied before." She tried a new tack. "Thomas is a great teacher and always willing to listen, to give a hand, to brainstorm. Students and colleagues love him and so do I. That's how I came to be here."

The dark eyes bored in on Janet like a woodpecker on a worm hole, and Reah asked, "Why did you need him to brainstorm with? Don't you have a man of your own?"

Janet could feel an angry flush exploding over her whole face. But before she could get out a word, the wizened fingers closed on her wrist and Reah cackled, "Never mind. I was only testing. I never needed one myself."

Her eyes filmed over for a few seconds, then she added, her voice low, "I do wish sometimes I could be young here and now all over again. I would do much different."

Finally, Reah said "Since it appears you are determined to snoop through our lives and since I like talking, I will tell you our story. Francine, she is a nice woman, but I don't trust her. She doesn't have all her duckies and never did. Fussy child, she was. And so possessive and image-conscious. You might as well get the story right from me."

Janet stayed past lunch which, in honor of July Fourth, had a theme of red, white, and blue, with foods that had little paper flags inserted in unlikely places. They moved from the living room into the corridor and back, for a change of view. At one point she pushed Reah's chair through the solarium where Reah could identify any plant Janet pointed to.

During the hours Reah cackled, mumbled, and sometimes even drifted off for a few minutes. She told some parts as though they had happened yesterday, others in a singsong like sections in a religious litany. Sometimes tears trickled down her wrinkled face and other times a smile radiated like a sunrise. But she did not brook interruption. Having decided to tell the story of her family, she needed to develop it in a certain way, with a particular rhythm. Janet listened and recorded Reah's story.

Reah told of growing up on Providenciales at the turn of the century, with a childhood of adventure and pleasure. She went exploring and fishing and she could pilot a boat by the time she was five years old. Being the youngest of three, she was pretty much left to herself. She knew nothing of the outside world, of electricity, schools, and big cities. When she was ten her father whom she took after in nature and appearance, disappeared in a boating accident. Many other island families were similarly fatherless and for her not much changed even though she missed him. She missed his smell of sea and salted smoke, missed the quiet days out on the ocean when he taught her, mostly by example, the ways of fishermen.

"He never spoke much. Now I think it was his reaction to living in a household full of women. There was my mother, Ruth, who liked to talk and argue with people. There was my oldest sister, Mary Elizabeth, who was always conspiring and plotting with friends, filling the house with strays and hungry neighbors. And then Sarah and myself."

Reah explained that Sarah, nine years older than herself, later became Thomas and Francine's mother. She had been quiet, read a lot, did her chores, and as soon as she could left for the mainland where she got married to Theodore Houston and had four children.

Some years after her father disappeared, Reah was sent to Jamaica to be put under the tutelage of an order of nuns. As she described it, "Thirteen years old, barefoot and untrained in the ways of the world." Frightened and homesick she roamed the cool stone halls in search of refuge. It took her months to realize that her feeling of deafness was linked to the fact that she could no longer hear the pounding surf. Human voices, yells, and laughter never could make her feel as alive as the ocean did at home.

Then Aurelia had rescued her. She had taken Reah, one year her junior, under her wing. With her help young Reah survived and grew into a proper young lady. When the time came to leave the boarding school she felt her heart would break.

Janet was elated. This had to be the mysterious Aurelia of the careful handwriting. In her letter she had asserted life to be meaningless without Reah, and now it appeared that the feelings of love were mutual.

Reah went on with her story. Her family had, in the time she had been away, settled near Jacksonville, Florida. Joining them there after graduation, the excitement of mainland living helped for a while, but she continued to miss Aurelia, and they wrote and visited with other whenever possible, for years to come.

When World War Two came, Reah got a job as a machinist in a navy shipyard close by. She recounted the events of those heady days with so much detail that Janet did not realize until later, when transcribing the tape, that Reah had not mentioned any male friends. Of course she knew from readings that those were most exciting years to be young and female. The first wave of the new Women's Movement was riding high, women were being educated, living away from their parents by themselves or with each other, going to clubs, dancing, and having men friends.

After a nap, during which Janet had made herself a list of topics she needed to check at the library, Reah was anxious, agitated, and not willing to talk about her life. She said everything reminded her of surgery and death. Janet tried to entertain her with anecdotes from her own past, but she found that her life in Minneapolis, even her tenure struggles, remained flat and all her recent memories led her back to Michelle. She told Reah about the cave, the bats, and the fresh-water pool, reveling in being able to talk about Michelle even if only indirectly, and soon they were talking of salt.

Reah said, "I know a lot about harvesting salt. Tracts on the processes and distribution of salt were what I learned to read on, besides the Bible, of course. My grandfather had been a salt raker for many years, did you know that?"

"No, I didn't. But I have seen the salt storage cellar in Hamilton House which he built, right?"

"Yes, in 1865. For my grandmother, Sarah, so she would have a real house to live in. I liked his old shack though, the place where he lived the first years, raking salt and saving his money to build the house. Later he and Sarah ran the store together."

Janet's heart beat faster. Here it was, the beginning of the story she had actually come for, and she had almost missed it, lulled into following a good yarn about old days spun by a master storyteller. She was sorely tempted to interrupt, but Reah continued, following her own thread.

"For more than three hundred years they exported salt off those islands! The purest, best, salt in the world. It's all coming back to me again—tracts on solar salt versus bay salt, peat salt, and of course, the mine salt. You see, Grandpa Dennis tamed me with reading."

After her father disappeared in 1910, Reah said, things began to change. Though the household carried on, it was clear that something had gone out of the girls' mother. Ruth began staying in bed for days at a time, and it was left to the daughters to look after the store. It was then Ruth's father had stepped in.

"A small, spry man Grandpa Dennis was, with rather soft skin and a thinnish voice. He hadn't taken much interest in the family till then. He locked himself into the bedroom with my mother for a week, and after that he stayed on in our house."

Life settled into an organized routine with Dennis at the head of the table and behind the counter of the store. Soon no one could imagine how it had been before. Ruth took up her life again, albeit quieter and with hardly any arguments about anything, and Reah continued exploring the island.

For several months Reah only saw Dennis at mealtimes but by the end of hurricane season of that year, Dennis took her in hand. Seventy years after the fact, Reah's voice still filled with awe and surprise when she told that part of her story. Janet thanked providence for the tape deck whose steadily glowing recording light allowed her to lose herself in the story.

Dennis had caught Reah one morning as she was on her way out. He packed her under his arm to keep her from escaping and asked her to spend the day with him. She had no desire to do so and loudly and vigorously made it known. He tied a rope around her chest and double knotted her wrists, leading her off like a trussed calf. Reah had been so incensed she had barely noticed the cheering of the island children they encountered. Dennis walked her along the shore to his old shack, the place he had lived before his marriage. It marked the western-most point of Hamilton land as they used to call it, a narrow spit reaching into the ocean.

When evening set that day Dennis and Reah had reached an agreement and for almost two years they spent the mornings in each other's company at Dennis's old house. He taught her to read and write. He taught her the shape of the world, he showed her how to use tools, how to work herbs for healing. And he told her stories.

The stories were what Reah missed most after Dennis died in his bed at the age of sixty-nine. Shortly after his death the family sent Reah to boarding school and that was the last time she lived on island for any length of time.

Reah's head sank to her chest where it swayed back and forth a couple of times, as if in dismay, and then slowly stilled. After waiting quietly for about twenty minutes, during which, for the first time in days, Janet allowed herself vivid memories of Michelle, she stroked the gnarled hand that lay on top of the lap rug and left. At the nurses' station she left a message she would be back the next day at the same time.

On her way across town she came upon a small, lush neighborhood park. Nobody was around and it looked so cool and inviting that Janet got out of her car and lay down beneath a leafy shade tree. Next to her head she could see a silky jade green patch of moss so soft and alive she felt like burying her nose in it. Suddenly she began weeping, soundlessly at first, then with sobs as though in mourning for her life. She cried and cried until she quieted, slowly. It was then she realized that the moss smelled like Michelle during love-making. Tangy and fresh, making her head spin, it was a bright green smell which made her long to bury her head between Michelle's thighs. Like an addict she missed her drug. And like an addict she could not remember how life had been possible before she had met Michelle.

No amount of reasoning diminished her desire. Not the fact that she wasn't the sort of person who found herself buffeted by lust, not the argument that she did not harbor such feelings for women. It didn't even help to remind herself that Michelle never wanted to see or speak to her again, or that she found it impossible to envision Michelle living here on the mainland.

As soon as she stepped into her motel room, the phone rang. Over the long distance static she heard the voice she had feared was lost to her forever. All she could find to say was,"Thank you so much for calling me back. How are you doing?"

Though businesslike and impersonal, it was still Michelle who began by reminding her of the party line, then said, "I'm fine. Janet. Would you do something for me, please? Talk to my cousin Montserrat? Ask him what he hears in Miami about the drugs here?"

"Why, what's happening?"

"Nothing. They sit here, the police sit here, no one moves."

"Sure, I will. Give me the number. But, tell me, how's Johnny?"

"He is OK. Billy looks after his boat."

"Michelle, I need to ask a favor. Can you see what you can find out about the partnership formed for the improvement of underwater research?"

"Whose?"

"The partners are Chester, von der Koll and the Prime Minister, according to the *Conch News*. See what you can find out about their purpose. Maybe that will tell us something."

Michelle agreed, without asking anything more. Then there was an awkward silence and Michelle said, *"Alors, au revoir,"* when Janet interrupted, "No, wait, Michelle! I have to ask you something else."

The connection had not been broken so Janet charged on. "Did you ever ask Rudy to take pictures of you?"

Just then, incomprehensibly, the buzzing line turned grave-like silent. Finally Michelle uttered just, "*Non*" in a tone Janet could not at all interpret.

"So, that picture of you on his office wall—?" Janet did not know how to finish the question. What she really wanted to say was "Who is it you're looking at like that?" But Michelle answered her anyway.

"I did not know he was taking it. Has he—" She seemed to have just as much trouble finishing her question, except now Janet clearly heard panic underneath.

She said, "Yesterday morning, before I left, he showed me some pictures he had taken—"

"So, now you know?" Michelle's voice was small.

"I can guess some things but I don't understand very much."

"We talk about this when you are back. Call my cousin soon. *Au revoir*."

Suddenly Michelle was in a hurry to get off the phone and Janet imagined her hearing the noise of Andre's car approaching. She did not allow herself to feel the ache of loneliness after the final click, but instead, dialled the international operator immediately. Surprisingly, the call went through within minutes, and, just as surprisingly, Sophie answered.

Not sure what she wanted of Sophie other than to prolong the connection to the island as long as possible, Janet asked to be updated on the drug story. Sophie told her about the plane which crashed that same Monday night on Middle Caicos. Since none of the airstrips were lit, it was not an unusual event, but it seemed a logical conclusion to assume it had been meant to pick up the cargo. No one had stayed around to be arrested. But later that day two Americans had been picked up on North Caicos. To date all that could be reported for sure was that the Police Commissioner had officially declared himself pleased with the speed of developments in the case.

She also told Janet that Annabelle had broken several ribs and had a huge bruise over half of her face. In audible quotation marks Sophie added, "She fell down the companionway," and, when Janet pressed her on specifics, said only "You know what I think of Chester. And then to choose a Frenchman, no less."

After they had said goodbye Janet worried that piece of veiled information like a dog with a bone. She finally decided that Sophie had meant Chester was a violent man. And if she, Janet, had been correct and

Annabelle indeed was having an affair with Andre, Chester could have found out and beat her up. That explained the comment about the Frenchman.

What, if anything, did this have to do with the other unsolved questions? Was there really a connection between the drugs, Mark's death, and Chester's violence? Or was she making it all up so she could stay in contact with Michelle? For sure, Johnny was connected with the bust, if for no other reason than that the police needed to polish their image. They had three suspects jailed, and seventy tons of pot under lock and key. Someone would have to take the fall for that one, no matter whose bales they were.

If the police were looking for a scapegoat on whom to hang an aborted transfer, Johnny was a tempting target; far from home, without connections, he was known to have sold square grouper bales previously.

With a sinking feeling she realized that left her next in line for being suspected. If he was cast as the drug dealer then she could be his middle man, his mainland contact. She, after all, had visited his boat within hours of arriving on Provo, had helped him transport said bale. She then had left the island when he was no longer able to do business.

Looking out the motel window onto the parking lot she thought, And what if it weren't only the police who thought this? The people who lost the shipment might want scapegoats, too, to offer up to their creditors and suppliers—and that would be B-A-D.

Panicking, she yanked the pieces of plastic-coated curtain across the window and, to ensure it stayed closed, pinned the halves with a safety pin. Probably somebody out there was watching her! She crawled under the bedcovers with a sudden attack of chills, and let her fears roam.

What if the drug people assumed she was in Miami to sell the seventy tons to the highest bidder? Considering her appalling timing, people could not be faulted for assuming she had been part of the bust. They would capture and torture her to find out who had betrayed them. They would kill her if she did not reveal who her employers were.

Unable to stand it any longer, she got out of bed and left the claustrophobic room. While she locked the door behind her, a car screeched out of the parking lot without any lights on, as though it had been waiting for her to emerge. Walking the few blocks to the restaurant, she looked surreptitiously behind her every few steps, convinced someone was following her. Unaccosted and grateful, she arrived at King Neptune's Castle, whose gaudy exterior she had admired since her arrival. She pulled the door open like someone just having run a race for her life.

Just then she noticed the man, opposite the restaurant, leaning against an abandoned building, his wraparound shades reflecting the bright neon colors of the Castle's flashing sign. Turning her head she saw two other young men, with the skin and facial structure born of Aztec ancestry, strolling toward her. She ducked inside the restaurant.

Get hold of yourself. No one is following you any more than they were an hour ago, before you talked to Michelle. If you're going to get this weird, you should not rent a motel in a cheap neighborhood. Berating herself made her feel less lonely. At least that way there was more than one voice to keep her company.

The question of who would have her followed surrounded her like the tentacles of an octopus. One possibility was whoever had left the marijuana on the beach. Another were the people who had heard about them being left and were looking to buy them cheap. The third set would be made up of the official groups dealing with narcotics, the DEA, FBI, ATF and CIA, or whatever acronyms stood for the legal arm of drug trafficking. Maybe the Franchise Tax Board had an interest in bales of pot, too? The Coast Guard certainly did! Janet realized what a sheltered life she had been leading, not really having any idea who dealt with drugs and in what capacity.

Two beers and a very satisfying plate of fried fish and chips later she decided to make up lists. She began one which she entitled "What makes me a suspect?" She got to six very good reasons before changing her mind about the plan. She folded the paper into her back pocket, paid, and left. She would instead return to her room and transcribe her first meeting with Reah.

The motel room was so cold and impersonal it made her earlier speculations seem as unreal as the movie which played soundlessly on TV. In it, manly, unshaven men in improbable suits committed various unlikely feats for unexplained reasons. The howling, crackling and booming of fireworks occasionally broke through the rumble of the air conditioner, but Janet hardly registered it. Reah's voice was carrying her back to the islands.

Chapter Nineteen

The next morning dawned sharply blue and unforgiving, and Janet found herself in her Ford Fairmont heading for one of the giant strip malls that pockmarked Miami. She needed to begin working on the lists of things requested by her island friends. Seeing the rows of shoes lining the walls of one store, brazenly outdone by boxes of bright, discounted shirts and shorts on the wall opposite, she visualized the shelves in Sam's store, so bare compared to the excess hawked here. When she began comparing prices she understood Corinne's desire for Miami goods. Even the basics such as toothpaste, writing paper or books, cost less than half of what you paid for it on the island, *if* you could find it.

Wandering around stores she felt twinges of last night's fear but argued with herself. What could be more innocuous than a woman shopping in a mall? There were lots of people, uniformed security, and besides, malls reminded her of her real life, one in which bad guys appeared on TV or in movies, and whatever they were doing never had anything to do with her.

Three hours later, with an incipient headache, a sugar high from all the churros she had eaten, and in a very bad mood from having been pressured, overlooked, and treated like one of a thousand shoppers (which, of course, she was) she parked outside the Manor House Retirement Home. The young man slouching against the side of his low-slung Chevrolet looked very much like one of those she had seen the previous night outside the restaurant. Deliberately not looking at him twice she, nonetheless, double-checked the locked doors of her rental car.

On her way in, she tried to describe the man to herself as she would to a police sketching artist. He was probably in his twenties. He had black hair, olive skin, was muscular and medium size, with no scars.

"It's about time."

Reah, as though ready to pounce, had parked her wheelchair next to the entrance. She looked, if anything, even more shrivelled, but her eyes flashed and her voice was steady. "Couldn't take sitting for that long, could you? Or did you stay out late last night? Went to go see the fireworks, did you?"

"No. I went out to eat, and back to work."

"Youth is definitely wasted on those who do not enjoy it. We could see fireworks from here. Only the highest ones of course and the finale. Mrs. Munson, the one with the blue hair over there, had to be tranquilized, she cried so hard because she could no longer hear them go off. Have you ever heard such foolishness! But then it is easy to say that when one still has one's hearing."

Reah wanted to be taken to the solarium and they set up in a quiet corner among lush tropical foliage. Without prompting Reah took up her narrative and her story was once again as vivid as if it had happened recently.

This time Reah began with a date Janet recognized immediately. "In 1859, a young man named Dennis Hamilton appeared on the island of Providenciales." As an aside, Reah explained, "This is how Grandpa taught me about history.

"The writ Dennis Hamilton proffered as his identification assigned headright and bounty of a plot of land to the loyal subject of the same name in 1790. It had been executed by the Territorial Deputation of the Government of the British Empire. Only, to his disappointment, Dennis found the plot no longer available. After the abolition of slavery in 1830, the land had been redistributed, and young Dennis needed to look about for other work. Thus he became a salt raker. It was horrible work."

"Did Grandpa Dennis ever say anything about the original Dennis Hamilton?" While Janet did not like to interrupt for fear of causing the thread to come unravelled, she had to ask.

Reah remained quiet so long Janet cursed herself for her lousy timing. But then Reah spoke musingly, as though teasing the memory from a very distant past. "Not really. Only I remember this one thing for some reason. It was his grandmother who had told him about the islands and entrusted the land certificate to him. I remember Dennis saying, as if to himself, 'And here I am carrying on her tradition,' but at eleven or twelve I didn't know what he meant nor did I ask."

Reah returned to her story. The first years of Dennis's island life were pure torture. The salt leached oils from his skin, which cracked and bled, stinging with the sweat and salt which clung to everything. Skin peeled continuously before it had time to heal and the dehydration made the shimmering flats seem like hell itself. Heat and thirst assaulted the workers; mosquitoes and black gnats descended in clouds from which there was no escape.

Most of the rakers were white men, the black islanders having established themselves as loaders and carters. Black men also delivered the exportable goods in lighters, those small local boats still in use, to the ships anchored off shore. Soon Dennis' fellow rakers began to drop by the wayside like the proverbial flies. Within six months half of the men Dennis had begun to work with were dead or had been shipped home near death. The ague got them, or Yellow Fever, and all of them suffered from dysentery. Those who caught the particularly vicious form called the flux, usually died within a few days.

But the money was good. The United States was fighting a civil war and salt was in great demand on both sides. The armies needed it not only to preserve food but also to cure hides for leather shoes for their soldiers, and for harnesses and reins for the cavalry.

So Dennis kept on. After a couple of seasons he managed to build himself a boat to go fishing when he was not in the salt fields. He fished and dove for conch, lobster and fish which he salted, dried and sold. He never went with women, he did not waste his money on rum, he did not take days off. He worked day in day out for five years. And then he began building his dream, a trading station.

Finally, in 1865, a woman came to the islands by the name of Sarah Maynard. Dennis met her boat in South Caicos and, before they returned to Provo, they were married. They moved into the upper floor of the new trading station as soon as they could, and within five months a daughter was born named Ruth, later to become Reah's mother.

"Dennis said those were the happiest years. He had friends, they played cards and visited. Even when he was old people still remembered him for his whistling and swearing. My mother remembered Sarah, her mother, as a very private person, even more than most women in those days. For the first year she hardly talked. She could not tolerate any violence, particularly aimed at women or children. She did not even like to be around Dennis when he had been drinking. He told me once, Sarah had had 'enough drunkenness in her youth to last for a lifetime.' He also used to say 'men and their inconsiderate wills are like hurricanes—as unstoppable but much meaner.' I now know he was talking from experience. But I did not understand it till much later."

Sarah worked as a midwife, bringing children into the world and assisting those who were leaving it. She died of the ague in the summer of '85 during a severe drought, along with many other people. Shortly after the funeral, Dennis moved out of the upstairs, back into his old home by the beach. Their daughter Ruth took over the store together with her young husband. For close to twenty-five years Dennis lived as a hermit in his beach shack, until Ruth needed him after her husband's disappearance.

When Reah had reached this point in her narrative she was clearly exhausted. Her head began lolling then she jerked back up, looked around wildly and wondered, "Where was I? What have I been saying? Don't leave me here. It's a zombie place."

The nurse had observed Reah's agitation and came over on silent, thick rubber-treaded feet. "I think we need to rest now, Miss Hamilton. You know it is not good when you overexert yourself. Why don't we tell your young friend to come back tomorrow?"

It was so clearly not a question which required an answer, let alone the starting point for a conversation, that Janet began packing her tape deck, papers and pens. Reah had squeezed her eyes shut at the approach of the nurse, and she did not open them nor respond in any other way to Janet's good-byes. Reah was gone, and watching the back of her wheelchair disappear down the long, dim corridor only underlined a departure that had already happened.

When Janet stepped through the automatic doors the heat smashed into her chest with the force of a shore breaker. Standing on the front steps trying to remember where she had left her car, Janet realized she was stiff from the air conditioning and gratefully let the heat loosen her joints. Her mind re-emerged similarly, slowly rising from the past century into the present.

She had been right about the Hamilton family! They represented a live thread from the royalist times into the late twentieth century. "Now I have a specific narrative to introduce the general, theoretical argument," she thought. "With Dennis the Second not being able to assume his land rights but instead becoming caught up in the island's main export trade, the Hamiltons offer a micro-economic illustration of a society in flux. There's the move from plantation owner, to laborer, to middle class service sector, to the unofficial governing elite."

Janet could not contain herself but sat down on the steps to make notes. A few minutes later, she impatiently got up, stuffed her notepad back into her carryall, grabbed her keys, and headed for the university library. Like a predator with a fresh track, she was caught up in the pleasure of the hunt.

Only once, stopping at a red light, she thought, Now—what happened to the scandal? Dennis died peacefully in his bed. True, they did send Reah off island right after his death, but that only makes sense. Finally having civilized the little savage they might want to enforce proper behavior. But, so—what happened? Who tore up the death certificate?

By the time the wide doors of the library opened to her she had forgotten the small concerns of one family in her urge to get at the bigger economic-historic picture.

Hours later, winding down from focused reading, she meandered the stacks at random and came across a monograph on the harvesting of salt in the Turks and Caicos islands, written by the British Governor in 1813.

The text, though dry and peppered with output of bushels and barrels, lengthily justified the need for slave labor in the salt procuring process. The writer's tone seemed so fervent and defensive, Janet began to suspect that he was writing against opposition either political or philosophical.

But the drawings that went with the text captivated her. Racist and cloyingly romantic, they were meant to be informative rather than artistic and contained 'natives' of the type which used to serve as wooden hat stands or doorstops during the nineteenth century. They grinningly swung adzes, hoes, and other implements of salt harvesting and generally behaved like the white man's fantasy of 'slave.' Nonetheless, the folio made Janet see the process of harvesting salt in vivid detail.

One picture showed a flat, arid island covered by a system of shallow rectangular ponds and low coral dikes no wider than footpaths. The picture reminded her of the hellish scene she had seen that day with Johnny. The ponds held rose-colored brine and a brightly dressed black couple, probably to help with the perspective, walked the path. The text explained that sun and wind made the brine strong, that lime dropped out of the water in crystals and was later collected to be mixed with coral for cement.

Another, drawn as an overview, showed the canals which led from the lagoon to the reservoirs, complete with wooden drop gates which allowed use of the tidal flow. And finally she found one which showed the horizontal wooden windmills Johnny had talked about. In the picture minimally clad 'natives' made as if to unfurl the sails, while mules and salt carts stood ready to be loaded. Interestingly, not one picture showed any white men. Janet wondered if the artistic sensibility required color-conformity or if it had more to do with the Governor's point about slaves and salt. She often wondered what someone like this governor did, once slaves were freed and his reasoning became subverted. Could he have drawn the same picture with some white men swinging adzes and smiling happily?

Whether he could have or not, she now knew that white men had, indeed, swung those adzes and loaded the mule carts. And the labor, no matter who did it, was backbreaking and often deadly.

She spent an extra hour in the section on trade and international development where she found a couple of interesting footnotes on an oil company called The Big Four, founded and owned by one Chester Taggett. Taggett was described as a man who envisioned a worldwide explosion of small scale, locally run explorational wells, supervised and supplied, presumably, by him. The franchise approach to oil, he called it.

Well, that confirms some things, she thought. But what exactly, I don't know. If nothing else, now I know his last name. Is it possible he's up to no good, maybe even breaking international law, using illegitimate means to muscle his way into oil exploration on a protected reef?

Chapter Twenty

Janet got to the yacht club bar at a quarter to five the next afternoon. She was early for her appointment with the man who, according to Michelle, would tell her what the mainland word was on the seventy tons of marijuana that had been found on Provo.

She was feeling flat and irritated. Having spent the morning at the library, her notebook bulged with background on the economic and political situation in the Caribbean during the middle of the last century. She had even formulated the introductory paragraphs for her book chapters, but she was not happy.

Something was missing. So the budding plantation owner concedes defeat and returns to the mainland, after which the next generation comes along. It finds itself dethroned and shuffled to the bottom of the political pile. The laborer works his way up to the middle class, builds his trading monopoly, gets married and begets progeny. The generations following ascend the social heap through tradition, intermarriage and foreign education, until they reach the top and Sam and Francine join in on the Sunday brunch of the Lords. *So what?* What was the point of all this?

What was she doing here? In Miami, researching obscure background and accumulating detailed knowledge on some family scandal only faintly related to a book that might never get published? In danger of losing her job, under threat of blackmail, madly in love with Michelle who might never to talk to her again, she was in over her head. And even if Michelle changed her mind, what kind of future could they possibly have anyway?

Her stomach growled when she thought of food; she recalled lunch— a plastic sandwich, fancifully named 'California Dreaming.' Its major theme had been alfalfa sprouts. Tonight she would treat herself to a nice juicy steak and a baked potato dripping with butter, topped with a good-size dollop of sour cream. As soon as she finished here. In the meantime, the salted pretzels and peanuts would have to do.

Remembering the sandwich made her consider why she had eaten in the car to begin with. After her long stint at the library she'd been heading toward Hollywood along the waterfront, when a mustard-yellow '60s Thunderbird had cut across her path and almost run her off the road. Its tinted windows made the occupants invisible but Janet was convinced it had to be 'them.' In utter panic she had wrenched the wheel of her sluggish car, run a red light, and had not stopped until she was on the toll road heading north. During a gas and bathroom break in a rest stop at one of the modern islands of consumerism and bad taste, she had purchased the erroneously labeled sandwich.

Now, safely ensconced in the bar, she reconsidered the adventure and, by the second Coke with a rum chaser and a new bowl of nuts, she convinced herself she had imagined the men in the chase car. If 'they' had tried to run her off the road and had failed, they had to be the most inept and bungling criminals around. 'They' should be able to succeed. She realized that while she did not mind casting doubt on the honesty of politicians and the efficacy of the police, it demoralized her to doubt the competence of the criminal underworld.

For lack of anything better to do she pulled the piece of paper from her back pocket and reread the list she had penned two days earlier. What makes me a suspect?

1) Landing on Provo, a peaceful nowhere place, and someone gets killed immediately.

2) Within hours of arriving I go sailing with Johnny and help pick up a bale of illegal drugs.

3) Another man is killed, presumably in connection with drugs; I discover the body.

4) Seventy tons of marijuana appear out of nowhere, dropped on said peaceful island. Hours after this event I fly off island to Miami.

5) There I pretend to visit an old lady, stay in some dive in close proximity to the airport and—

6) My phone records show calls to San Francisco, Minneapolis, and Gaylord, Minnesota, as well as the Turks and Caicos Islands, all the first day.

Sighing, Janet lay the list aside. In the last two days alone she could add late night excursions to empty movie theaters and visits to the library which, of all of her activities, had to be absolutely the most suspicious. Everybody knew that criminals and spies most often met their contacts in libraries. And, of course, today she was meeting with a man who was known to have down-island drug connections.

She was just getting to the point of complete frustration with the way she had handled things in the last few days when Montserrat, Michelle's cousin, walked in the door. Part of a Caribbean fraternity Janet imagined like a sort of an African-featured mafia, he was tall, the color of wildflower honey and well-proportioned. While he was busy greeting people on his way through the crowd, Janet managed to remind herself that, whatever else she had been doing the last month, she had also met Michelle.

Thus she managed a smile when Montserrat finally joined her. "What may I get you?" she asked instead of a greeting.

"Oh, Charles knows," Montserrat nodded at the bartender who seemed extraordinarily grateful for being acknowledged by name.

"The usual Black Russian, Monty?"

"Yes thanks. And," turning to Janet, "let's move over there to a table for privacy. Thanks, Charles."

As soon as they were seated, Montserrat turned his dark liquid eyes on Janet, studied her for an interminable moment, and said, "What's your interest in this?"

"None," Janet heard the whine. "I don't even smoke the stuff. I'm doing some research on a book and I'm meeting with you because Michelle asked me to."

He shook his head thoughtfully. "Hm. Lovely Michelle. Always curious. But what's her interest?"

"I think she wants to prove that her brother had nothing to do with the drugs. And she said there was something strange going on."

Montserrat inspected her again, then said, "Ah." His tone suggested he'd come to a conclusion. Janet could feel a blush spreading up from her neck. Before she could refute his "ah," he spoke again. "No, brother Mark did no business with drugs. She's right about that. Now, what do you know?"

After a rather short time Janet's report was complete. While talking she had become aware of the fact that this mystery, the question of whose drugs they were, did not really interest her. She wanted to know the mystery of Michelle, and how to get von der Koll off her back. They seemed directly connected, though whenever she tried to think about the links she became utterly confused.

After a pause Montserrat spoke up. "Here's what I hear. You want nothing to do with this stuff. Word is the Turks and Caicos government is involved, the island fathers themselves. You get back there, tell Michelle to keep her lovely nose clean, bail your friend out and tell him to get his boat into international waters. I hear that unless they move the stuff soon, the politicians are in trouble. A full scale investigation is threatened which would involve various Commonwealth countries and heads will roll. That means they'll fry the little people first!"

Looking troubled, he sipped his drink. "Messing with this size shipment means powerful people, possibly one of the cartels. The best thing for the island would be if someone had dumped the stuff to force a political inquiry and expose the island's well-hidden dirty laundry to the whole world. At least it would not mean an all-out turf war."

"You mean a shoot-out on the island?"

Montserrat just looked at Janet without answering. She asked, somewhat sheepishly, "Do you think someone could be following me?"

"Well your timing is bad enough. Tell me."

She told what she could but saw him becoming exasperated with her vague descriptions. She faltered, then said, "What do they want?"

"As I can't guess from your description who they might be I can't tell you what they want. There's no question but many people keep tabs on the Turks and Caicos. Too much money's going through that place not to be noticed. And you are sort of in the middle of things." He thought for a moment. "Probably thought to be part of the "new" triangle trade, that of guns going to South America while drugs travel to the US and money ends up in the Caribbean. The Cali Cartels as well as the Mafia and the Cuban underground have been sniffing to muscle in on the Prime Minister's hold on traffic."

He set his empty glass carefully onto the ring the condensation had made earlier. "Here's what I will do. For Michelle, mind you. I'll have some friends keep an informal watch. Look for a red bandanna like this one. But don't talk to anyone or you'll blow their cover. They're just last ditch, OK? And remember, whoever can afford to lose seventy tons of merchandise you can't afford to cross."

Several steps away from the table he turned back and grinned, "And in case of doubt, call the police. You are, after all, white and female— police is your friend! You should have no trouble with them... I'll give you a ring Monday. *Salut, ma vieille.*" The unexpected verbal nod toward his French speaking background made Janet conscious of his generally cosmopolitan North American accent. For whatever reason he had successfully lost all traces of island speech.

Watching his back disappear she felt strangely bereft. Trying to get used to the idea of being a watched woman she ordered a straight rum. Her stomach grumbled but her appetite was quite gone.

When she arrived at the motel she noticed a dark-haired sleek young man leaning nonchalantly against the graffitied wall of the building across the parking lot. Seeing him, so like the other slouching, lounging young men of her recent past, she lost her composure. She got out of her car, walked halfway across the parking lot and yelled across the street, "Just leave me alone. I don't know anything, you hear. Go away!"

His gestured response, indicating mental deficiency and confusion, made her wonder if she were imagining things and whether she might be more drunk than she'd thought. Embarrassed, she returned to her room but, just in case, blocked the door with the heavy armchair, after having chained and locked it.

Only then did she open the Fed Ex package she had found by the door. It had been mailed in Minneapolis and, as expected, contained a very scuffed and tattered Bible. Thomas had also included a small packet of greeting cards, the flowery Victorian, kind. Janet looked through them quickly. They were written to and sent by two girls named Deborah and Sarah. Janet put them aside with a slight sigh. More family members? To judge from the cards, Deborah and Sarah were roughly contemporaries of Dennis Hamilton the Younger. It was time to make a chart, get an overview. Time for the family genealogy.

The Bible still held the shipping line chit, permanently affixed to the Song of Solomon. The archaic language distracted Janet for a few moments but then she turned to the front page.

In different-colored inks and various handwritings, some ornate and precise, some unsure and clumsy, the passing of a family was laid out. The Hamiltons took shape before her eyes, through their births, deaths, and marriages. Before she could make sense of the whole, the phone rang.

Janet hardly recognized Michelle's voice it sounded so tinny through the ether and her accent was neutral, hardly French. But she insisted she was doing OK. Since she volunteered nothing else, Janet found herself giving her an account of suspicious men and freeway tailings, and though she meant to sound amusing she knew she sounded afraid. Michelle asked, "Why did you not call the police?"

"You know it's easy to get paranoid in a strange city, especially when you stay in a cheap motel. Anyway, your cousin said he would get some of his friends to look after me."

"Well, that should make you feel safe," Michelle said with amused sarcasm. "*Eh, bien.* So? What does he know?"

Janet retold Montserrat's suspicions of political intrigue, including his theory about the bales being planted to force an inquest. She added "It seems so unbelievable to just drop seventy tons—you might as well dump several million dollars out the window! I mean, with that much money you could buy yourselves all kinds of publicity and inquests, don't you think?"

Michelle did not respond for a while, then she said, "It seems exaggerated, yes. But if Monty says so…maybe you catch crooked politicians like other criminals, with a sting operation."

"So now you're saying these drugs were planted by the DEA, or maybe the ATF, and—" Some other conversation interfered, like a rogue audio wave rolling over their line. Janet hardly noticed, still puzzling. "Who were they trying to catch? The Prime Minister, or the drug dealers?"

Michelle's silvery laughter sparkled in her ear. "*Ah non, ma cherie.* I think a sting is to catch the monkey with the cookie in hand. Here all we have is a cookie and no monkey, no paw in the jar, not even a catcher. And the police have the cookie anyway. It's confusing when all we have is pot, no dealer, no buyer."

The man and woman whose phone call crossed theirs seemed to be having a fight. Janet wondered if they heard their voices as loudly as she heard them. Now Michelle was talking again. "Do you remember the von der Koll house, the voodoo ritual?"

"Yes, what about it?"

"You heard of the anti-Paradise group, right? Of the fact that the club is to be built on sacred land? Several people have come forward with not very veiled hints about people who do not respect history."

Janet could almost see Michelle's eloquent shrug and thrown-up hands, and her relief came through the phone wires. "The horrible von der Koll doll we found? It means someone is trying to make him listen. And, as Mark was against the ugly club project, too—"

"Do not say such things over the telephone," Michelle interrupted loudly. "But if you want to know more about the island, join the meeting on Saturday. You will be back, right? Oh, and the police want to talk to you."

This sounded ominous but Michelle did not seem worried. "I promised Monsieur Cromwell I would tell you. He is interested in your contacts, he says."

"Contacts?"

"You know, the people you see in Miami?"

"Oh, so what do I tell him? Aunt Reah, your cousin, and the librarian?"

"*Eh bien, oui.*"

After they had hung up the room closed in on Janet. The island, next Saturday, and even Michelle seemed as far away as eternity. Missing Michelle drove Janet out of the room.

She got into the car, heading for a bookstore she had seen advertised on the library bulletin board. The parking lot was empty in front of the small building. She locked the car and walked to the door, her back prickling. But no one followed and inside the store was cozy and quiet. One woman was there, sitting behind the counter reading. Dressed in khaki pants and a tee shirt that read *Amazon* in purple letters across her bra-less chest, she glanced up, smiled and returned to her book.

Instantly, Janet found herself wondering why this woman needed to be so blatant about her sexual preference, judgment creeping up her spine like a line of ants. It wasn't that being lesbian was wrong, something to be hidden. It was more that she did not want to be confronted with the necessity of a public stance. She could remember arguing that people should not define themselves according to whom they had sex with and that gender was an artificial construct. "We all have the potential for archetypal androgyny and with it comes the freedom to make love to soulmates of either gender," she had repeated often, only slightly self-consciously. Thinking back on some of those speeches now made her cringe. How pompous she had been about something she really knew nothing about!

Seeing this lesbian so comfortably proclaiming the fact that she preferred women suddenly brought back the visceral memory of making love in the cave and she began to speculate whether the other woman, too, knew earth-shaking orgasms of the kind she had discovered with Michelle. It made her feel conspiratorial and slightly silly. But it also made her more determined about her present mission.

The place was well stocked with feminist texts, non-fiction, classical women writers and modern fiction. Behind a display of photographic art, coffee table books and records, Janet spied the reason for her visit. A large bookshelf protruded into the room, wholly dedicated to lesbian books.

Just when she had reached that shelf she heard someone enter the store and a second woman appeared by the lesbian section. She was young, wore her hair cropped short and seemed very sure of herself. Janet felt suddenly self conscious. What if that woman talked to her, or decided she was a fake? Janet wasn't sure if there were a protocol, a certain way of speaking. Now, having decided she might have been fooling herself, the thought of being caught "posing as a lesbian" made her anxious.

But the young woman seemed oblivious to her presence and concentrated on the books she had come to buy. Darting glances at the other's selection, Janet's fear changed to recklessness and excitement and she saw herself on the threshold of a new world. When Janet finally left the bookstore she carried several volumes, among them the classic love tragedy by Radclyffe Hall.

Back in her room she dripped some of the take-out *sopa de mariscos* down her shirt and lost a piece of squid inside the bed covers. But she felt hopeful. Michelle was talking to her again and together, she was sure, they could deal with Rudy. It was as though the nightmare was over. Tomorrow Reah would provide the remaining answers and in three days she would fly back to Michelle and they would fix whatever had gone wrong.

By the time her thoughts returned to drugs and criminals she had convinced herself that, not only had she imagined the men following her, but that the conspiracy theories were all wrong. Why could it not all have been an accident? A hijacked boat, the grasshopper which had carried the stuff, had simply dropped off its cargo and—its part in the operation over—was taken off shore to be scuttled. The plane was supposed to land, load, and disappear before anyone was the wiser, but it crashed. Easy to do in the dark without landing lights. Either the boat crew missed the message that the plane had crashed, or the crash happened after the bales had been unloaded. And so it had happened.

So far so good. Now it was time for lists—lists of things to do before Tuesday morning and a list of questions to ask Reah tomorrow. Last but not least she compiled her thoughts on the mysteries of the salt rock, as she had begun to call the island's set of goings-on. They were laid out in the form of questions and answers and as she addressed the envelope to Thomas and finally crawled under the covers, she barely noted that it had turned Sunday long ago.

Chapter Twenty-One

"Did Dennis have a twin sister?"

Janet leaned over the table at Wolfie's so she could make herself heard. It was as though half of Fort Lauderdale, the hard-of-hearing part, had come to Sunday brunch, and the cavernous room bulged with people and conversations. Reah, like a child, was all eyes and her head practically swivelled in excitement. "Let's order coleslaw and some of the sauerkraut Wolfie's is famous for."

"How about lox and bagels?"

Almost petulant, Reah said, "I've looked forward to a pastrami sandwich for months."

"Reah, how about you order whatever you can imagine would taste good and I'll take home what we don't eat. That way I won't have to go out for the rest of the day."

The elderly waitress with her frilly pink apron and beehive hair looked down through her heavily mascaraed eyes and chewed her gum rapidly. "Whaddya-want?"

Having ordered, they sat back in the pink plastic booth and observed the hubbub for a while. Janet felt wrung out and limp. Her phone had rung at seven waking her out of a deep sleep. It was Michelle, saying that the British Governor had announced a Dependency-wide inquiry into narcotics dealings and official corruption. As the High Commission was made up of officials from various other island states as well as British representatives, the inquiry meant the chance for serious housecleaning.

"And so maybe Mark will receive justice in the end!" she had happily concluded. Janet had been too sleepy to ask how that fit in and had simply enjoyed hearing Michelle's voice. Its liveliness and excitement had warmed her all over despite the six hundred miles distance.

On her way from the motel room to the car to pick up Reah, she had come across a young black man using the parking lot to practice a complex solitary dance, accompanied by his boom box. The flash of red in his back pocket made Janet perk up and notice. Montserrat had promised a red bandanna, and here was one of her "last ditch protectors." His arms and legs flailed or jerked, his body gyrated, and altogether it was a breathtaking sight of controlled contortion. Dressed in black he gave absolutely no sign of having noticed her nor of wanting to. She had driven off smiling and, for the duration of her laps at the YMCA pool, she had felt curiously cared for.

Now she focused in on the present and noticed that Reah's attention had begun to waver away from watching people. Janet pounced and repeated her question. "Did Dennis have a half sister, maybe?"

Reah's face scrunched up in consternation and she turned her head to fully face Janet. "Now why would you think that?"

"Thomas mailed me the family Bible, you know, where people used to mark births, deaths and other important events. And remember that chest I found in the attic? The one with the initials DRH, dated 1843? Well, the only birth in that generation of Hamiltons, according to the Bible, was in 1843. Only it was a girl, Deborah! So I've wondered, maybe Dennis wasn't legitimate and that's why he's not recorded."

Right then the food came, huge platters and bowls of it. If Reah managed no more than a taste from each dish, she would still not leave hungry. Janet settled in for a long enjoyable visit with food, the main challenge being not to stuff herself too soon.

After a time of tasting, loading plates and oohing and aahing, Reah said, "I will tell you a story about myself."

She took another bite, considered, then continued, "After you have listened carefully, you can ask me more questions if you need to. Agreed?"

Janet only nodded, busy with an unwieldy bite of bagel, lox, onion and capers. Reah's tale occurred during the war and involved a young woman, a drunken husband, a pregnancy, and Reah.

Maria worked with Reah at the shipyard. They began going for drinks after work, sometimes taking in a movie. Somewhere along there Reah learned that the husband had been beating Maria pretty much since their wedding but—as Maria said—her father had done the same to her mother. For a while, when her husband was off at training camp, Maria moved in with Reah to save on rent. Over the span of a year the two women became close friends. During the time the husband was on active duty they lived together too. Then he came home, invalided out of the army, bitter and drinking more than ever.

"We had been living together for the six months he was gone. Maria had gotten pregnant during his last leave. We were so happy together, like a real family, Maria, the baby and I. I could feel it move when I put my ear to her stomach. After he came back things got bad. She had to return to him and he kept beating her. She came to me one day and begged me to run away with her. To save her. And—"

Here Reah dropped her hands into her lap and her eyes looked vacantly out into the past while the tears ran slowly, unchecked, down her wrinkled face.

"I did nothing. I put her off. I...was scared. Of him, of being one of those women everyone hated and talked about. I did not want to live my life on the run. I...delayed and looked for excuses."

There was a pause which went on so long Janet thought maybe she had gone to sleep. Just then Reah's lips moved and she whispered, "Two weeks later she was dead. Beaten to death by her husband. The baby died with her. They said it was a little girl and she could have lived if someone had helped her be born."

Reah's face was scarcely human there was so much pain in it. She looked directly at Janet and said, "I killed Maria and our baby. Because I did not love enough. Because I feared too much. I have paid for it for forty years, but soon now I will be with them again."

Silence wrapped the table like a blanket. After a while Reah asked to be taken home. "You can ask your questions in a little while, maybe," she said.

Janet dropped Reah back at the Manor House and returned to the car frantically writing down the story as well as she could remember. The background noise had overpowered Reah's voice and all the tape delivered were clanking dishes, the roar of human voices, and here and there a word.

What a heartbreaking story. For forty years Reah had held on to it, and for forty years she mourned the love of her life! Had she suffered it all in silence, or had she told someone before now? All because she was a woman, rather than a man. Talk about 'the love that dare not speak its name!'

When the explosion came, Janet dropped her notebook and covered her face. After her heart had restarted, pounding painfully but regularly, she began hearing the rain. Only then did she realize the end-of-the-world blast had been mere thunder—albeit right overhead. For a while she watched the spectacular celestial fireworks. She felt the urge to run back in to Reah and tell her—what—that she was forgiven? She, Janet, would make up for her cowardice; she would let the world know that love in all its forms was sacred?

Of course, the hundred yards to the entrance would drench her completely and anyway, Reah would probably be asleep. Besides, there was nothing to be said that Reah hadn't already thought of a million times. And who was she to talk about bravery? She, who had run away from Michelle at the first sign of trouble from von der Koll!

Why had Reah told her that story anyhow? Was she just trying to get it off her chest? How did it fit with Dennis's story? Maybe Reah meant to hint about Michelle? Janet missed Michelle so intensely that all she wanted was to be back on the island. It was time to stop by the airport and confirm her flight for Tuesday morning. She would call Reah later in the day. She started her car and eased into the road, the wipers going madly without much visible effect.

Splashing through the hub-deep water in her rental car Janet wondered about Michelle's other lovers. She might be with one of them now. That conviction grew slowly, imperceptibly, like an expanding fungus. That was why Michelle didn't want to confront von der Koll with Mark's evidence, why she was so controlling about who Janet should, or should not, talk to.

One of those other lovers was the one she had looked at with such tenderness, in the photo in von der Koll's office. Maybe the the one she was with this very minute.

What do I really know about Michelle? Janet asked herself. Peering through the waterfall coursing down her windshield she resolved to be coldly analytical. Michelle had an older brother whom she didn't know very well as they grew up on different parts of Martinique. There are other siblings, a mother, father and grandparent, but Michelle didn't speak of them much. In fact, she didn't talk much about anything personal. She has a French husband whom she doesn't particularly love and whom she might have married in the hopes of moving to Europe. She paints, she sings and she is beautiful. Janet chided herself impatiently, Come on, Janet, you can do better than that!

OK, she knew that Michelle made love to women, had done it before. She knew that Michelle was a good cook, that she had an eye for beauty in all forms—that she was educated, liked to read, knew much about African religions, and didn't want to have children. But what does all that mean?

"What do I guess, then? I guess that Francine has issues with Michelle because of her lesbianism. I think Michelle, too, is being blackmailed by Rudy von der Koll."

Saying those suspicions out loud, even to herself, shocked her. Not as much as realizing she'd known for some time. Luckily she was stopped at a red light.

Thoughts began to flash by so fast she could not think them all through. Why should Francine care about anyone's tendencies? What does von der Koll have on Michelle? Can it be anything but a sexual liaison— as he has on me now? Would he use the same pictures to blackmail both of us? Had he already shown them to Michelle? Thinking of those pictures tempted her into remembering Michelle's passion, the feel of her skin, but the light changed and she sluiced on across the lake that was the road.

What else did she know or guess about Michelle? She was curious. She was passionate about achieving justice for Mark. And just possibly playing a dangerous game with von der Koll by dangling some knowledge she had acquired through her dead brother's papers.

Did Michelle have anything to do with the seventy tons of pot? No. Not likely. On the other hand, something connected with either Mark's death or the drugs or both had to be going on between Michelle and the banker, Bob Chappell. Why else would she not confront him about the fight at the bar, why refuse to ask his wife what Mark might have meant with the comment about her not getting enough attention? Was Mark Mrs. Chappell's mystery lover, the one she refused to name? Too many unknowns. She shook her head, trying to clear it.

And what had Michelle found in Mark's apartment? What letters was von der Koll so intent on, and why had Michelle not told her about them? She knew about the one from von der Koll's wife. Was that all? Trying to remember von der Koll's exact words Janet was sure he'd talked of 'letters and papers.' Maybe Michelle had found business papers in the apartment and had threatened to make them public? It was the only explanation for what Michelle could possibly have to threaten him with.

Janet turned off the engine in the dimness of the short term parking lot at the airport, still caught up in her thoughts. What did she, Janet, mean to Michelle, really? Or the other way around? Was she willing to resign her job for Michelle, or rather, for her right to love a woman? Would Michelle leave her husband and go away with her? Where would they go, what would they do? If she lost her job, how would they earn a living? Could she emigrate, as Dennis had done, and make a life for the woman she loved? But she couldn't do anything but teach. Would they end up hating each other within a year?

She trudged toward the elevator. If Reah's story were happening now, and it was Michelle who was pregnant and needed protection, Janet would bring her to Minneapolis, would fight for her, for their child, and would create a life for them. Wouldn't she? Could Michelle live in the snow? How would it be to wake up every day next to her?

She turned a corner so caught up in the fantasy of Michelle's dark head on the pillow next to her, she did not hear the man's question at first. What penetrated was the smell of breath mints wafting over her left shoulder, and the feeling of someone very close.

"Who're you working for, bitch?"

Then she noticed there were two more of them. One stood squarely in her path, his right hand hidden under the flap of his bulging jacket. Face unreadable behind the black sunglasses, he said, "Just give us a name and you'll never see us again."

Five swaggering, jiving young black men materialized from behind a parked van. They sauntered up, surrounded the frozen scene in the middle of which were Janet and the man breathing down her shoulder. And as suddenly as it had occurred, the picture dissolved. The three men accosting Janet were gone and so, too, were the black youths, five red kerchiefs flashing like warm signal flags in the gloom of the parking garage.

Janet stood alone amidst abandoned cars, enveloped by the roar of plane engines. She began walking in the direction of the airport lounge as if sleepwalking. Only when she was inside the freezing terminal filled with stranded travellers waiting for air traffic to be resumed, did reaction set in. She slid onto a bench and stared at the damp rubber tiles. "I froze. She whispered. "I absolutely could not have said a word. What would have happened if those guys hadn't shown up?"

Who were they anyway? Where did they come from so suddenly? The whole thing was unreal, like a slow-moving film.

Rerunning the scene in her mind, she clearly saw the red bandannas in their back pockets as they walked away. So they were Montserrat's men! A warm feeling of gratitude welled up for the man she'd only met once and, immediately, it expanded to include Michelle. He was, after all, her cousin. Michelle saved my life. An absurd thought. But she liked it because of the way it made her feel.

But who were the thugs? A faint memory nagged at her about the one who'd stood in front of her. She had heard his voice before. Propped against an institutionally gray wall and staring at a wet shiny black floor inside the chilled airport terminal she tried to remember. First to emerge was a feeling of heat, then the image of a shattered wooden airplane prop mounted on a smokey wall. The airport bar in Provo! That's when she'd heard him say, "Don't think we're not watching." Back then she'd never seen his face, only his broad back, one of a line of backs hunched over their beers. He could have been any of them, with their battered leather jackets slung over the bar railing.

And she had frozen—could not have said a word if her life depended on it! Which it well might have. She almost wished for a Catholic past, so she could prostrate and flagellate herself in atonement. As it was, she was condemned to sit on a bench in embarrassment.

After several minutes the normality of people rushing around, penetrated, and Janet got up to look for the airline which would get her away from here. After several false starts she found her way to the small airline counters way in the back corridors where nothing ever seemed to happen.

Bahamas Air came first, with its double counter and romantic posters of roving bathing beauties, it looked like an official airline. Still, its counters were empty and the service shut down like most of the other ten or so booths following.

Way in the back, one of the last counters was Island Air. When Janet got there it was empty. Not closed empty but moved out empty. A few booths down, one uniformed bored looking black woman doodled behind the counter of LIAT.

"Excuse me, I have a ticket on Island Air for Tuesday. Their booth was right here last week. Do you have any idea where they went?"

Without looking up, the woman said "They out of business."

"What!"

"You heard me. They out of business." The woman raised her head, probably to enjoy the sight of someone with their mouth hanging open.

"But—it was only a week ago. How do I get to the Turks and Caicos now?"

"Cain't get there from here," she said, slapping her thigh and roaring with glee at the old worn-out joke.

Janet took a few deep breaths. She would not cry in front of this woman and neither would she yell at her.

For a while the two women stayed this way, Janet staring at the LIAT wall relief map, a brownish chain of islands depicting the Lesser Antilles which did not include the Turks and Caicos, and the woman looking at Janet.

"If you want to find out who be flying there, axs for Bobby. He be usually in the upstairs bar, in an Arawak Air uniform shirt. I hear they going there now."

Janet thanked the woman and trudged back along endless corridors. As if her path were preordained in this empty timeless space of impersonal, futuristic airport corridors, she watched the film of her life on her interior screen. Her career-focused years, the ease with which she had passed professional challenges, never really worrying about advancement. Personal crises had touched lightly and people were blithely accepted as friends, lovers. She saw how through it all she had considered herself principled and brave enough to stand up for her beliefs were it ever required. All it took was a few photographs to sink that illusion.

She thought of how she had avoided falling in love by being too 'choosy,' had avoided intimacy through busyness, and how she had kept lovers at bay with work commitments. She thought of Reah's regret, of Michelle and the cave. And she thought of her inability to stand up to the strangers—even if only to say: I don't work for anyone. I don't have anything to do with the drugs, so go away. She did not like the image of herself she was faced with.

By the time she spotted the bar she had come to a conclusion. For better or worse, she was going back to Provo to do what she could to help expose von der Koll. If he outed her as a lesbian, as he had threatened, she would deal with it. It's time to stand up for something! I need to be able to look myself in the eye again. In the time it took her to cross to the bar, she marvelled at how much lighter the mere idea of action made her feel.

As soon as she entered the smoky space she could see the man in the white shirt with its blue Arawak Air logo at the other end of the room. He was on his fifth drink, if the carefully aligned empty glasses were anything to go by. When she approached his table he generously gestured her to a chair but continued to gaze at the televised baseball game.

"Who is playing?" She asked even though she would not have known any of the teams.

"Who cares? It's a replay, anyway."

"Listen, can I talk to you for a minute?"

"Go ahead. Seems to me you're jawin' already."

It only took the cost of one drink for Janet to find out that, indeed, Island Air had gone belly up and that Arawak Air had taken over the cargo route to Provo. They agreed that, in exchange for her useless Island Air ticket and two quarts of Jim Beam, Bobby would take her down on Tuesday morning, regular time.

"But why do you want my ticket if it's useless?"

"Oh, useless to you. Not me. I am collecting chips and I know who will owe me mucho favors. Nothing to do with you."

Janet was happy to accept the dismissal. She found her car in the parking maze after only twenty minutes of increasingly frantic search, all the while expecting the three men to pop from behind some car or pillar. But no one followed her, her key finally opened the door of one of the many identical Fairmonts, and she sank gratefully into the cheap plastic driver's seat. She drove back to the motel without once looking in the rear view mirror.

Once in her room, locked in and barricaded, she dialled the Manor House, still acting on remote control. It was time to get the answers Reah had promised. She couldn't figure out the mystery of Dennis's birth and, she still had no idea what 'The Scandal' was she was to be enlightened about.

Reah was awake and available; their call was relatively quick and one-sided, with Janet doing most of the listening. When it was over, Janet carefully replaced the earpiece as though she were afraid of it.

She lay back and repeated the sentence that had come through the phone wire as though on high amplification: "Because you see, he was not a man. Grandpa Dennis was a woman."

The problem with the family genealogy was not a mystery twin, and was not an impostor! What she had found in the Bible, the birth of one Deborah Ruth Hamilton was the whole answer. On August 1, 1843 on a farm along the Charles River a girl had been born, and she, Janet, had held the key to the mystery all along, if only she could have seen it, if only she had changed her glasses.

The chest with the initials DRH was, indeed, a girl's hope chest. Sixteen years after the birth of that little girl, Deborah had re-emerged on a tropical island forgotten by history as Dennis Hamilton, businessman and, later on, proud family man. Armed with her grandfather's land deed, she had arrived on Provo in 1859.

What terrors or hopes could have driven a sixteen year old girl to leave family and country to try her luck as a prospector on a barren salt rock of an island? Clearly, she would not have been safe travelling and working as a woman, so it made sense for her to pass as a man.

And several years later her oldest friend and companion Sarah came to join her. They married, raised a child named Ruth and lived, for all intents and purposes, normal lives. Until Dennis died, at which time the secret came out. Thus the death certificate!

Maybe the doctor who wrote out the affidavit of death could not make himself turn her into a woman after all those years. But, being an official, he also could not pretend she was a man. So he left the space blank.

But who tore the certificate? It could not have been Reah; she was only twelve. She said she remembered that everyone was very upset after grandpa's death and that they buried him down by the ocean near his old shack. At the time she assumed that was what he had chosen.

"Much later, after Maria and the baby had died and I was walking the world like a zombie, my mother told me about Grandpa. She said that the scandal almost ruined his funeral because the priest refused to bury him in the cemetery. People were so angry, and his friends felt betrayed. But Mother still loved him. She told me she had given all of us his last name, Hamilton, because she owed him her life."

"If only mother had told me about Dennis earlier. Or, if only I had not been so afraid."

Janet did not know how to comfort her. After a long silence interrupted by nothing but laborious breaths, Janet heard her say, "Don't let her get away, the one who showed you the caves. She made your eyes glow when you talked of her."

Now, in the silence of her motel room, Janet cried. For Dennis and Sarah, for the fear that must have been a part of their lives. For Reah, for her guilt in not having acted, her lifelong aching after Maria. For Michelle. And for herself.

Oh, Michelle, what am I going to do? It had seemed so clear this afternoon. Now she wondered how she was going to convince Michelle to be open, to trust her. What chance did they have even if they exposed von der Koll? What chance did she, Janet, have to vie for Michelle against a husband, a settled life and a society that respected her, a community she professed to need? What would she find when she got back? Determination mixed with fear, longing, and self pity. By the time she got up to look in the mirror, she saw her self look back puffy-eyed, soggy and utterly confused.

Chapter Twenty-Two

When the plane bumped along the short landing strip this time, Janet had not the slightest urge to laugh. Arching her neck she looked for Michelle among the people on the ground. But it was Billy, peeling and reddish, who waited for her in the same place as the first time, three weeks earlier. Along with the hot tarmac burning through the soles of her sandals, this comforted her oddly, despite her initial disappointment. Here she was again.

Janet marveled that just three weeks ago she had been a somewhat jaded academic with a book project and generalized anxiety about a tenured future. And now? A woman in love, fighting for her future and trying to solve simultaneous mysteries involving murder, drugs, and a century old scandal.

Watching the dusty brush pass by along the rutted road she thought for the first time in days, of Francine. Maybe she should write her a note. Something like, "As you might have heard I have been visiting with your Aunt Reah and have, thus, discovered *The Scandal*. So there!" Maybe not. What about: "I hope you have forgiven me for trespassing and trust that you will come to see how important it is to publish the story. If for no other reason than for its lovely parallelism—the lives not chosen: Dennis/Deborah married the woman she loved and they lived happily forever after—until her death, that is. Reah, on the other hand, gave in to social pressure and did not rescue Maria. She says she has been waiting for her own death so she can join her love on the other side."

But Janet decided to postpone this problem for now as they passed the police station.

"Yes," Billy confirmed grinning. "They're still taking turns guarding the stuff. Still smoking as much as they can."

"Maybe they'll smoke it all and the problem will be solved."

"Do you know what the Prime Minister wants to do with it?" Billy slapped his knee in anticipatory delight. "Burn it! Can you imagine how many people would be stoned for how long? We'd have all of the Caribbean downwind from us, just breathing!"

Janet joined in the laughter. The picture was too tempting. But all too soon she was back in her maid's quarters and things began to look overwhelming again.

First, with no little trepidation, she ripped open the letter-size envelope Billy had handed her along with the room key. However, it was not from Rudy von der Koll, but Michelle, who apologized for not meeting the plane. She was off island with Andre, back Wednesday. She suggested though they meet for a swim the coming noon.

So many things have happened I want to tell you in person, but this one story I HAVE to write to you immediately. You heard that Annabelle broke some ribs a week ago? She said she had fallen, on the boat. Only she told Andre the truth. (I think you noticed that they were having an affair? C'est normal, enfin! It is OK, only, people talk and make things worse.)

The truth is that Chester beat her because he found out about her affair with Andre. She was very angry with him for that and wanted revenge. So, next time she sees Andre she gives him the radio log of Serenade—where you can see all his calls and you can guess who he makes deals with. The international police want that record very much but they can't get it from him because he is in Turks and Caicos waters. I make a copy of it without anyone knowing. Andre gives it back to Annabelle when she asks, after changing her mind. Because, really, she is afraid of Chester. And I think that is good survival technique. But maybe we give the copy to the police Commissioner? Anonymously (so Annabelle will be safe.)

About the partnership, I have found out that Chester will withdraw financing of the Club unless they change the specifications of the airstrip runway to allow for bigger planes. I will tell you how I found out if you tell me what it means. There is much we need to talk of. À demain! Michelle.

P.S. Yes, you were right about von der Koll and I was afraid for you when we met him by the beach after having visited the cave. It is the same place the photo in his office came from. I thought if I never saw you again you might be safe, he would leave you alone. But when you told me about his threat your last day here I knew it was too late. That staying away would not help. And I have missed you so very much.

Janet read the letter several times, trying to focus. So Chester could be directly linked with the Paradise Club. She remembered from the model that the Club was to have its own airstrip. What would they need a bigger landing base for—to transport drugs and not just people, to land heavy cargo planes rather than the light private island hoppers? And why would Chester get involved in something like this?

And then, of course, there was also the P.S. So this was the beach where she had been making love with someone, and Rudy von der Koll caught her with his camera, just as he had caught her and Janet later?

In the picture Michelle certainly had looked like someone who had been well loved. Michelle had said over the phone, No Janet, don't. Was Michelle trying to ease the way into that conversation? Why only now? Another secret Michelle kept, or just an oversight?

Deliberately, Janet pulled back and wondered about Annabelle, about why she would, after having received a beating, go right back to her batterer. Was *Serenade* still in the marina?

About to tear her hair from impatience Janet left the room in search of Sophie, Billy's mother. She was at the reception desk with Corinne. Having remembered to bring her Miami purchases along, Janet felt entitled to interrupt their meeting. While they were oohing and aahing, Janet asked, "Does anyone know what's happening with Johnny in jail over on North Caicos?"

It was Sophie who answered. "I've been to see him once and he appears OK. Worried about his boat but I think they'll let him out soon. The police chief says they don't have enough evidence."

More vehemently than she had planned, Janet said, "I don't see how they could arrest him on such flimsy evidence, anyway."

Sophie shrugged, "You do need to understand that boat people are notoriously unreliable. If the police do not arrest them they simply sail off into international waters."

With her orders of Grape Nuts, 35mm film, and a set of foul weather gear loaded into her arms, Sophie directed Janet to pick up the new slide projector she had also ordered and follow her into the family's living quarters. "Here, have a seat. How about a beer?"

Janet sipped and looked out the large windows at the reef while Sophie added up the money she owed Janet for the things she had purchased.

"Talking of boat people, what about *Serenade*?"

"Well, yes," Sophie answered with a smile. "You have a point there.

They sure aren't sailing off into international waters. But then there's several waters *Serenade* can't sail into without immediately being apprehended."

"Oh, really? On what grounds?"

"Tax evasion, unlicensed international trade, bribing of officials, you know, the usual."

"How come you know all this?"

"It's not like Chester's ever seriously tried to hide it. Of course, he always gave good reasons for what he did. And don't forget, this is a pirate hideout where resistance to governments is honored. Has been forever. And, of course, Chester's safe. If the commissioner tried to pin anything on him he'd simply sail, too. But basically, Chester's got the sense that he has the right to do what he does. Someone will do it anyway so it might as well be him doing things right."

Having concluded her calculations, Sophie counted out money. She rested her chin in her hand and added, "But beating up women is not OK in my book, piracy notwithstanding."

"Did Annabelle tell you?"

"No. I don't think she told anyone. How did you hear?"

"I heard it from Michelle."

"Well, anyway, it was obvious. You hear a few 'I walked into the door stories' and you begin to see the pattern."

"So what's happening there?"

Tiredly, Sophie flicked her wrist as though fanning away flies. "Oh, nothing. Of course. She's back with him. They are keeping mum. Sometimes I just don't know."

They sat for a while, sipping beer. Sophie snapped her fingers and said, "By the way, Morris Cromwell wants you to call on him. And Rudy von der Koll has been asking about you."

"Any particular reason?" Janet was pleased to note her voice sounded normal, almost bored.

"Not that he told me. Missing you, I suppose." Sophie grinned at Janet conspiratorially, and Janet returned a somewhat forced grin. They fell silent again.

"How's Charlotte?"

"How should she be? Eaten up by remorse and isolation."

Janet looked at Sophie with a frown. "What do you mean, remorse?"

"Oh, nothing specific. I hate the kind of blindness that passes for tolerance around here. The old, 'If I don't know about it, it's not happening.' Francine is one of those, old enough to know better. There is a poisonous self-hatred in Charlotte's despair that, to me, goes beyond a 'normal' affair."

"You're driving me crazy with these hints. What remorse, and what is a normal affair?"

Sophie did not answer directly. After a while she merely said, "Please understand, I'm not saying this for titillation. I believe you truly want to find out who killed Mark Sanders and you very well might. But for that, before you go charging into people's lives, you need to know as much as possible about them and the world they live in."

Sophie's tone became somber, almost ominous. "Also, remember, you might end up discovering things you'd rather have left alone."

"Sophie, are you threatening me?"

"Don't be daft, Janet. Do face it. What do you really know about any of us?"

"I'm sorry, Sophie, that was a dumb thing to say. And, of course, you are right. It's just—I want to *do* something, find the truth, fix things. I don't know."

"Well, I think we all want to be Superwoman at some point. Only the lives we make for ourselves whittle us down to size. Take me. I didn't plan to run a resort while Carl…"

Sophie's voice faded and she looked ashamed for what she had been about to say. While Carl what? Made drug deals in the back room and played international tycoon? Sophie went on as though there had been no interruption, "Oh bugger all. Time to get on with work."

Janet sighed and heaved herself out of the chair. "You're right, I guess I better get the police over with, too. Thanks for being straight with me. See you later."

That evening Janet did not join the few new arrivals at the Welcoming Bar, though she'd seen them in the plane, nor did she appear among the regulars at the round table. She needed the time to plan. Turning over the box of books she had filled before her departure she came across the bundle of letters she had "borrowed" from the attic. Armed with her new knowledge she compared them with the packet of notes Thomas had mailed her in Miami. Now it was obvious that the sweet, girlish notes mailed between Deborah and Sarah were the precursors of the love letters of Dennis Hamilton and Sarah Maynard.

Again, Janet was struck at the harshness of this life they had chosen–the lack of water except when hurricanes drowned the land, the exhausted arid soil, coupled with the loneliness of two women passing as a regular couple among a few hundred compatriots. She packed the letters in a large manila envelope and vowed to do all she could so they would get the public recognition they deserved. So they would not have died in silence, their love obscured forever.

Which left more present, immediately pressing problems. Cromwell, the police chief, had been polite and thorough, writing down the names of the people she had met in Miami. He even took the description of the three 'parking garage thugs,' as she had taken to calling them, without much comment. Though he refused her request to visit Johnny in jail, which (since she was his supposed contact) did not surprise her much, he did not treat her as a criminal. Perhaps neither Johnny nor she were on the prime suspect list any longer. He asked her again about the garge incident. Then, abruptly, he seemed to switch tack and asked, "Did you know the local boy who was killed out by the old school?"

"You mean Corinne's brother? I never met him. He died shortly before I arrived on island."

"Yes, that is correct, isn't it? So you never met him?"

"All I know are rumors."

Cromwell inclined his head, raised an eyebrow and remained silent.

"Well, I'm sure you've heard all this before," Janet said. When he didn't react she went on. "He was supposed to have worked for Chester. On *Serenade*?" Cromwell did not react but kept looking at her.

She suddenly remembered that Chester was supposed to have Cromwell in his pocket. Oh well, too late. Might as well go for broke. She told him about being blackmailed by von der Koll. He made some notes, then said, "I'll be following this up. Send anyone willing to press charges to my office as soon as possible. In the meantime please don't leave the island without telling me."

Feeling as though a great weight had lifted she began to plan her moves. Strategizing helped push the thought of Michelle and their future to the back of her mind.

When the knock came she was ready, her bathing suit underneath her clothes. She opened the door and, for an eternal moment, forgot how to move and stood gaping at a glowing apparition backlit against the brilliant sun. When Michelle's cool lips met her cheeks—left, right, left, Janet could feel a smile spread as she thawed.

They headed for the nearest beach, shy with each other, their conversation restrained.

Michelle had found out the information about Chester's requirements for the runway by listening in on a phone conversation.

"It is an island honor code not to listen in, but it happens often. Von der Koll talked to another man whose name I didn't catch. The only reason von der Koll talked so freely was because he was having a fight with the guy who insisted that such a large private runway would cause unnecessary trouble in parliament and that von der Koll needed to get this across to 'that stubborn bastard.' And von der Koll kept saying, 'It's in your best interests, and if you don't come through he won't put up the money.' What does it mean?"

"I don't really know yet. I think it's a safe guess that this was a conversation between two of the partners in the Paradise development concerning a third. You recognized von der Koll, the other on the line was likely to be the Prime Minister, Norman Windham, so 'the stubborn bastard' would refer to Chester. But I can't figure what Chester would get from this partnership, or even why he would deal drugs when he's got a lucrative business already. It just doesn't make sense."

They fell silent for a while until the balmy water freed them. Without looking directly at Michelle, Janet blurted the question that had been tormenting her for days, "Who were you with on that beach?"

"What do you mean?"

"That picture in von der Koll's office was taken down by the cave, and he used it to blackmail you, right?"

Michelle looked neither ashamed nor angry. She nodded as though agreeing with something internal and said, "He hung the photo there to remind me of the power he has. He took pictures of Charlotte and me. We were making love in the open, on the beach, and he spied on us. I admit we were stupid, but we were also unlucky that it was he who saw us instead of someone else."

They stood several feet apart in clear blue-green water up to their armpits, their arms floating freely. Janet was struck dumb and her insides felt like a pressure cooker. What a fool she had been! How blind! Charlotte had as good as told her who her mystery lover was and she had been oblivious.

Michelle was talking again, monotonously, resignedly. "Von der Koll said he would leave Charlotte alone, not tell her husband, if I paid him. Because, he said, the affair was not her fault, she was 'just a dumb woman.'"

Janet thought she would die if she couldn't smash something—maybe the lovely face next to her, maybe her own. "So it's true, you've slept with everyone's wife? Just as Rudy said. How do I fit in? I'm not even anyone's wife."

"Don't do that Janet."

"No, don't make excuses. Spare me that, at least."

Michelle's eyes flashed and she put her face up close to Janet. "It's easy for you to go about being judgmental. What do you know of me, really? Do you think I like living this way, never to love openly, to be afraid, always? Oh, what use is talking?"

As though exhausted, Michelle let her head fall back in the water. The air was filled with the sound of waves crashing against the surrounding reef. After a while the pounding rhythm calmed Janet so she could return to the woman next to her. She watched the graceful curve of Michelle's long neck and the vulnerable pulse beating at its base and she was filled with the need to kiss there. But the urge to commit violence had been too recent. Instead she said, "About Rudy—when he came to see me that last morning he told me you were threatening him. What did he mean by that?"

"After I'd been to Mark's apartment I wrote him a letter. I told him I knew what he was doing, blackmailing others, and for him to stop. When I saw him by the beach that day with you he was showing that he still held the power and I was scared."

Michelle's voice was so resigned, Janet's need to hold her became irresistible. Michelle let herself be enveloped and lifted off her feet. Without thinking Janet rocked her and murmured against her neck, "You are safe. We can deal with this. Let me love you."

After a while they sat on the beach making small talk. Janet told Michelle about Miami, her pursuers, and of Montserrat's red-bandanna'ed body guards. It seemed funny, now. On her last day in Miami, Montserrat, as promised, had checked in. "And he told me that after Saturday, his men had only found one more sign of surveillance. One man who turned out to be an exhibitionist, lurking in the hopes of flashing me!"

Michelle laughed so infectiously Janet wished she had more stories to tell. But there was no time. Hesitantly, Janet said, "How long were you and Charlotte lovers?"

"It does not matter. It is over. Don't you see, now it's about you and me."

With effort Janet held back the responses that threatened to spill out.

Michelle spoke again. "I did not tell you, but in Mark's apartment I also found photos of Mark and the Reverend, naked, having sex! I always thought Mark disapproved of me with women. I am so sorry! If only I could tell him how I wished…" Her voice faltered.

"Why didn't you tell me about them? At least you wouldn't have…" Janet breathed deeply and said, more quietly. "How come Charlotte knew to talk to Mark? Did you know that Annabelle has been spreading rumors about him being gay, saying that his death was due to a lover's quarrel?"

Michelle's voice was barely audible. "Finding the photos was shocking. But not…because of them. They were beautiful, *tu sais?*—Only to think that von der Koll was watching while they were doing this private thing, like he did with us."

Michelle looked away and then said, "You know Charlotte hates what we were—what we did. Von der Koll has made her feel ugly." As if she just thought of it, she added, "I believed I was the only one he blackmailed. I should have known that was extremely stupid, but—*eh, bien.*"

"Have you talked to Charlotte yet?"

"*Non.* Why?"

"She has been paying money too, the whole time. And she said to tell you she was so sorry. She thinks Mark's death is her fault."

The look Michelle gave her was so full of mute animal pain, Janet could not face it. She turned away and told her scheme to an empty horizon. While she spoke of her terror when she first saw the incriminating photographs, Michelle's hand wormed into her own, and they sat for the rest of the time with their fingers entwined.

She restated the main points of her plan. "I hope to make von der Koll think that I have several letters to Mark by people he blackmailed, telling their stories. All you told him was you had proof of blackmail, right? That I will go to the police with the file—unless he exchanges the letters I have for all the negatives and prints. That will make him leave us alone and, hopefully, make him back off from doing it to others, too. For a while."

But Michelle remained downcast. "Even if you did, no one would believe you. It's black people, queers and foreigners against one of 'the Lords,' an island worthy."

Lightly, Janet said, "Except that von der Koll is about as foreign as they come." When Michelle didn't react Janet became concerned. "Look, we're just trying to get von der Koll on the defensive and maybe the provocation will get him to tell the police who killed Mark. He said he knew, remember? Or maybe the real murderer will be rattled enough to make a mistake—I don't know! But it's time to heat the pot and we both know von der Koll is guilty as hell."

"Remember the papers I found at Mark's apartment? I gave them to the anti-Paradise group, Mohammed actually, to see if they could come up with any explanations. I haven't heard so it's probably nothing. I think they had to do with the resort and I hoped we could use that ammunition to put pressure on von der Koll." Then Michelle shrugged, her momentary animation gone. "Oh, I do know better! This will not work. *Enfin*, it has long been a white man's island…"

Janet knew she couldn't afford to listen. "Look, if it won't work we'll know soon enough and by then we might have a better plan. But for now I want to go ahead with it."

Chapter Twenty-Three

Corinne, resplendent as usual in brilliant colors, did not approve of the idea of looking for Rudy. "He be around soon enough, just like the plague." But she agreed to pass on Janet's request to meet him in his office the following afternoon.

Just then Sophie came careening around the corner, saying, "Have you heard? The High Commission has arrived and is convening next week. As their authority extends over the whole dependency there's hope they will get to the bottom of some of the worst excesses. They might expose dirty laundry all the way up to the Prime Minister, you know?"

"Speaking of which, he is in on the Paradise project, isn't he? I saw this piece in the *Conch News* from a year ago or so, with him all smiley with von der Koll and Chester."

"Oh, yes. You can't hide something like that on this size island, though they're keeping the details very quiet. I mean, it's smart for von der Koll to get someone high up involved. It's really scary. You can only imagine the kind of scam they can run once they have government officials on their payroll. Wouldn't it be nice if the commissioner managed to clean up that whole mess at the same time?"

Before she continued on into the dining room, Sophie took up the topic once more. "There's those who deal in strategies and power. Carl is one of them. And then there's people like me. We operate in the gray areas, dealing with people and their needs, without the grand principles and theories, and usually we don't make it big, in politics or financial dealings. Carl accuses me of having a timid mind while I feel he's becoming cruel and heartless. But what else is there? And who knows what will come out at the final reckoning?"

As Janet walked back to her room she thought of Sophie's departing words. I think you're being too generous to Carl, she said to Sophie in her mind. He's leaving you to take care of the human element while he's doing deals. That's an unfair division!

Janet spent the next day in a fog. While her body ached for Michelle and her thoughts circled her mind like rats in a maze, she could do nothing but wait. First Michelle needed to bring her the famous letters, the ones von der Koll wanted back, and then she had to wait for the time she was to meet him. The empty time stretched endlessly, the proverbial calm before the storm. Once her plan was put into effect, things would begin to move fast.

When Michelle joined her at the table, a coffee cup in one hand, a buff colored envelope in the other, she looked wan but determined. "It is not safe for you to see him alone. I want to come with you!"

"No. This is between me and him. He's threatened my reputation. Anyway, the answer is absolutely no." While speaking, Janet had pulled the papers out of the envelope.

"Oh, yes," Michelle pointed at a set of stapled pages, "the radio log. I almost forgot. What do you think?"

They pored over the columns of numbers and symbols of a secret language. Janet said, "Well, obviously, here's the date and time of any call, along with a caller symbol. The comments table seems to be divided into calls concerned with dates, with dollar amounts, and with some other category of numbers. This part seems almost too blatant—shipping orders, as in running a delivery business? Of course, we don't know the code and without it everything else is meaningless. Not to mention the fact that there's no proof that these pages come from *Serenade*."

Michelle riffled through the pages pointing. "Here, and here, and here, regularly calling WH5181. And this one, he also calls once a week. Why do you say the pages don't come from *Serenade*?"

"You know what I mean. We'll have to think of someway we can use these. But for now, let's look at the letters."

There were three letters, still in their envelopes with German stamps on them, addressed to Mark Sanders. Katrin von der Koll wrote in a precise tight hand and her style was short, almost abrupt. But they were love letters, nonetheless. And reading them, Janet felt goosebumps rise. The hopelessness of the cool measured phrases spelled many of Janet's fears.

Katrin's point was that, though the islanders had learned to live with mixed-race society, their tolerance was clearly delineated. That an older white woman and an island boy would not do, and that, even if they dared oppose island rule, Rudy would destroy them with slander and lies. As he'd done to others before. Her final letter ended with the words, "I loved you. I will always love you. But we had no chance and I could not let him ruin you. Be safe."

Janet shivered, then refocused. "OK, so here we have names. Do you know any of those people?"

Michelle nodded and pointed out, "The island doctor. He became very isolated and is hardly outside his house any more." Her finger moved to the next name. "She moved off island, to Antigua, after tales circulated about her and young boys. This one, Malcolm Prescott, was the Reverend here, before the present one. I heard he committed suicide."

They agreed on four possibles, four people mentioned in Katrin's letter, who might have agreed to tell their story to Mark Sanders.

"Now, we go see him."

"No, Michelle, the answer is still no! I'm going alone."

"But he threatened me, too. And he killed my brother—why would he not kill you?"

"Because I'm not threatening. I'm offering to deliver what he requested and look, I need you not to be there. Please?"

Michelle changed tacks, "You are not delivering what he requested. And if he discovers that you are lying about additional letters to Mark…"

"Look, we talked about this yesterday. It's the only plan I could think of and it's what I'm going to do. Besides, I don't think he would harm me physically; he just wants to demonstrate his power. Just help me this once?"

They locked eyes but whatever it was Michelle saw made her back off. Finally they agreed to meet in Janet's room right after she met with von der Koll. They would go together to the public forum from there.

If she failed, she would be simply back at ground zero, having to depend on von der Koll not to deliver the incriminating photos to her dean. The letters he wanted, from his wife to Mark, were the only source alleging blackmail. Janet had no proof he had tried to blackmail her. He had threatened her verbally only. She shook herself. It had to work. She had no better idea and time was up.

"Did you enjoy yourself in Miami?"

Janet noted that he wore his suave facade. She was grateful for the delay, still hoping she would know exactly what to say when the moment came. They exchanged several observations concerning the mainland before von der Koll introduced the topic by saying, "I think you have something for me?"

Barely breathing, Janet handed over the manila folder. He flipped it open, scanned the letter, then read it again slowly. Having reached the end he said, as if to himself, "So this is how he knew…"

"I have more, other letters to Mark from people you were blackmailing. You must give me the negatives and prints or I'll go to the police with those letters."

His opaqueness scared Janet more than anything she had seen of him. There was no way to prepare, so long as he gave no clues. Did he believe her? Was he angry, surprised? She tried to keep breathing, forcing air through her open mouth so she would not make any noise.

He looked up, scrutinizing her thoroughly, from head to foot. "What did you think you would achieve with this little trick?" He closed the folder, tapped it with his right hand and said, still looking at her, "Did you really think you could threaten me with imaginary letters?"

Janet didn't trust her voice, so she merely shrugged.

His voice became tight and the consonants began to spit. "You actually thought I'd believe you? You probably even thought I cared about this." With that he waved his wife's letter to Mark in front of her. "Didn't you realize the point of it all? Even after I explained it?"

He hurled the manila folder on the floor and stepped over it, advancing toward her. "OK, so you want to keep your job? Fine! A deal is a deal. But you tell your girlfriend not to make any waves here or the pictures go to the newspaper in Minneapolis without delay. Long after you've gone home. Got that?"

Janet had kept their distance constant by backing up. Now she stopped and said, "What about Mark?"

Rudy von der Koll looked at her, his head cocked as though he was listening to some other, internal voice. Amazement came through in a sudden dawning, and he said, "You really think I killed him?" Then he turned to the Paradise Club model which still took up the center of his office, shimmering in all its primary-colored glory, and he absently caressed one of the miniature buildings. "And then, in your fantasy, after our little chat I confess to you, in tears, about my misdeed? I didn't kill him. Not that I didn't think about it."

When he faced her again, the contained man had turned icy cold. He began herding her toward the door. "Look, just go back where you came from and leave us alone. This has never been any of your business and we don't want your interference."

By now he was almost on top of her and Janet did not wait to hear any more. She was still out of breath by the time she reached the resort.

Michelle was waiting in Janet's room and opened the door as she reached it, whispering, "You are back." They simultaneously looked outside and Janet slipped into the dim room, turned and locked the door. Then she leaned up against it, belatedly dizzy with fear.

Michelle said, "I was so afraid." Almost blindly Janet reached for her and they came together with no room for words. They kissed feverishly and their hands tore at each other as though they might never get another chance. Hunger having built for a week, fear and excitement fanned their desire which burned away all other reality.

After a while Janet pulled back, saying, "My God, Michelle, I've missed you so much. But we need to go. The meeting starts soon." Michelle became utterly still, her head buried in Janet's shoulder.

Smelling the scent of Michelle's hair, Janet forgot her resolution and gave in to her need.

Janet stepped back and, while steadying Michelle by the shoulders, she began slowly to unzip Michelle's shorts. She buried her head in the curly black patch with a moan of hunger.

Her hands tightly clutched the flesh of Michelle's buttocks and pressed her close, thus offering her parched lips and tongue a taste of Michelle, dripping wet and smelling of fresh green moss. And Janet craved more, much more.

Once on the bed Michelle's legs opened wide and invitingly and Janet's tongue burrowed deep inside the warm cave, her cheeks caressed by the hot swollen vulva. Michelle's hips moved in sync with Janet's tongue and her breath became labored. Janet ran her tongue down along the silky thigh and Michelle responded to the lightest of her caresses.

Janet explored the perfect smooth skinned, caramel-colored body like an archaeologist at a precious dig. From the crease in back of her knees to the quivering tendon of her forearm, Janet played the body in front of her with a tingling pleasure of power.

Kneeling over Michelle who was face down, her hands cupped around her lover's breasts, Janet pulled Michelle up until they were aligned thigh to thigh, belly to back, arm to arm. Nuzzling the back of Michelle's neck she felt like crying out in frustration over her lack of extra arms; she could not reach Michelle's vagina without relinquishing one of her soft breasts with its puckered nipple and the impossibility seared her.

Michelle slid back down onto the pillows and began caressing herself slowly, provocatively. Janet watched for a mere minute before her need became too much and she accepted the invitation. With a groan Janet reached for her. With one hand at Michelle's belly just shy of her clitoris, Janet ran her tongue down Michelle's back until her hips rose in response. She laid the other hand lightly, tauntingly, between Michelle's legs.

Almost instantly Michelle reacted, the tantalizing undulations of her hips becoming feverish until she bore down hard on the fingers. Janet, burying her hand deep inside her vagina, covered Michelle's body with her own and the shudders and vibrations passed through them both. Only then Janet noticed that silent tears coursed down Michelle's face.

She held Michelle close and, without moving or sound, Michelle cried. When Janet shifted, in preparation for a question, Michelle merely tightened her hold on Janet's waist.

Janet began to stroke Michelle's back rhythmically, soothingly and Michelle cried harder. After a while her sobs became audible, her whole body convulsed. Her despair was so deep, so solitary, Janet became scared. "What is it, Michelle? Why are you so sad? Tell me, does it have to do with us?"

But no matter how hard she pressed her, Michelle merely shook her head. She would not, or could not, explain.

"Oh, shit!"

Michelle shrank away as though Janet's voice had been a direct blow. Automatically Janet stroked her, calming her like a wild animal. "No, no, it's not you. I just realized we missed the meeting! Time got away from us."

Michelle hardly reacted. She still seemed miles and ages away. Her eyes were dark and empty. Janet pulled her close, stroking and smoothing her until she felt Michelle come back to life under her hands.

In an attempt to distract her from the misery as well as the guilt of having missed the public forum, Janet told Michelle the tragic tale of Reah and her lover Maria.

With only the whirring of the fan and the night noises of lizards and crickets as background, it was easy to speak of love and public commitment. Later, in bed by herself and remembering the realities of their lives, Janet felt moments of cold fear course through her bones. No fear was as intense, though, as the terror she had felt looking at Michelle's eyes when they had said good night. And even now, the sense of unalterable loneliness she had seen there made her pull back.

Chapter Twenty-Four

The resort was abuzz when Janet walked to breakfast. She heard the staff all talking about the forum. Janet only caught snatches of various conversations, accented from flat American to island lilt, but they combined into one rather ugly picture.

"He act like slave master, cutting off anyone who say against Hell's Plan."

"I heard he called Mohammed a liar and a conniving nigger."

"No, he called everyone in the room niggers, after those who called themselves 'The Young Guns' began shouting for a public vote."

"I say we kick out the white man one and all."

"Why let him insult we?"

"Is it true that the ground he bought is sacred?"

"Well, as I heard, it used to be burial grounds. The man he cheated out of the property is illiterate."

By the time Janet reached the reception hall she was impatient with her role as passing ear and she hailed Sophie in relief.

On full speed forward, Sophie started talking as though in mid-conversation, "You can't imagine how rude von der Koll was. And, by the way, where were you? I thought you were going to join us at the forum?"

Her arms full of folded linens, Sophie was too intent on her memory to notice Janet's embarrassment at the question. "Mohammed and his people made this great plea, first, just to move the club somewhere else, because of the plot's history as a slave cemetery. Then as von der Koll practically laughed at them, they started on him harder, accusing him of having stolen the land from an illiterate old man. But the surprise of the evening was Bob Chappell who came out against the project, vowed to support the people's coalition and to withdraw the bank loan. I almost fell out of my chair and, to judge from the stunned silence in the room, so did many others."

"Did he say why?"

"No, he refused all further comment, sat down and looked stoic. But he must have warned von der Koll about what he was going to do because that guy—I have to admire his style—didn't flinch but coolly proclaimed he'd signed on another funder, that rumors and old wives' tales would not deter him. 'This is business in the best Luddington tradition' he said.

"That was too much. Talk about inflammatory! The room erupted and years' worth of discontent broke out. After a period of wild shouting, with everyone accusing everyone of anything imaginable, things settled on more organized attacks. They accused 'the Lords,' the white overseers as they called them, of pandering, corruption and racism. They blamed von der Koll for the death not just of Mark Sanders but also of Corinne's brother."

"How did it end?"

"Well, about as expected. The police, meaning Cromwell, quietly moved people out with a touch here, a private word there. Last I saw von der Koll he was surrounded by the core members of the anti-Paradise coalition. It looked as though he was baiting them, flaunting their power-lessness." Sophie sighed. "God I hate that man. Well, bye—got to run."

Janet did not see Sam until he was right at her table. Looking as mournful as she remembered him, he somberly presented a legal-size tan envelope on which she could read her name in a spidery script. "This came on a private plane for you." To her astonished look he added, "People send mail that way in between the weekly shuttle."

"Anyway I collected it and, as I don't think Francine is ready to see you yet, I brought it down here directly." Waving away her profuse thanks and attempted apologies, he said, "She is a good woman and we have a good marriage. I am sorry she's so worried about some long dead scandal but I respect her wishes. I hope you will keep this in mind, too, whatever you may have discovered."

Janet took the envelope down to the beach. Inside she found a short note by Reah, that read:

I've decided, having come this far, I might as well trust you all the way. Besides, I would not want any stranger to find these letters, should anything happen to me. Do with them what you think proper. —Reah.

There were two other envelopes inside. Carefully Janet removed the handful of flimsy pale-blue pages from the first one. Dated February 12, 1865 it was written in the small, regular script Janet had learned to recognize as Sarah Hamilton's, born Maynard. The February letter! The one that had been missing, the one that would explain what "the misfortune" was.

Janet forgot to breathe in her excitement.

Addressed to Darling D, Sarah talked of the weather, the state of their feed supplies, the pain of missing her friend. And then she reminded Darling D of the night she, Sarah, had spent in D's hayloft. Drily and almost apologetically, she contrasted those nights with the years since D had left, when she no longer had the same escape possibilities.

"And so he caught me, many nights since you left. He who brot me forth into this world has forct himself on me those many tymes and made a new life in me."

Her father, a habitual and vicious drunk (even though Sarah had never called him that) had obviously molested his daughter from a young age. After Deborah had left and Sarah was alone, his attacks had become more frequent. That meant for four years Sarah had been repeatedly raped by her father and now she was pregnant.

Janet felt suddenly cold, despite the tropical sun. For an unmarried woman with her lack of social position there would be no alternative other than leaving the community for the city to practice prostitution, or emigration. She could not hope to find a man to marry her in the tight Puritanical community they lived in, having lost her only asset, her virginity. And even emigration was not an easy option, since as an emigre with child she had to be able either to produce a husband or a certificate of the untimely death of said entity.

Or she could stay on in her father's house, daily facing her rapist, her disgusted and disapproving brothers, and her suffering and powerless mother. The prospects were grim and Sarah's letter was full of despair.

The last envelope contained only one sheet of paper which read:

My Darling Sarah:

I have begun to build a house for our family, for you, my wife, and our child. The world may not understand us but God knows we have tried to live right. And now fate has given us a sign that we belong together.

Arrive only, and I will greet you with the greatest beauty this world has to offer, equal to your own. Look for me with an armful of flamingo feathers. Each feather, with its thousands of tendrils will show you the exces of my love and reminde Us of the many days we shall love each other and live in Harmony. Forever and ever.

Your loving friend, Deborah Ruth Hamilton.

Janet's tears fell unnoticed into the sand where she sat. No wonder those letters had been hidden. No one had ever used the name Deborah after the young man known as Dennis Hamilton had arrived in

Providenciales. By using it, Dennis had made herself extremely vulnerable. The punishment for women passing as men, particularly, if they also "layde" with a woman and were found to "have counterfeit the office of a husband" was death by hanging or fire. Dennis/Deborah was relatively safe as long as he/she stayed on the island by herself. But once she stood up in front of that South Caicos magistrate, claiming to be Dennis Hamilton and taking on the responsibility for a wife, she risked everything.

If found during their lifetimes, these letters could have destroyed more than fifty years of subterfuge. They could have killed Dennis; they could have destroyed the child's life once people found out who Ruth's father was. Why keep them? Maybe the two women wanted their child to know the truth? Wanted a record of extenuating circumstances for the sin they were living? That they lay with each other as man and wife only because Sarah needed help. That they had been driven to it by a pregnancy caused by her father's ongoing rape.

Now there was a "familiar sin!" What a pity death by brain stone could not be visited on this perpetrator! Of course, the courts would have let the raping father go free and, instead, would have punished Deborah and Sarah for impersonating a family.

How brave of them, how sad and lonely. She tried imagining the kind of love required to sustain three people in an unknown world with lives requiring silence. A love that by definition never could be announced to the world! She would not betray their legacy! So the world had not been ready for two women in love. Knowing about the lives of Dennis and Sarah she had a responsibility to those who came after her.

And this was something she needed to do for herself, too. Though von der Koll seemed to be occupied elsewhere, his threat had not disappeared. Why would she trust his word about not exposing her anyway? How could she ever be really safe again, unless she took direct action?

She wanted to call Thomas Houston, in his position as her department chair, not as her friend, and tell him of her decision. Only the phone system being what it was, she felt she had no right announcing potentially explosive news to anyone who cared to listen in. So she settled for writing a letter. After many false starts, pages of crossed out lines and paragraphs, she finally had a version she felt she could live with.

It read:

I learned from your aunt Reah that Dennis Hamilton the Younger was really a woman She became a man, in part, because she had to—being a pioneer and all—but in another part, because she was in love with Sarah, your great-grandmother.

I'm certain you also remember the laws concerning homosexual acts being punished by death? Well, in our enlightened age, we instead have ostracism and hate crimes—which I don't really need to tell you, your being an historian.

But I needed to remind you, in order to preface what comes next. Someone is threatening to have photos published of me making love with a woman. I wanted you to know it from me, first.

We both know what that means in terms of my future as a teacher. So—I wish I didn't have to make this kind of decision but here it is: If the story breaks I will offer my resignation. This will save the department and myself pain and much unwanted publicity.

As my friend, I want you to know I am quite taken with the idea of writing a book on these women, the stories of women in love. You know, a sort of Surpassing the Love of Men, *but with the sex left in it. I feel that this is where I can take responsibility. For all of us, Dennis and Sarah, Reah, and myself, too.*

And don't misunderstand me: such levity as I've managed is mere survival strategy; you know how I love my job! Gone—for what? —Janet.

She would give the letter to Corinne so it could go out on the next plane. Relieved, she stretched and yawned.

"Miss McMillan?" A uniformed police man stood about six feet away, stiff in his ironed and starched uniform. "Would you please come with me, Chief Cromwell needs to speak to you."

Chapter Twenty-Five

The police chief stood outside the real estate office, saluted Janet and said, "Rudolph von der Koll was found dead here this morning. He was woolded, do you know what that is?" Without waiting for a signal from her he continued, "A traditional island punishment, in which the brains are squeezed out of the skull, literally. It is rather unpleasant in its effects. I'm sorry but I need to ask you a few questions right away."

He motioned her into the von der Koll office. The scene was striking and unreal. Blood and brains splattered the wooden floor and rose in wide swathes along one wall, part of a pattern which included hair, feathers, the skins and bones of small animals, as well as pieces of coral and some pebbles.

Until the warm smell of blood, urine and feces hit her, Janet saw it almost as if she were looking at an art exhibit. Suddenly the room seemed stiflingly hot and the black rings at the periphery of her eyes, like shutters in a camera, grew until the whole scene disappeared.

When she woke she found herself on her back next to the table which held the Paradise Club model. The wooden floor was cool against her cheek and the whorls of grain next to her absorbed her mind until, hesitantly, she had to accept the police chief's voice.

"Yes, I'm fine. I'll be ready in just a minute." She took the ice cold bottle of soda and held it gratefully against her forehead.

Pulled up by strong black hands Janet leaned against the island model and noticed, without understanding at first, that the miniature island in front of her was clear, wiped free of the Paradise Club as though by the hand of God. She understood when, steered by her elbow toward the back of the office, she came around the table and saw the body. Von der Koll looked immense, his head mercifully covered with a cloth, the rest of him much taller than he had appeared upright, and over his body, sprinkled like so many colorful children's toys, lay the model houses, miniature trees, pools and tennis courts of his project.

Chief Cromwell did not let her slow down. He said, "Please, Miss McMillan, help us clear up this one thing and we can get out of here and continue outside." The darkroom door stood open, the trays for fixing and developing were set out on the counters, scissors and glue, photographic paper and pieces of prints lay all over the work table. It looked very much as though death had interrupted Rudy at work.

"Please don't touch anything. Just tell me what you can of the photos on the counter. There are boxes full of negatives and prints, but this seems to be what he was working on last."

Janet thought she had come prepared for the worst. After all, the fact that the police brought her, a foreigner, to a murder scene had to mean that to them she was connected in some way. But when she stepped up to the work bench she gasped and bile rose in her throat.

There were prints of her, Janet, engaged in acts of bondage and bestiality. She was clearly recognizable, in the foreground against shadowy figures, human and animal. In one shot she kneeled on all fours, being sodomized by a large dog while performing cunnilingus on a woman whose face was shadowed. Even in her repulsion and horror she recognized the beautiful body splayed for all to see and she remembered the feel of that silky vulva she had kissed and stroked, only hours ago.

"But—" she stopped. What could she possibly say? Should she deny the animals, the men, ropes and handcuffs and "only" cop to the lesbian sex. Better to leave it all in the realm of fantasy, reject any part of it. Only how to explain the photos at all?

Helplessly, her gesture taking in the whole darkroom she said, "I'm sorry, this is—is horrible and," she gave up, shook her head, and said, "All I can tell you is, I have never done these things."

Chief Cromwell stood unmoving at the door of the darkroom and past him Janet could see the harsh light of midmorning glancing off the blue and green island model. After a deep sigh the police chief pushed off from the door lintel and said, "Well that's what I thought. But it does support your accusations."

From a file on the counter he pulled some prints, the first of which he slid across in front of her. It was grainy as though it had been enlarged from a very small piece of negative. There were two men. One, seen in profile, was Chester. The other one, squarely facing the camera, wore wraparound sunglasses on his wide fleshy nose and had a leather jacket slung casually over the left shoulder. Janet gasped. "The guy from the airport."

"Are you sure?"

"Dead sure. I'd recognize that thug with my eyes closed!" Cromwell looked at her as though to object but changed his mind. "I hope you'll be willing to ID him in an official statement. We've been wanting him for some time."

"Well, who and where is he?"

"He's a private pilot and he does pickup jobs." Cromwell cleared his throat, shifted uncomfortably, then slid the other two photos in front of Janet, and went on. "He's also the man last seen with Corinne's brother. We've never had any proof of illegal activities." He pointed to the left print. The same man was loading brown paper packages into a Cessna, helped by two younger black men. "What with the date and time on the print I think we'll prove an undeclared shipment."

Janet pointed to the third print where the pilot was intently talking down at a slight young man with lustrous dark skin. "Corinne's brother?"

"Right. Well, thanks to von der Koll's extensive documentation we might just have a case." He gestured back to the main room in theatrical acknowledgment.

"Meaning, von der Koll didn't trust his partners, even," Janet mumbled but Cromwell did not give any sign of having heard. "So where is the guy?"

"He's not on island right now. Stayed in Miami, I suppose. We'll apprehend him as soon as he shows up. Which will probably be in a couple of days. Mid-month is the usual pattern. But now I suggest we get out of here and you tell me everything you've left out so far."

When the chief finally dropped her back at the Old Turtle Janet went for a long shower. Despite scrubbing her skin raw she could not get the morning off. She kept seeing bestial collages, splattered brains and blood, the swiped model of the island.

She finally gave up and turned the shower off.

Fortunately Sophie knocked at the door. She came in with a large drink and joined Janet sitting on the bed. She'd already heard. "What a horrible way to die. But then that man's created enough trouble to get himself killed many times over. You might not know this, but a woolding is the closest thing to popular justice we have. In part because it takes a number of people to execute it, which means they have to agree that the criminal deserves it." Sophie took a gulp and shook herself. "Well, at least this may have solved the question of who murdered Mark."

"Why?" Janet was still trying to assimilate the idea of popular justice.

"Didn't Cromwell show you the file with the pornographic pictures? I figure von der Koll caught Mark at something and flew into a murderous rage. Then he kept the pictures as proof that he had reason to kill."

"Jesus, Sophie, how do you know about the pornography?"

"Well, like I've told you, islands and secrets don't go well together." But she looked curiously at Janet, as though gauging the extent of her misinformation. "The other possible reason for von der Koll to have killed Mark is due to letters from his ex-wife to Mark about people he blackmailed. The way the police figure it is that Mark talked about that to von der Koll and for that he got himself killed. Then von der Koll went to Mark's apartment and got the letters back."

Janet's heart skipped a beat. The letters—she'd forgotten to tell Cromwell about them.

She began sweating. Her voice sounded hoarse to herself but Sophie did not seem to notice. "Why would he keep those letters? Seems rather incriminating?"

"I don't know. He might have planned to use them in revenge against those mentioned. I hear they're mostly women who'd stepped outside marriage. Bastard! But why would they pay, rather than face their husbands with the truth, I can't understand."

"Why don't the police think one of the people he blackmailed murdered him?"

"Cromwell said it didn't make sense for someone, after paying money quietly for some time, to suddenly go murderous. Plus, that's when he reminded me about a woolding needing several people to make it work. Well, though it is a horrible way to die, I must say that, if anyone deserved it, von der Koll did, if the allegations at the meeting last night were even half true."

Janet, nauseated at her memory of the bloody office, hardly took in the latest news but raised her glass to Sophie and took a large gulp.

After some thought Sophie said, "I'm sorry to be coldblooded about this but I am glad we've got some breathing space on the island. I'm sure someone else will soon come in to build some giant resort, in this era of mass tourism. At least, for now, we can relax. And with the Commissioner's probe going, for a little while the big crooks might just keep a bit of a low profile. Which reminds me," her voice was much more animated suddenly, "They released Johnny from jail and he's back, getting *Rosinante* ready to sail."

"Does this have to do with the high court investigation?"

Sophie shrugged. "Oh, they won't be ready to act for some time. No, I think it was simpler. They let him out this morning.

"Remember the two Americans they arrested the morning after the plane crash? Well, yesterday, the two broke out of jail and escaped off island.

"It seems a Cessna radioed trouble with its cargo door on takeoff on North Caicos, taxied to the end of the runway and opened said door. Two men jumped from the low brush, were seen hauling themselves into the cargo bay and the Cessna took off. The description fit the escaped prisoners. So there was no longer any reason to hold Johnny."

"Wait, how does that figure?"

"Johnny was supposed to be the island connection. Now that they lost their main suspects, there is no point in holding a potential witness— which is all he could have been anyway."

Janet's mind had begun whirling while Sophie spoke and now she finished her drink in a hurry, telling Sophie she had to go to the marina to say goodbye to Johnny. By the time she got a ride out to *Rosinante*, Johnny, in fact, was practically done. His wan face was flushed with exertion as he stuck his head out the companionway.

"Hi, how are you," Janet said. "I hear you're getting ready to leave. Sorry, that was inane. How are you, really?"

"Oh, as well as can be expected. They were quite fair in the brig, *Rosinante* was looked after, and now it's over. I'm glad to see you though. Sophie told me you'd been off island."

They sat in the cockpit and Janet doggedly overlooked his signals of impatience while she told him some of the recent developments.

"I'm still not sure he killed Mark Sanders and I don't know how anyone will ever find out now. The police are more than ever convinced they've solved the crime.

"But I feel I need to make one last effort to solve part of the riddle. While I'm not sure that von der Koll personally bashed Mark's head in, I am certain that Chester is one of the reasons you landed in jail and that's why I'm asking for your help. I think the partnership was responsible for the drugs. Such a shipment warrants major involvement and the guy in Miami practically told me that the Prime Minister was involved. I cannot prove anything yet but I have a plan. No, don't shake your head until you hear me out. Look, even if I'm wrong, no one will get hurt. You least of all."

Johnny became quite still while Janet outlined her idea. "I noticed that *Serenade*'s dinghy is tied at the marina. So with any luck they're both on shore. If not, we'll find out as soon as you hail them. If you could just create some diversion with *Rosinante* for a few minutes while I skip below on *Serenade*, I might get something to tie Chester to the drugs, or to von der Koll's murder, or God knows, to anything … Since you're checked out, if anything goes wrong, you'll be long gone by the time it all hits the fan. Are you game?"

After several minutes of risk weighing and backup planning, Johnny agreed. As long as she promised she would not act on whatever she'd found until he had time to reach international waters. "I can promise that. Plus even if I wanted to act immediately, I don't think you have to worry," she said, "after all, I'll have to walk to the resort after you drop me off at the customs dock."

Janet went below to stay out of sight while he took the sail covers off, hoisted the anchor, and finally puttered toward the narrow reef entrance, past the boats lying peacefully at anchor in the windless afternoon. Just abeam of *Serenade*, *Rosinante* developed engine trouble. Johnny hailed *Serenade* but no one responded, so he quickly tied some fenders to his topside and put a springline on one of *Serenade*'s forward cleats. Janet, meanwhile, staying in the lee of the rather tall cabin, climbed onto *Serenade*'s deck and snaked her way into the cockpit and down the companionway, out of sight to anyone on shore. As she had hoped, the boat was open. Thank God no one ever locked their boats in the tropics.

She could hear Johnny raising the cockpit access to his inboard diesel, ostensibly to repair the intake airlock which had threatened to freeze the engine just now. He would putter for ten minutes or until he saw someone approach, whichever came first. That was all the time she had.

The cabin, luxuriously furnished with fake leather settees and a miniature fireplace, seemed rather impersonal, like a floating Hilton suite. Calm down, Janet admonished herself, there is no time to waste. Quickly she opened the doors that led from the salon. Forward lay what could only be described as the master bedroom, a huge double bunk with bedside lights and a quilt in primary reds and blues which went with the gilt-framed still life bolted to the bulkhead. The only concession to this being a sailboat was that the bed, which took up the whole width of the cabin, narrowed toward the bow. To port a door led into the head, complete with a shower with golden faucet. Aft of the salon was another door to what seemed to be a guest suite, again with its own amenities.

She nodded to herself. Not bad, if you had to live in a small space. Now where would he keep important papers? Just aft of where she stood a radar screen suddenly gave off a small bleep and she realized it was scanning, constantly. On the fifty mile range it had just discovered a fast moving object. The navigator's table. Of course! The first cabinet she opened showed a beehive of round holes in which nautical charts were rolled like so many ancient papyrus edicts. Rulers, circles and pencils sat in a lovely wooden tray ingeniously engineered to fold out from the sextant box. She recognized single side band and ham radios, guessed at several scanning receivers and satellite navigation instruments. But no papers.

She lifted the wide expanse of lovely varnished light wood which positively invited complicated navigational calculations and found, underneath it, a solidly built waterproof file cabinet. She unscrewed the flange which kept it sealed. The files were in alphabetical order, mostly labeled with an acronym and looking very business-like. For a moment she wondered if Annabelle still did Chester's filing for him. Riffling through the folders she recognized "Big Four" but didn't find anything under von der Koll. Then it struck her: PCP, of course. The Paradise Club Partnership. Despite the fact that she was sweating in the still afternoon heat, the orderliness of what she found there chilled her. There were pages of profit projections, cost and investment schedules, liability and equity calculations. And finally, there was a lovely colored chart showing a distribution network which led from Colombia via Providenciales to Florida and Texas, with lines out to the Bahamas and Virgin Islands. The points were labeled with numbers and letters and the lines were of varied thicknesses as well as colors. It looked somewhat like the maps airlines printed in their inflight magazines to show off the varied ports of call.

This was it! Cool as anything, a simple business proposal! Janet turned over the map, trying to find the explanation for the numbers and letters. Instead she came across the proposal for the Paradise Club resort. A glossy two-page spread, the project was called "a different kind of resort." There was the private airstrip Janet already knew about, ostensibly for those who planned to arrive in their personal Learjets. In addition the club would offer its own plane to pick up and deliver guests. It also boasted a fleet of boats, condominiums for VIPs, as well as the usual first class hotel accommodations with elegant dining and dancing facilities. And of course tennis courts, fitness clubs, sailboats, jet skis, hot air balloons and dive boats. Blah, blah. Janet flipped the brochure closed in disgust. What was the deal here? So far, all she could see was that local resources would be completely bypassed, but otherwise? Not particularly illegal, if rather exaggerated. How were they planning to make all this pay for itself? Buy-ins? Timeshare? It didn't make sense. Her fingers kept turning pages. Aha, finally, the partnership papers.

Janet skimmed through reams of legalese about equal shares and distributions. Nothing that explained the extravagant profits promised, nothing about what the partnership proposed to distribute from South America. She turned back to the financial projections. It was there, all right: millions of dollars of profit, annually, to be shared equally. No matter how elegant a resort, returns did not run in such magnitude. She had to be right—the distribution map was, in fact, for a drug delivery highway. OK, but why? When they had a perfectly logical business front, why would people like Chester risk messing it up? Or the Prime Minister of an—admittedly rather small—island chain? There had to be something else!

She heard a knock on the hull, three shorts and two long. Johnny's signal that she had been below for nine minutes. Baffled she stuffed the file back into its slot. Her eyes travelled over the headings of file folders and she picked up a few promising ones, merely to put them back in disappointment, until she reached one labeled TCEx. It contained a single, handwritten piece of paper and she almost overlooked it in her hurry.

On this day, June 14 1982 I, Chester Taggett, promise and agree to transfer my share of the Paradise Club Partnership free and clear to Norman Windham. The transfer is to take place not before the club has been running for six months, and no later than twelve months after the operation is showing profits in the range projected in the PCP financial contract.

In return for which Norman Windham will assure me, Chester Taggett, guaranteed and exclusive access to the underwater exploration of any and all territory within the Turks and Caicos dominion.

The letter had been written by Chester, because Norman's scrawl, loose and loopy stood out against the tight flat words of the text and signature. Norman Windham? Of course, the Turks and Caicos' Prime Minister.

She became aware of frantic knocking on deck, directly over her head and realized it had been going on for a while. Now she even heard Johnny's voiceless hissing: "Jesus, Janet, get out of there, they're halfway here!"

Janet jammed the file back into the box, dropped the navigation table top and scrambled up the companionway. Never raising her head above the cabin top she rolled onto the deck, pulled herself over to *Rosinante* and dove headfirst down the gangway. The powerful outboard motor on the rubber dinghy whined as the propeller spun empty because it was being driven so hard. But nothing covered Chester's enraged bellows. "What the hell do you think you're doing there? Get that tub away from my boat! I swear you scratch my topsides and I'll sue your ass right back across the Atlantic, you penniless bum!"

Janet heard light footsteps above her head as Johnny untied his spring-line. The engine tut-tutted in forward and the footsteps returned as he pushed *Rosinante* away from *Serenade*, pointing her bow to the opening in the reef. She could feel the boat turning while she heard Johnny shout, "So sorry mate but I had to tie up for a couple of minutes. Sure glad you were moored out here. She developed an airlock and lucky for me it was before we hit the tight reef passage."

Janet had been holding her breath, certain Chester would board *Rosinante* in his rage, beat up Johnny and discover her down below. Once he guessed she had spied on him, he would— she didn't want to think farther.

But the outboard slowed down and then Chester's voice grumbled from higher up, practically next to her head. He had obviously climbed on board his own boat and now spoke from the foredeck. "Well that's all right, then, I guess. Engine trouble in the reef opening is bad. You off?"

Johnny must have nodded, because from farther back Annabelle's voice said, "Have a good trip."

Janet sank onto the port bunk in relief just as the waves began to rock the hull. Only after they'd traversed the passage and were rolling uncomfortably in the swells, invisible to the anchorage, Janet stuck her head above the cabin.

"I guess that was as close to an apology Chester has come in a long time," Johnny chuckled. "Did you hear how hard even that was? 'Well, that's all right then,'" he mocked in a bad imitation of Chester's growl. "Seafaring etiquette still works! Of course, he didn't know how right he was to be pissed. So was it worth it? Do tell."

Chapter Twenty-Six

The first thing Janet did after arriving back at the resort was to call Michelle. Andre picked up and told her Michelle was at Charlotte's house, and to meet her there.

When Janet arrived, the door stood open and she walked directly in. The dark hallway was empty and, at first, she thought, so was the living room. Only after her eyes adjusted did she notice the moonlike face of Charlotte bright against a maroon-colored overstuffed chair.

"I came because Michelle asked me to meet her here. Sorry to have walked in; the door was open."

Charlotte did not move or respond so Janet continued. "I did want to tell you that I found out why Rudy von der Koll killed Mark and it had nothing to do with you. He could not stand the fact that Mark had relationships with men; it was too frightening for him. It seems that his homophobia took over."

Charlotte covered her face with her hands and a sob escaped from between her fingers. Just as Janet had reached her chair, intending to comfort her, she heard Michelle say from the door, "No, Janet. You are making it worse."

The tableau froze in time. Only the grandfather clock ticked ponderously behind Janet's back.

"Charlotte, I know it was not Rudy." Michelle's voice was tender but decisive, and it held a tension which Janet felt excluded her.

Charlotte finally removed her hands and, looking at Michelle, mutely shook her head.

Janet thought Michelle would go to Charlotte, touch her, hold her, but instead Michelle moved farther off, backing away as if to give Charlotte breathing space. She said gently, "I know. You can tell her."

"Bob killed him. He told me a few days ago. When Janet came to talk to me that time, before she went to Miami, I was afraid it had been Rudy von der Koll, that he killed Mark because I'd talked to him about the blackmail. Only it was so much worse."

Michelle sat down across the room on one of the garishly flowered sofas. Janet picked one of the straight chairs by the table, feeling as though she were invisible, outside of their circle of energy, a mere spectator.

"Mark died because you and I made love." Charlotte's voice had taken on a proclamatory solemnity. Each word of that sentence fell, slowly and ponderously, into the middle of the silent room.

After several moments, as though to let the horrible truth of this confession sink in, Charlotte continued, her tone now rather flat and uninvolved. "Mark went to meet Bob by the pier. Not about the boat loan, as Bob had thought, but, something else. I've tried to figure out why he would do such a thing.

"Bob thought he was trying to tell him that he and I had had an affair, which, to quote my husband, 'I didn't want to hear but it would have been easier than what he did say.' Because Mark told him about you and me." Nodding at Michelle she continued. "Bob could not stand to hear it, could not stand to imagine it, and so he hit Mark with a coral rock. Even when he told me the story, he kept apologizing for what Mark had implied— because to him that, rather than murder, was the real crime."

She sank deeper into the chair and said, very quietly, "So you see, I am very responsible for his death."

Janet felt a surge of emotion which pressed the words out. "But you didn't kill Mark. Your husband did, because he couldn't stand the idea that his wife could be a lesbian—"

"Janet!" Michelle's voice cut in sharply. "Quiet! Is it not hard enough already?"

"But, Michelle, don't you see—"

"Please, would you come with me for a minute?" With her head Michelle pointed at the door. Janet got up and preceded her out through the corridor.

"Can't you understand that she does not wish to be reminded of making love? That shame and guilt is all she remembers of the time with me? Calling her lesbian makes it worse." Michelle was like a different person, utterly focused, etched with hurt and a hopeless kind of love. Janet saw this, and her own heart ached with the pain of loss, jealousy, and ultimately, compassion.

"OK, I'll be quiet and let you handle it. I am sorry! For you and her. But tell me, how long have you known that Bob murdered Mark, not von der Koll?" Janet's voice had risen almost to a wail.

Michelle furtively squeezed her hand and let go almost immediately. "I learned much in the last hours. I came to see Bob this morning after I heard about the monies for Paradise Club because I understood why he had withdrawn so publicly.

"It was the papers—those I discovered in Mark's apartment? Mohammed took them to Bob Chappell who finally realized that, yes, the project contained much illegal money. He confronted von der Koll and they made a 'gentleman's agreement:' Barclay's would not fund the project and Chappell would not disclose the reason until after the public forum. Von der Koll, for his part, would clean up his act. Mohammed agreed to keep the silence till after also."

"But what does that have to do with Mark?"

Michelle, as though in pain, shifted her shoulders. "Charlotte is right that Mark died for trying to tell Bob Chappell about us. But wrong about why Mark went to him. Mark meant to tell Bob about the Paradise Club scam, from the papers he had. He must have trusted him, despite everything else."

Her voice turned flat, "He was wrong. Bob was still too angry about the fight to listen to what Mark tried to say. So Mark apologized first for provoking him. He swore he hadn't had an affair with Bob's wife and that—" here her voice broke but she went on, "that he knew because it was me who had been lovers with Charlotte. And that's when Bob killed him."

"Poor baby. I'm so sorry." But when Janet stepped forward to take her into her arms, Michelle stiffened. Janet sighed. "What do we do now? Go to the police?"

"Maybe we don't need the police?" Michelle shrugged her eloquent shrug of chaos and impotence. "Charlotte hates herself for what we did and it is eating her. I have found the person responsible for Mark's death and he is taking responsibility, making restitutions. Locking Bob in jail would not bring back Mark or make me any less responsible."

Janet looked at Michelle in horror. "But this is lawlessness, letting murderers get away, people playing with justice. I thought you'd want—"

"Justice! You talk to me of justice. Is destroying Charlotte for revenge, justice? Mark is dead and I have cleared his name. Do you know what police means here on island: Cromwell! He is one of us but his hands are solidly in the white man's pocket."

"But only this morning, he—"

Michelle interrupted, "No. Justice is what we make it. You never did understand us. It is not the same here as on the mainland. You come here, you research, you inspect us like bugs, and then you want us to follow your rules." With final emphasis she said, "This is not a book."

Janet felt as if she had been punched. What was Michelle saying? When had she, Janet, become the enemy, the one on the other side of "us" and "them"?

"Do you know what the police would do to the white man bank president who struck down an island boy, particularly if he claimed it was in self-defense? Do you know what their stories would make of Mark's memory? Yes, I wanted to know. And I want justice. Just maybe not your kind."

Janet wanted to ask, what about me, what about love? And wanted to say nothing is all right. She wanted to find the passionate lover Michelle and tell her of her resignation letter. She wanted to ask will you come with me when I go back, will you be with me forever? But she felt alone in the hot noon sun, on a deserted pockmarked street looking at a dark doorway and had no choice but to follow Michelle inside. The living room was exactly as it had been when they left and Charlotte looked as though she had not moved, had not even noticed they had been gone.

"Charlotte, why did Bob change his mind about the Paradise Club project?"

Janet thought, but Michelle knows that. Why is she asking her, in that tone of voice?

"Bob wanted to do something, make amends for this terrible accident in a way that would really matter. Everyone knows how committed Mark was to the anti Paradise cause, so a few days ago Bob spoke with some of the leaders and after that decided to withdraw. You know, for the future of the island?" Her voice rose as if for a question.

Michelle was right, Janet realized. Charlotte won't turn her husband in. They've found a way to live with it. Will I?

The outside door slammed shut, heavy steps came down the hallway and Bob Chappell himself entered the dim room. Behind him, almost invisible, followed the slight form of Andre Ferrand de Devilleux, resort chef, diver and husband to Michelle.

"Ladies," Andre bowed and moved to the sofa where Michelle sat, sitting by her and taking her hand in his.

Bob had gone to stand behind Charlotte's chair, large and heavy over her thin frame, but rather than looming his posture looked penitent.

Michelle said, "We were speaking of the public forum."

Andre, his eyes lighting curiously, turned to Bob. "Is it true that you pulled the financing right there in public and that von der Koll—God have mercy on his soul—had constructed a complete laundering scheme and had planned to hire all off-island contractors?" When Bob nodded Andre muttered "*Bravo*" around the cigarette he was busy lighting.

Michelle said, "Please tell Charlotte the whole story. It is time for truth."

Bob looked down on his wife's head while he spoke. "I withdrew from the project for the reasons I told you. But the person who first tried to talk to me about the scam was Mark. This was why he asked to meet me. Only I was so angry at him that his words didn't sink in till later, after I saw the papers Michelle had retrieved from his apartment. I went to see von der Koll and we compromised, for the time being. I thought it was for the best.

He rubbed his eyes hard, then added "And I'm so sorry about Mark. I didn't mean to kill him. I just lost my mind. And to kill him for telling me the truth! You shouldn't have lied to me," he cried out to Charlotte who sat like a stone statue, looking at nothing.

Andre interrupted and like a public defender addressing his jury, spoke to the whole room. "This is not necessary. Bob told me what happened and it was an accident. It's over, *non*? We think of how to go from here?" He turned to Michelle, "The past is gone, forgiven?"

Michelle's face was a blank mask, her eyes dead, but she did not turn away from Andre. Janet looked from one to the other and it was as though they had all shut themselves off from her.

She couldn't stand it. She said, "You can't do this—sweep everything under the rug!" Her voice was dangerously high and seemed, even to her, rather wavery. "People have died!" She sputtered but couldn't decide what needed to be said first, second, or last, so she subsided. "Do you really think you can get away with this?"

The room was deathly quiet. Tension grew until it was as visible as the dust motes in the still air, thickening until it was too dense to breathe. Cold sweat dribbled down Janet's body and she felt as though she were going to scream or faint.

All at once it seemed to her that Michelle's eyes showed a spark of returning life. Simultaneously the room seemed to expand, the air thinning. It was as though even the furniture let out a breath. Bob Chappell sighed and took a step toward the hallway. "You're right. We have to talk to Morris Cromwell."

Andre spoke in an authoritative voice, "The island is at a crossing point. Mark's cause has succeeded; his life was not wasted. Von der Koll is gone and, with him, Paradise Club, while the High Commission inquiry is in full swing. It is time to start building a different island. But not with more police interference! Let it lie."

Michelle seemed to thaw, uncoiling herself as if for an argument but Bob broke in first. "No, look. Janet is right. We've got to clean this up. Andre, I know you hate police involvement but you can help me by putting in a good word, being a witness. Charlotte, would you go call him, see if he can come join us right away?"

"Michelle, I appreciate your trying to let me do penance privately, and everything we talked about this morning still stands. Only now, Cromwell will be a part of the solution. It's the only way, really."

To the room at large he said, "As I told Michelle this morning, I'll help defray the cost of the defendants in the case of von der Koll's murder. After all," here a crooked grin momentarily showed on his face, reminding Janet of the man in the bar brawl, "they did my family a service, removing the blackmailer, one might say." Immediately he flushed red and had the grace to look embarrassed. "Sorry!

"I'm also having papers drawn up to form the Mark Sanders scholarship. It's purpose is to help promising young islanders..." He faltered. "As I suggested, I'm hoping that you, Andre, would be on the judge's panel for the coming year... I'm no good at this. It's all written down. But anyway, it's for young island residents with artistic talent and dreams and, of course, the first recipient is, as is only right, Michelle."

Except for Janet, no one seemed surprised. Even Charlotte who was just returning from the hallway, took the announcement in stride. Andre released Michelle's hand and said, "Finally you get to Paris. See what you think of the old country, *non*?" With hardly a break he added, "And you know you did not, truly, want to live in Minnesota."

Janet's face burned and her mind was spinning. How had he guessed, and what did he think about having a wife who loved women? She looked closely, but his narrow leathery face did not reveal any emotions. No one else's did, either. Charlotte sat with her eyes downcast. Chappell looked vaguely at the grandfather clock across from him, while Michelle remained open-mouthed, as if in shock. Had they all known?

A scholarship to Paris? What about love, a future? Janet shook herself mentally. This was all too much. She had to get out of here. But first, she had come to report something. Grateful for a direction for her thoughts, Janet focused on telling them her findings and conclusions concerning Paradise Club and Chester's part in it. She talked of being followed around Miami, reminded her audience of Johnny's arrest and release, then told how she boarded *Serenade*. "So I'm convinced the partnership was set up to run a fancy resort, while using the grounds for a, government sanctioned, drug transfer center. As a business proposition it could hardly lose. There was no risk of getting caught, what with the private airstrip, deep water pier and internal security. The profits projected were phenomenal. Which probably was what seduced Windham, the Prime Minister. In return for which Chester would get exclusive offshore oil exploration rights. Once it was set up and in operation there was no way to connect these three men to anything illegal. Unless you had a way to trace the drugs through to the money and the Bahamian bank, back to an individual.

"But while the setup is obvious, what I found is no more than circumstantial evidence, at best. Chester and Windham's agreement only spells drugs if one takes into account the projected earnings. The map with the colored lines between Central America, Texas only means delivery routes if…etc etc. You see? And, of course, I don't have either the map or the IOU, figuring that if Chester realized someone had been into his papers he'd simply disappear."

"*Salaud*!" Andre exploded, blowing a dense cloud of blue-gray Gauloise-smoke into the air. "They were planning to destroy the reefs! Had I known about this I would have killed von der Koll myself!" He subsided into cursing loudly in French. Rather than abating, his anger seemed to grow with his words and Janet noticed Michelle flinching. She thought she detected her name among the flood of unintelligible phrases but she wasn't sure. Finally Michelle put her hands over her ears and closed her eyes. After a couple more minutes Andre wound down.

Janet continued, trying to sound uncowed. "We do have one thing, though: the copy of the radio log that Michelle made. In the hands of the right department, the DEA or whoever is running the choke point, the document will help the government build a case. They can trace those call numbers, they can spy on his transmissions." Sounding wistful she added, "at least I think so."

The room stayed gloomily silent. Janet couldn't tell whether they were convinced or merely stunned. Then Michelle asked, "Will Cromwell be able to arrest the man who killed Corinne's brother?"

At the same time Charlotte said, "Are you telling us the Prime Minister knew all about this?"

Andre began muttering against governmental interference.

Bob Chappell's voice cut through the melee. "Janet, are you saying Cromwell implied your tail, the pilot, worked for Chester?" Janet thought back to the photo of the two men, and of Cromwell's obvious discomfort. "Come to think of it, yes. So, maybe he isn't in Chester's pocket like everyone thought."

Andre dismissively said, "Ah, he has the High Commissioner breathing down his neck is all. He is a bird doesn't change his feathers. No, we don't want him to hear this story so he can warn Chester."

Bob nodded. "Maybe it would be best if Janet were not present when Morris arrives? He can't help much with the problem of Chester and we might not wish to test his loyalties too hard." He looked at everyone in turn, and added. "Are we agreed?

"After all, Janet, your method of gathering evidence could cause any police chief a bit of a dilemma, and the sooner you take that log off island the sooner we can begin to rebuild here."

Janet looked at him open-mouthed, unable to assimilate what he had said.

"Janet?" he repeated. "What I mean is we should not mix up the cases. Morris Cromwell is engaged in clearing up three murders on the island. An international swindle in which he may be somewhat implicated is best kept separate."

Janet looked around the room but found only blank faces. She got up and almost stumbled over the threshold. Did I just get sent home, like a kid—while the grown-ups do business? As though my presence on island was the problem! But before she could turn back and tell them exactly what she thought she felt a light touch on her shoulder.

Shadowy in the dark hallway, Michelle said, "Thank you for trying. Not that it will make much difference…"

"Oh, Michelle, are you just going to accept that bribe and—" When she heard the indrawn breath she said, "I'm sorry. That was crude. But why?"

"You do not believe me when I tell you why."

"Please. Let me try."

"You think I make excuses when I say the police does not arrest a white man banker for killing a black man? But I am right. You will see. Certainly Paris is a bribe but what do you think I should do? I have found out who killed Mark. And, at least, I will not have to live among these people for two years."

"Oh, Michelle, you were always so extreme. Mark's death was an accident and I'm so sorry," Charlotte said from the doorway to the kitchen. "If only I had told Bob the truth long ago Mark would still be alive."

"Maybe," Michelle said. "Only Mark himself lived a lie about his life, about *l'amour*."

"And if he hadn't used your relationship as a trump card in his debate with Bob he might not have gotten killed," Janet added. The air in the hallway suddenly seemed to chill and both women looked at her as though she had said something rude.

"Ladies, please. Morris will be here promptly." Without waiting for a response Bob left the room, and Charlotte quickly disappeared back into the kitchen.

Michelle reached out and took Janet's hand. *"Je t'aime,* Janet. You know that, *non?* Whatever happens, I will never forget how it felt to really love, with my whole self." She let go and stepped back. "You think—talking love is just words? Yes, I loved Charlotte and I have been lovers with other women but this is the first time I have been me—in love. And it has changed me. I love you." Then she walked toward the living room while Janet turned away from the house.

Love! Janet fumed to herself. Whatever happens, I'll always love you. Easy for her to say and then she walks back in, to hubby! Katrin von der Koll wrote the same stuff, 'I'll always love you,' except at least she was honest, adding 'but we don't have a chance.' Reah thought she'd killed her lover because she was afraid, because she hadn't loved her enough. God, what a mess love is!

The walk back to the hotel took about twenty minutes…but it seemed a pilgrimage through a lifetime. Janet raged and kicked pebbles until her toes hurt. Then she kicked some more and finally she just trudged through the dry noisy heat.

Maybe Michelle had a point. The ways of island justice certainly seemed different than those at home! Who would ever think of inviting the police chief for a chat over lemonade while the murderer decided what should or should not be a part of the confession.

Michelle accused her of coming here and studying the islanders like bugs. "Island culture depends on taking care of your own, not depending on some white man's law. Just think of von der Koll." Sophie, too, had said something similar. "You don't live here. What do you really know about any of us." And though her mind was busily making up defenses and explanations, a small voice kept echoing, You don't belong, you're just visiting. You don't understand...

But how could Michelle act this way? She let these people get away with murder and folded up for a measly bribe. After all that brave talk. Well, let her! She, Janet had work to do, a life to live. With von der Koll dead she might not have to resign from her job. She had books to write, a tenure committee to face. In no more than two years she should be installed in her new permanent office up on the third floor, her own bronze plaque solidly affixed to the door. A full member of the academic community with a safe future and a pension plan!

The realization washed over her in a wave. Her life stretched endlessly ahead of her—safe, yes, but also gray, meaningless, and empty of love. These last few weeks she had been alive like never before. She had had a promise of being whole, a taste of love. Until now, not knowing, she had not missed it. But now she knew she wanted more of what she had glimpsed, what Dennis and Sarah had had.

And yes, Michelle was right. Janet did not understand how it was to be a black woman who loved women, how it would be to go against the injunctions of island society while being an integral part in it. But if she let herself remember how scared she had been after von der Koll threatened her, she found it easier to sympathize. And slowly her heart softened.

By the time she stepped onto the sandy track she had reached a conclusion. She would not just run. They deserved another chance. Paris was not half as far from Minneapolis as Provo was—and not merely in geographic terms.

Dennis's shack listed to one side, the wooden walls had turned soft and silvery, and the door hung on one hinge. There was a trace of a coral wall which probably used to demarcate a garden from the wilderness but which now only served the lizards as sunning spots.

When she came around the corner of the house she could see the gray block of granite, so foreign against the background of white coral and turquoise water. Dennis Hamilton's grave sat in an outward corner of his former garden, overlooking the ocean he so loved.

Someone had tended the grave not long ago. The letters carved into the gravestone were clear, the space around it swept. "Dennis Hamilton, Father, friend and husband. You will be remembered." And the date "1843-1912."

Janet rested her hand on the sunwarmed stone. "Yes, Dennis, you'll be remembered," she vowed. "I'll tell your story. And mine." When she looked down, she noticed that behind the granite slab, someone had formed a nest of red and black coral. Inside the nest, surrounded by chips of shells, lay half of a chambered nautilus, smooth and immaculate. The warm glow of mother-of-pearl from the shell fragments, reflected off its creamy outer skin.

She picked it up and caressed it. The sun shone through it and lit its center like an eternal light. Like a promise of hope. For one short moment she pressed the shell against her heart before she put it back down.